TARA BRAZEE

All Together Now

RABBIT ONE
PRESS

For Mom and Dad
Thanks for not being evil!

Contents

Acknowledgments

Yet another Outrider Adventure! Be honest, did you think I'd stick with this self-published book thing this long? Write your answer below (and never show it to me):

When I first started dreaming up this superhero team, the first three adventures came together rather quickly in my head. One crazy summer vacation where a group of friends turned into heroes. I thought "wouldn't that be fun" and scribbled out a few ideas for scenes and a very shaky timeline.

Now the third of that initial set is out and I don't want to stop. If I get my way, I'm giving these teens the stars. Do I know exactly what happens next for them? No! That's part of the fun, for me. And part of the torture.

All that is a problem for Future Me to solve. I love giving her work. For now, let me thank the people who helped me get this far along.

My dear family, who have been incredibly supportive all through this venture of mine.

My best friend Stephanie, I stole your name so you always get a shout-out. Also you let me ramble at you about story stuff even when it only half makes sense.

The lovely Tavern and the End of the World, the bestest Discord server there is. If I didn't have that little writing community, I probably wouldn't have kept going this long. With extra thanks to Kierian and Shannon for giving this a read first and helping make the story even better.

Finally, I want to thank Deanna Howerter from Terrace Books in Columbus, NE. She is an incredibly lovely person and talking to her always makes me less nervous about this whole author thing. Also, thanks to Kojak (the bookstore cat) for existing.

1

Information Overload

Mina tried not to laugh as the hologram version of herself spun both blasters by their trigger guards, leaned heavily on her left leg, and took aim at an unseen opponent. Hologram replicas of the rest of the team locked into similar positions on either side of her. She could feel the "insert catchphrase here" as the scene froze as Emma raised her hand.

"Do you honestly expect us to stop fighting, group up, and hit a pose at the same time?" Emma asked from her spot on the floor in the training room.

"I'm gonna need a count or something to stay on time," Steph added from beside Mina.

"You guys are overcomplicating it," Sean said as he walked through the hologram taking up the middle of the room. "We use a trigger phrase or something. Someone calls out the first part, everyone gets lined up, then they finish the line. Just like that, we look awesome."

There was the catchphrase Mina expected. She'd leave those up to the others, if Sean didn't already have a list.

"Jonesing for those good angles, aren't ya?" Henrie asked from beside Emma. Mina could tell from how their arms pressed together that they were leaning against each other.

"Nek, please demonstrate for the non-believers once again." Sean waved at the hologram now behind him.

Nek's colorful waves bounced along the panel across the room. "One moment."

The hologram reset to the beginning, showing the six of them walking toward a central point. Fake Comps zoomed around, their small blasters taking shots at invisible targets. Comp2876 buzzed through on its own path, playing itself in the scenario. 2876 didn't send off any bolts, but Mina caught tiny *Pews!* popping on its screen as it flew by. The team stopped in unison, stared (presumably) at the same spot, and held their weapons as if ready to charge toward an enemy. As they stood at the ready, an explosion went off behind them. Comp2876, hovering between the fake Mina and Zane, scrolled a large *BOOM!* across its screen. The training room filled with fictional smoke. Nek was working hard to sell the effect.

This time, Steph raised her hand as the hologram paused. "Where does the explosion come from again?"

Sean gestured to Mina. "I figured we'd leave that up to our head honcho."

"You make one bomb," Mina muttered loud enough for the rest to hear, "and it's your thing for the rest of your life."

Her comment got a light laugh before they drifted back to the general timing issue with Sean's plan. She returned to working on her home project, a twice daily check-in on her home's security cameras. No sign of her parents in their home lab today, still busy at Hephaestus getting everything ready for the Expo. There were also no signs that they'd readjusted the camera angles, so she moved them all another fraction of an inch. One more day, maybe two to be extra safe, and they'd be in the clear to slip in.

As vomit-inducing as the idea of going inside her parent's home office without permission was, they needed the intel. Nek had offered to hack into her father's computer and retrieve anything there. That plan held little worry of detection, but her mother's physical records remained an issue. Mina knew there'd be information there neither would trust being digitized, most notably if her mother was doing any more digging on the Guardians. They'd held off on performing the break-in this long because her parents' schedule was a mystery. They'd rarely ever been in town for this long. Her moving the cameras wasn't even a part of the original plan they'd come up with. Nek was going to loop footage, but one day while checking the feeds, she nudged a camera by accident and closed out of the program in a panic. When the change went uncorrected, she kept up the small shifts. The task brought her a similarly small feeling of control. These were her parents. While she was incredibly grateful to have her team behind her, they were her problem to solve.

She checked her armband. The mini-fab in her workshop showed twenty minutes left on the pieces for her new Lockpuck idea. Mina wanted to call them Lockpicks, but the final prototype ended up being the size of an air hockey puck because of the necessary internal hardware and the others insisted on changing the name. Her newest bit of tinkering adhered to any electronically locked device and cracked it. They'd gotten the program processing rather quickly, but runtime varied by the level of difficulty. To cut that down in the future, Nek built an internal database to store all those broken passcodes, allowing the Lockpuck to learn and advance each time they used it. They'd preloaded any data they could find online for code cracking and the decryption the Comps crafted to beat Capri's work on the Pawns.

That same bit of programming was being used and expanded upon by a set of Comps working on the hard drive retrieved from Capri's old Pak once Henrie took ownership of it. She thought they resembled a little robotic cult huddled around the drive in the workshop next to hers. Mina considered making an excuse to leave and pop in on them since she couldn't see their progress via the framework. Nek was concerned about countermeasures that could impact the entire swarm. They'd severed the five assigned to the task from the framework. There was also a docking station installed in the room so the Comps could take shifts recharging without leaving. She liked to poke her head in and make sure they were all holding up okay. Their reports to Comp2876 made it seem they were getting close, but she didn't want them overworking themselves.

Even though her curiosity was driving her mad. Mina didn't know what would be on that drive. She hoped for actual answers, but all they could do was wait. The house heist put her stomach in knots, but at least she got to decide when that happened. Not to mention, the heist was providing her an opportunity to test new tech in the field.

The Lockpuck worked on everything around the ship she'd tested, but Mina wouldn't feel satisfied until the job she'd built them for was done. If that went off without a hitch, Nek would print more for everyone else. Another part of the database was the small portion of useful programming they'd pulled from the mind altering box they'd stolen from Mina's parents. Nek cleaned up their work, in the hopes it'd work faster if ever needed again. No one else was getting mind-controlled for long if they could help it.

Added bonus being that the more they all used them while on missions, the less they'd need to call on Nek for the assist. Taking something off their plate for once seemed like a nice idea.

A series of pokes ran up her side. Come back to Earth. She straightened up and tried to gauge how long she'd been vacant.

Zane laid out on the floor, his head near her. "It'd be cool to pull off once, for sure. You really think we can do that every time though?"

They were still on the timing issue, so not horribly long. Zane might have even poked her out of instinct, with no one else noticing.

Sean walked through the hologram toward him. "Practice makes perfect. 2876 already has the moves down."

Glad to assist! 2876's display exclaimed.

"What about when no one is around to see the cool bit?" Emma asked. "I mean, the general public is usually hiding or running away when we're in the suits."

"Yeah, I ran through downtown as a smoke monster and there are barely any pictures of it." Henrie's tone sounded casual, but she twitched and rolled her shoulders. She looked like she was trying to relieve some tension there.

Mina assumed a memory was causing phantom pains along the healed, but scarred, injury down Henrie's back. She'd only caught flashes of the marks during their training over the last weeks because Henrie rarely left her back uncovered. Emma slipped her arm behind the other girl to massage a spot between Henrie's shoulder blades. Henrie's head rested on the wall as her shoulders relaxed. It was good that Emma didn't have to be covert about giving extra attention to Henrie anymore, and that the rest of them didn't have to pretend to ignore the obvious. Those two officially made the jump to "a thing" last week when Zane missed the morning warm-up because of family plans; leaving the two girls alone in the gym until Steph stumbled in for her workout orders and caught them making out on a bench press.

Mina didn't know how much normal dating time they got in, but they appeared to be getting along fine. That gave her more data related to her personal interests, as she hadn't asked Steph out yet. She couldn't shake her fear of being a distraction or a complication, muddying allegiances by getting romantic emotions involved. One quiet night alone on the ship, she'd slipped a hint of that worry to Nek using the other two girls as a cover. They'd assured her plenty of Wardens in the past were romantically involved with fellow team members and no harm came of it. Mina intended to ask more questions, but Nek mumbled something about "even Rin managed" before they changed the subject.

Her eyes shifted to Steph, who'd clearly also caught Emma and Henrie's little exchange and was smiling to herself as she swiped at something on her armband. Mina pulled her legs in tighter, using her tablet to hide her own grin.

Another poke on her calf pulled her attention down to Zane, who'd squirmed closer to her. She knew her body blocked him enough that Steph couldn't see his face. He mouthed, *Your month is up.*

She mouthed back, *Stop.*

Ask. Her. Out.

Mina dropped her leg into his face. He gave a muffled protest and wiggled away. Once on his knees, Zane pointed two fingers at his eyes and then pointed them at her. She laughed, "Oh yeah? What are you gonna do?"

In one quick move, Zane grabbed her ankle and was on his feet. He pulled her along, sliding her toward the center of the room. "Suit up."

Mina handed her tablet to Steph before she was out of reach. "You're going to fight me?"

"It's a matter of honor." He let go of her leg once they came to the middle.

Sean's hologram fizzled out around them.

She remained on the floor. "But you? Fight me?"

"I can do surprising things." In a blink, his suit rolled out from a pocket, his grin disappeared behind the helmet. He lifted a foot, pausing long enough to let her know he planned to slam it down on her.

Mina laughed and activated her Pak. Her own suit covered her in time to catch the kick. With a little extra boost, because he would forever out-gun her, she gained enough leverage to knock him off balance and send him stumbling. Clearing enough room for her to stand.

"Widen your stance," Henrie called over.

She should have expected there'd be something to critique. Mina pushed off her minor annoyance and did as she was told as Zane circled for his next attack.

"If I pin you," Zane whispered, ignoring the fact that he was on their personal channel, "you ask her out today."

She shifted to follow him. "Can you stomach the idea of knocking me down?"

"For love? Yes." He lunged at her stomach.

A simple move to dodge, but he was nearly twice as wide as her. She leaped to make sure she cleared his path, putting a little spin in her landing for flare. Sean would appreciate the spin. Zane's bull charge sent him directly at the wall, but he caught himself before the collision.

"Ole!" Sean cheered.

"Keep your guard up, Mina," Emma said. Both coaches were standing now, officially back on the clock. "Remember, Pawns don't come at us one at a time. Have to be ready for the next one coming in."

Advice immediately made useful by Zane coming in with a swing aimed for her head. She pushed his arm away and dodged again, but realized too late that this was what he'd wanted. Zane grabbed her arm and twisted it behind her back. He used his other arm to keep her bent forward, putting just enough pressure that she felt a small tug in her shoulder.

"Say uncle," he said, now for the group to hear.

She tried breaking off to the side, wanting to use a wall to run on, but he was ready and countered her pull with his own. He wrangled her to the middle of the room, rotating them so that she now faced Steph, who'd also stood to watch their tussle. Steph, who must have sensed Mina's eyes on her through the helmet visor, gave a small twist of her hips.

Oh, right. Mina twisted her hips toward him instead of away and threw her free arm back to bring her elbow into the side of his head. Zane took the hit easy enough. Her elbow was more hurt than he was, but she'd won enough freedom to break his hold. He clapped in acknowledgment of her maneuver. The coaches remained quiet. She took that as a bigger win.

His next attack came low. He swung out a leg to take her feet out from under her. She didn't even need an assist on the jump to clear that one. Mina realized this could go forever if he was going to take easy shots at her. She knew she was the weak link with hand-to-hand fighting. Some of the critiques were warranted, but she felt she'd improved enough to handle a sparring match. Her personal belief wouldn't stop him from pulling punches. What she needed was a way to end this before he tripped her up and gave the coaches something else to lecture her about. There was no way she could overpower him. She had to outplay him instead.

He was just so big. She needed to get bigger. Or at the least, higher. Give herself space to think before he could close in on her again. Mina took a run for the wall. She turned on the adhesive feature as she leaped and continued running around to the ceiling. Putting herself well out of his reach.

"Say uncle," she called down to him.

"That's not how uncle works." He stood directly below her, hands on his hips.

"Running away doesn't mean you won," Henrie called up. "Just delays the fight."

Mina crossed her arms, blocking her armband from the eyes below. "I'm utilizing the field."

Zane sighed and jogged toward the wall. Mina only had seconds, but all she needed was to flick through a menu. The options of her personal framework commands scrolled before her eyes via the heads-up display. She thought *Aid* and the task went out to the entire swarm working around the ship. Comp2876 jerked to attention below her, but didn't move. As Zane rounded to the ceiling and started her way, Comps began to pour in from the tunnels that ran through the walls. More came from the doorway and buzzed between them. Mina thought *Block* and a wall of Comps formed between the two upside down Wardens. She stepped close enough to nudge two aside to see him.

He raised his voice to be heard over the buzzing. "You're going to make me fight Comps?"

"You can't," Nek said. "Well, you could fight them, but they can't fight you. Programming keeps them from harming designated Wardens."

"I can't hurt these guys." Zane tried to grab two and move them aside as Mina had, but they shook and remained in place. Her command kept them on task.

"Blocking and harming are different," Mina called through her gap.

His arms fell to his sides. "That's not fair."

"You started this!" She wanted to stomp her foot, but knew she needed all the sticking surface she could right now.

"Fine. Uncle!"

Mina dropped her command on the Comps. They all disappeared from the room as quickly as they'd come, going back to whatever task Mina had pulled them from. There were spots in her vision as they walked their way around to the floor, but she blinked them off. Once right side up again, Mina dropped her helmet and stuck her tongue out at Zane. He shook his head at her as his own helmet pulled away.

Steph met them in the middle. "You should have expected she'd think of a crafty way around you."

Emma appeared on her other side, suit on and ready. "Okay, couple things to go over."

"Starting with," Henrie cut in, "the robots can't solve everything."

So she hadn't impressed the coaches. They'd just started taking notes instead.

She was about to respond to the robots comment but Sean busted into the middle of them, his own suit rolling out. "No! No. We're going back to my thing. Everyone get in line."

"Wardens." Nek pulled into a bundle on the panel nearest them. "I must interrupt our break. The drive is open."

"Really?" Mina grabbed her tablet from Steph, a flashing notification informed her that the secluded Comps had rejoined the framework after reporting their task's completion. The swarm immediately began digging through Capri's files, their organizational system built before her eyes as they filtered, sorted, and tagged. Comp2876, who now hovered stiffly in the air, was also doing their part to categorize the files. "She was kind of a digital hoarder, wasn't she?"

"It's extensive," Nek agreed. "I'm not fully sure where to begin."

"We should read everything," Henrie said.

Mina watched a file labeled *Rin Messages* fill with more entries than any other member of Capri's old team. She was suddenly certain there were notes in there she'd feel awkward reading. Ones that would feel more like prying than investigating. Being concerned about Capri's privacy was a bizarre feeling, given that she'd taken over Henrie's entire body and nearly ruined her life in the pursuit of tracking them down. Strange to extend a courtesy that wouldn't be returned, but all the same, Mina didn't think any of them should read those particular messages before Nek got the chance. "Nek needs time to sort everything out. We won't know what we're looking at."

Henrie popped up the hologram display from her armband, also watching files load in. "Pretty sure I can point out all the monsters she put in my head just fine."

Emma put a hand on her arm. "Maybe that is a good reason to give Nek the first pass. They can flag anything you might, you know, not want to see again."

Henrie gave an angry laugh as she continued to swipe through files. "Think Capri had a 'For Torturing Henrie' folder somewhere in here?"

Nek sounded distracted as they answered, "I'm not finding anything."

"Maybe we can spot check for certain questions we have?" Sean asked. "For example, who was the Palpatine to her Vader?"

Comp2876 shook back to life and flashed the answer, *Elder Warden Asher*.

Mina didn't know how 2876 knew the reference, unless it was doing pop culture studies on the side, but set her intrigue aside for their more pressing matters.

Nek churned as a bright ball of colors. "He led the committee that funded the expedition."

A hologram appeared next to Mina and she immediately pulled away. This Elder Warden Asher stood near seven feet tall. Overly long arms, that ended in hands sporting two extra fingers, were frozen in a gesture as if he'd been mid-sentence. His suit was activated and displayed four muted yellow stripes along his body. Outside of the arms and fingers situation, his pea green skin was the only thing that made him look non-human.

Nek also moved further away from the image. Their waves were low and tight as they spoke. "He always held an interest in the team during their career. Since the beginning. Messages insinuate he chose Capri as a target early on."

"Groomer," Emma grumbled.

The hologram came to life, Asher's voice was low and soft. She imagined the latter was forced, that he enjoyed making people lean in. "Our next steps are imperative, and you are a vital part of this. I wish not to overwhelm you with this information, Warden Capri, but the future of our mission highly depends on you setting an example. Be it by them joining our new venture or demonstrating that our own weaker numbers will not hold us back any longer. You will create the foundation for our stronghold and command a new legion of soldiers to fight in our cause."

Sean gave out a long, "Boooo."

Comp2876 copied the gesture with *Boo* scrolling across its screen for several seconds.

The image blinked out, Nek understandably not wanting to display him any more than they had to. Mina wondered if they could make a hard light version to use for target practice. She scrolled through the files, finding the one with his name. "There are a lot of messages. I bet saying basically the same thing. Boasting her importance to the cause and such. Insisting everything depends on her."

There were dozens of saved videos that, judging by their thumbnails, were different speeches from Elder Warden Asher. Capri idolized this man.

"Have to keep the gaslighting consistent," Emma said.

"So that's our real bad guy," Zane said. "He's gotta be dead. Right?"

"Yes," Nek said. "Unless he's also been in stasis for five hundred years."

Steph paced the room. "Okay, so Capri is prideful. We know this. I can see how that angle worked on her. She was also immensely loyal to the Collective though. How did one guy turn her on everyone?"

Nek spun tighter, turning white on their edges. "There are other names referenced in some of these messages. Other Elders and members of active Warden teams. Capri knew she wasn't the only one, but she did believe her role was uniquely important."

"Why would any of them agree with the Collective moving in such a harmful direction? They were all about protecting people, right?"

A groan came from Henrie. "Found them. Nek, you should play these."

Emma seemed unconvinced. "Maybe that's something we do in private?"

"No, you need to see this stuff." Henrie locked eyes with Mina.

She looked away, unsure why Henrie was taking the time to try intimidating her. Outside of the constant critiques, they'd been getting along well enough since their one short standoff directly preceding Henrie joining the team. Mina knew the first pushback had been about Henrie wanting answers, so what was she so desperate for them all to know right now?

Nek moved to spin above Henrie before they spoke again. "Capri's training started when she was young. She grew up on a central Collective planet. Her region held a very high rate for Warden graduates. I wasn't aware of the lengths they pushed their candidates to produce those results. These files are enlightening, even for me."

Videos appeared on the surrounding walls, most of them resembled the sort of body cam angles their suits recorded. In front of Mina was a group of children, the same blue shade as Capri, huddled together under some kind of shelter. The camera tipped up as two of the kids worked together to stab a long pole at the center of the shelter's roof. The structure convulsed as the pole speared into it. Thick orange liquid began raining down on the children below. What Mina initially took for support beams revealed themselves to be legs as they stomped and thrashed about. The creature she'd wrongly taken to be a structure was trying to attack its unseen assailant. The video was muted, but Mina could see many of the children were screaming.

She turned around to escape the monster movie. On the wall across from her was Capri, only a few years older than she'd probably been in the first recording. Another pre-Warden memory, showing her and a reptilian-ish being smiling at their reflections in a pool of water. They waved and Mina fought the urge to wave back. Just as a small tag appeared on the video, marking the other person as Rin, her reflection disappeared. Capri spun and captured her companion held high by strands of plantlife over what appeared to be a tangle of vines. The mass bunched together and Mina saw an opening split along the top. Blaster shots came in from offscreen, but as Capri charged toward the monster, the clip shook too much to make anything out.

"Nope. Not that one." Henrie flinched away from something Mina couldn't make out on the other end of the room. "Not yet."

Mina feared there wouldn't be a safe spot anywhere in the room. Instead, she observed her team. Steph and Sean were holding hands as they watched a video Mina couldn't see around them. Emma watched as Capri typed furiously away at a console, while others around her fended off a horrific beast that reminded Mina of reanimated roadkill. Henrie stayed near Emma, but kept her eyes on the floor. She'd demanded they all watch, but couldn't look herself. Mina's stomach turned. She feared she might be sick until she caught sight of Zane. He wore a small, sad smile on his face. She rushed to his section of the wall, hoping he'd found some scrap of good in all this.

They stood before a video showing other Wardens who came before. Capri and two others were in their suits as they dug through rubble to uncover someone else from their team. More tags appeared, Wardens Caro and Jarden. The rescued person, Camden, was crawling out of a control room. Mina didn't know what kind of destruction was required to bury a Guardian. Beneath that was a slideshow; the current picture featured

Capri sitting rather close to a stern-faced Rin. The first Warden leader of Outrider sported flecks of orange across her otherwise dark green face. Those cheekbones definitely aided a meaner stare than Mina would ever muster. There were several visible scars cutting across her scales. Mina wondered if any came from that vine monster.

The videos shifted and replaced themselves as the group slowly moved about the room. Mina heard Emma giving soft encouragement to Henrie, asking her to look at something less horrible. At some point Zane wrapped his arm around hers as they watched different clips play out before something either better or worse replaced it.

Zane stalled at a video featuring Capri, who appeared covered in bruises and excitedly rambling to someone offscreen. Small captions ran along the bottom. Capri was describing a new feature for the Comps she'd finally got the programming working for. Someone else must have recorded the video and sent her the file. Zane put a hand out and the video froze with Capri smiling off to the side. "How old is she? In Earth relative years. Do we know?"

Nek appeared nearby, low waves filling the panel. "In this video she was newly eighteen. At the time of the crash, she was twenty-two."

Steph spoke lightly behind them, "She technically still is."

"Oh." Zane stepped back from the video, his arm pulling away from Mina's. The scene played out and got replaced by a different clip.

"All of this," Henrie said, sounding as if she'd been running, "is so fucked."

"Nek, drop the feeds, please," Emma said. The images blinked out all at once around them.

"I said it wasn't good," Henrie huffed out.

Emma stepped closer, but didn't touch her. "Capri was brainwashed, remember?"

"Yes! By the Collective themselves first. And then by the secret, evil Collective afterward. I can't," Henrie looked at Mina, the edge she'd carried before now completely gone, "I tried, but I can't."

She pulled out her Pak and threw it to the ground before running from the room. Emma scooped up the Pak and went after her, calling back, "I'll talk her down. Hold on."

Mina didn't think she looked too certain. She'd seen how Emma watched those clips herself. There'd been a shake to her hands, her own quiet rage building before Henrie's panic took focus.

"Is this all sorted on the framework?" Zane asked.

"Yes," Nek answered. "Comps are still organizing, but you can go through anything they've sorted so far."

"Cool, yeah. Might be easier to process one bit at a time. I'll be in my room." Zane brushed by Mina. She tried to grab his hand, but he pulled away. He stopped short of the door to turn back to her. "I'm okay. Just need a minute."

"Do you want to talk?" She started after him.

He held up his hands. "A minute alone, okay?"

"Sure. Sure." Mina watched him leave. Thinking she'd catch that slow gait become his familiar rush to find the nearest trash receptacle because his nerves were at their end. There was no hurry to his step. He simply walked away from her.

"I'm going to head to mine, too." Sean nudged her arm. "I'll check in on him."

"Thank you," was all she squeaked out as he left.

Steph held out a hand to her. "Let's take a walk. The training room feels stuffy."

"Sure. Yeah." Mina took the offered hand. Normally she'd be obsessing over the fact that Steph had casually offered out her hand, but her brain remained caught on the image of Zane disappearing around a corner. Before they left the training room, she caught a flash behind them. She turned to see the videos once again playing along the walls. Comp2876 floated in the middle of the room, looking at Nek's panel. Their waves stretched thin around the entire room. Mina wasn't sure how she could tell, but she knew Nek was watching everything.

2

Ope

This was an unusual scenario. Comps continued to sort Capri's hard drive, but the framework felt quiet. Outrider hummed a little softer this morning. Comp2876 knew most were assessing the messages and videos that brought so much to light. As they worked, Comps were tagging files for their own personal reviewing.

The confirmation that the organization they were created for, or chosen by, was not wholly the honorable force they once thought sat heavily on the framework. Dark shadows lurked behind every mission and victory that brought their team here. A twisted Collective had taken shape without anyone noticing. Not one logged note of concern that Comp2876 could find in their recovered database. The most aggravating piece, for 2876 anyway, was not knowing what had come of their scheming. Comp2876 did not believe such a vengeful mission could have succeeded. Surely someone stopped them. Someone must have tried. Their team had, when Capri made her attempt at bringing them to her side.

Perhaps that's what waited for them in the planetary systems they once protected. More bodies and wreckage. Unpleasant. Comp2876 did not want their new Wardens anywhere near that. Better that they were so far away. Better they never knew.

Nek's presence around the training room shifted from one clip of fighting to the next. Comp2876 noted they'd linger on anything depicting Capri's childhood. They weren't happy with how little they'd known about her upbringing. 2876 thought it might be time to sort through the other Warden's saved data, something they'd all been avoiding, and see what they might have endured in the name of the Collective.

Comp2876 tried pointing Nek toward one of the happier bits, a Comp recording of the team waving to a crowd. *Not all bad!*

"The stars are vast and full of dangers." Nek drifted by an encounter with the Empyre, gear driven copies of the Wardens fighting the actual team. "We will stand against whatever evil awaits among them."

2876 knew the phrases, they were from Collective information packets. When in regions unfamiliar with Wardens, they would print pamphlets in local languages to explain the Collective's presence. There were pictures of the team doing just that floating around the room. The procedure felt odd now, seeing the act from so far on the outside.

Not all bad.

"I didn't know. I didn't know how hard they pushed them as children. I was training myself. I didn't know they were so…" Nek's attention fractured and spread across the ship toward their Warden team. "They won't believe me. I wouldn't believe me."

Good team!

"They shouldn't be here. We're creating the same problem. Look at Warden Henrie. She–"

Comp2876 did a very strenuous thing, they cut Nek off via their direct line with the soundbite horn Warden Mina refused to use. That was not something Comps could normally do. 2876 enjoyed being Secondary. Nek scattered on the panel from the small scare. They pulled back together as low, muted waves near the door. *Too much data. Overworking.*

"You're…you're right, 2876. Thank you." The feeds blinked off one by one around the room, eventually leaving them alone. The last picture, their original team standing with arms wrapped around each other in the loading bay of their newly acquired Outrider, remained for a long second before disappearing. Leaving a photo negative of itself behind that slowly faded away. "Since we came back online, it feels like one new bombardment after another."

Need rest.

"Warden Mina has gotten to you too."

Warden Mina is right.

"There is much to analyze from Capri's–"

Comp work. To prove the point 2876 delegated extra Comps to those exact tasks. Data filled the files at increased speeds. A catalog of tags and cross references came together on the side as the Comps created them. They'd inspect every inch of information Capri's drive provided them, good and bad. *You have a team.*

"I am responsible for everyone and everything on this ship. You and the framework and those…Wardens. Those very young Wardens that I asked to come here."

Even Comps need to recharge. You are not artificial.

"The team needs to be watched over."

2876 pushed its designation through their channel. *Secondary. Task appointed.*

Nek gave a little laugh. "I should have named you Secondary long ago. Maybe we would have…well, that doesn't matter. Order received. I will leave you to mind the team."

Comp2876 watched Nek fade from the panel and felt them pull away from the multiple points on Outrider they constantly observed via the framework. Once their full self resided in their housing below the deck, 2876 sent a trio of Comps to monitor any readings coming to the consoles up there. Comp2876 headed out to check on their team.

Wardens Emma and Henrie were the first pair located as they'd stepped into the gym after leaving the training room. While Warden Henrie appeared in control of her breathing, she remained agitated. She moved away from Warden Emma as 2876 entered the room.

"…don't want that anymore."

"It's safer that you have it," Warden Emma insisted.

"This," she pointed to the Pak and then waved at the wider room, "all of this, messes with your head."

"No, Henrie, I think there are other things messing with your head." She looked remorseful at having spoken those words.

Warden Henrie gave a weak shove to the punching bag. "You saw those videos! What they did to her, to all of them."

"It was horrible, yes. I recognize that. No one is ignoring that. But that isn't us. That's not what we're doing here." Warden Emma moved, 2876 believed she was trying to corner Warden Henrie in the back of the room to keep her from getting away. Comp2876 quietly shifted to flank her other side.

"What are we doing here? Huh? Outside of racing for punchlines and pretending this all ends once Capri is in cuffs?"

"Mina said we'd start making plans for other threats once–"

Warden Henrie shoved the punching bag harder. "Because we have to always listen to what Mina says. Or what Nek says. Not me though. I'm just the crazy one."

"That is not true. We are listening to you, but you make it a little hard when you're always trying to prep for doomsday." Warden Emma stood her ground with the Pak held out. "Capri will come for you again. You are safer with this on you."

Warden Henrie put herself partially behind the punching bag. "She'll only care if I have it. She'll leave me alone if it's gone."

"You think so? You think she's going to let the person who took this from her walk away without any sort of retaliation?"

Warden Henrie flinched. "This whole thing, Em, they were bad people."

Warden Emma sat on a bench, the glowing pink Pak beside her. "Not Nek. Not," she looked up to Comp2876, "our Comps. I don't think 2876 has a bad wire in its whole casing."

Thank you!

Henrie stepped around the bag. "Maybe not them, but the ones that made the Collective."

"We're not the Collective. You weren't here for it, but Nek declared us not a Collective mission day one of doing this."

"All of this came from such a corrupt system. I—"

"It's not like we don't have any experience operating within a system that is corrupt and created with our best interests very much not in mind."

Warden Henrie hunched over the seat of a stationary bike. "Em, I'm not okay yet."

"No one is expecting you to be."

"I am."

"I know."

"The therapy helps with the normal stuff, but I still…I feel angry all the time."

Warden Emma sighed and picked up the other Pak again to toss between her hands. "Here's what helped me. You find better ways to focus, better mediums and outlets. More than punching things." Warden Henrie raised an eyebrow at her. "I know. I know. Pot meets kettle, but listen. Physically throwing yourself at problems doesn't solve everything. You gotta spread that energy around. It's, um, this whole balance thing. It's been a while since I talked this out. You work on your whole person. Body, mind, and soul kind of stuff. Keeps you from losing it when the situation could be seriously dangerous. Keeps you from taking that anger out on the wrong people."

The two Wardens shared a look, Comp2876 thought something in Warden Emma's tone said more than her words had. She continued talking as she stood from the bench and walked across the room to Warden Henrie. "You stop fighting the people trying to be your friends. Let them in like you have been letting me. We're the only ones you can tell this all too. Talk to us. You don't have to dump everything if you're not ready, but any little bit you unload might help. You've told me parts, and that didn't suck, yeah? Trust that they will keep you safe."

"I can try."

"And," Warden Emma pressed the Pak into Warden Henrie's hands, "I need you to keep yourself safe too. Okay?"

Warden Henrie wrapped her hands around the Pak and nodded. "I, um, I need to get off the ship for a bit."

"Let me give you a ride?" She held out a hand.

Warden Henrie let herself get pulled around the bike. Warden Emma tapped on her armband, Comp2876 saw on the framework she'd selected the waypoint for Warden Henrie's home. They both gave 2876 a little wave before being teleported off of Outrider. 2876 waited long enough to confirm their safe landing, then moved on to the next set of Wardens nearby.

Wardens Zane and Sean were having a somewhat similar conversation as 2876 arrived. Warden Zane laid out across his bed, staring at the ceiling. "It's cruel, what they did to them."

"You are absolutely right." Warden Sean leaned in the doorway. He tipped to let Comp2876 in the room.

Warden Zane poked his head up. "She didn't send you after me, did she?"

Warden Mina did not ask me to come. 2876 opted not to mention that Nek had assigned the task.

"Okay. Okay, good." He dropped his head onto the bed.

"I have to say." Warden Sean crossed his arms. "I didn't think it was possible for you two to be at odds."

"I know how she'll want to handle this. She'll push on to the next thing, jump on her next project. I'll try to get her to talk, but she'll somehow have already worked everything out in her head. She can compartmentalize like that. I can't. Not with this. I can't take that information in and be all 'sure, okay, what's next'."

"She didn't seem 'sure, okay'. She was rocked the same as the rest of us. You didn't see her face as you were leaving."

Warden Zane pulled a pillow over his face. "Don't tell me that."

"I mean, you gotta think about how much of herself she's poured into this. How much this all means…to her." Comp2876 noted that Warden Sean's hands curled into fists at his sides. "Finding out this place has bad roots, that could really throw a person off."

Warden Zane sat up, eyeing both his bathroom and bedroom doors. "I should go–"

"No, I shouldn't have said that. Sorry. I didn't come here to guilt you. Stay here, focus on you. Steph was with her when I left."

Warden Zane faintly smiled and rested on his headboard. The two stood in silence until Warden Zane let out a long sigh. "You know, the evil organization thing doesn't even faze me. That's what corporations do with only one planet to work with. Add in the countless solar systems they could reach? Of course they become overly militarized and expect you to hoorah until you're blue in the face. Or blue-er in the face, for Capri. What gets me is their ages. I don't know how, but I got it in my head that they were way older than us. Twenty-two, Sean. Capri is brainwashed multiple times over, riddled with PTSD, and mad with her own grief. And she's twenty-two."

"She can't even get a good rate on a rental car here yet."

"Five years between her and us. Are we going to crack like that in five years?"

"Many would insist that agreeing to do this was already the crazy part."

Warden Zane glanced at the photos shoved in his vanity mirror, most featured Warden Mina and himself. "I'm not quitting. I'm not leaving her in this. It just…we all know my constitution isn't the strongest."

"Everyone has a dump stat."

"Sean."

"No, man, I get it. Trust me. I am churning this all over, too. I'm…I'm still working on how I feel, honestly. It's changed, for sure. Maybe we can rename everything? Or, I don't know, reclaim it for good. We don't even know if there is a Collective out there to worry about anymore. We do have a problem here though, Capri and those Lenians. As unfortunate as the origin story of all this getting here is, we can't leave Nek alone to fight them off."

"You're right. Yeah. I still need time to settle with it. If that makes sense."

"Take your time, man. I need you out there taking those hits." Sean poked Comp2876's underside and tipped his head toward the hall. "Let's give the guy some space, bud."

2876 followed the request, seeing Warden Zane lay back on the bed as Warden Sean closed the door behind them. Comp2876 waited until they were down the hallway before asking, *How are you?*

"Oh, good. I'm good." Warden Sean nodded for what felt too long by 2876's estimation. "Just a lot."

We are processing everything as well.

"I'm sure! Yeah, I bet. Hey, did Emma get Henrie talked down?"

Warden Henrie reclaimed her Pak. They have returned to Hurst.

"Yeah. I might do that too. Want to check in with Em myself."

She appeared steady.

"That's my cousin. She always does." Warden Sean tapped on his armband, setting himself up for a teleport to his home. "Tell the others they can text if they need me."

Comp2876 watched another Warden waypoint shift to Hurst. Their leaving was fine, they all retained their Paks and none spoke of resigning from the mission at hand. At least Warden Henrie had stopped talking about such things. This was fine. 2876 shut down its instinct to report to Nek.

They had fully withdrawn from the ship for the first time since Outrider was restored. Nek needed time not attached to the framework. 2876 realized the same went for the Wardens. Making this ship, this cause, everything to the team was part of the downfall of the original Collective. Making their sole purpose to maintain order among the planets led Capri directly to her ruin and the others to their end. Comp2876 swore to do better by this bunch, to protect them. For now, that meant letting them back away. They all learned a lot of dismal information this morning, but 2876 remained optimistic their team would overcome it.

With that in mind, 2876 pushed off down the hall to find the last pair of Wardens. Another Comp noted on the framework that they had just stepped inside Warden Mina's workshop. The reports sent to 2876 mentioned the two had not conversed much on their walk. Comp2876 joined them as Warden Mina pried the final Lockpuck pieces from the mini-fab and arranged them on an assembly mat. Warden Steph sat on a stool, silently watching her work.

Warden Mina smiled at 2876 as it scanned her components for errors. *All in good standing!*

"Thank you for checking." She retrieved her various tools from around the room, laying them out on the mat. Warden Mina sat and shuffled the pieces around, putting them in straighter and straighter lines, but not beginning her assembly. "I can't stop doing this."

Warden Steph tipped forward on her stool. Her face made it clear she'd been waiting for this. "No one said you had to."

"What if you all quit? Henrie just did, and it's not the first time. I think Emma might follow if she left for real. And you know Sean would be next. You have plenty of normal life things to focus on. Zane, he…he would–"

"He would never leave you. And I–"

"I could make him leave." Warden Mina gripped a portion of the casing tightly. "If I saw that staying here was hurting him. I'd make him leave."

"You would not."

Warden Mina waved toward her workshop's framework interface, showing the camera feeds for her parent's lab. "Being horrible is probably in my DNA. And I've never known why he stuck around me anyway. Why any of you do now."

Warden Steph left her stool and stood next to Warden Mina. She placed her hands on either side of the other Warden's face, turning her head toward Warden Steph. Comp2876 had not moved after the scan and was afraid to now. 2876 watched Warden Steph lean in, barely registering a hushed "I know why I'm here" before the two Wardens shared a kiss.

Pings went up around the nearby framework as 2876's data filtered out. It frantically shut down the communications before the information spread to the entire swarm. There was no need for gossiping Comps to bother Nek.

As the two Wardens parted, a smiling Warden Mina looked up at Warden Steph. "I, um, hmmm. Well. I'd been meaning to ask…"

2876 removed itself from the workshop via a low tunnel in the wall, neither Warden noticed its departure. The team was officially all accounted for. While they all carried their share of worries, the task was complete for the time being. Comp2876 could select other work to distract itself. Perhaps somewhere on the other side of Outrider. To keep itself from hovering or bothering the three left onboard. Something needed to be dusted, surely.

3

Now Who's This Guy?

There hadn't been noise from Capri's room in a while, which made Gregory anxious. Maxwell maintained his argument for keeping her fully comatose, but Gregory elected to remove the sedatives they'd been gassing her with that morning. His thinking was that they'd given her plenty of opportunities to burn off the rage from losing her Pak since returning to the base. She had to be more level headed by now. He checked the newly reinstalled feed, the fifth replacement in the last handful of days, nestled in a corner of her room. Capri's deep breathing confirmed that for the time being she remained unconscious on her cot. Balled up under the single thin blanket she used. Gregory knew the base was cold for her kind. Without that suit regulating her temperature, she had to feel that now. Perhaps he'd send a Pawn through the vent with yards of fabric off the walls in the suite, that would be an actual good use for the material.

His next thought was questioning why he cared. Good karma, he settled on. The hope that someone would do the same for him, if he ever lost his mind and fell into such a fit. He moved the feed to inspect her side of the door. There were no new marks. She'd stopped throwing things, herself included. Only items that were too heavy for her to lift, or too sturdy to break, sans the suit remained. Leaving only the larger cabinets that were bolted to the wall, and the workstation set in the middle of the room untouched. He'd watched her almost smash the workstation a time or two, but she always held off. Even Capri at the height of her fury couldn't destroy the data she'd stored there. The cot was the only outlier, which he wrote off as a primal survival instinct.

"Who's Councilor Aldrich?" Maxwell called over from his side of their floor. Why he preferred yelling to using the convenient voice channels, Gregory had yet to understand.

"A stranger to me," he responded through said channel, to prove a point. "Why do you ask?"

Maxwell again shouted across the way, "Look at your tablet."

Gregory grabbed the device and muttered, "Can never simply answer a question."

A notice flashed brightly in his messages. **Councilor Aldrich will arrive within the hour.**

So kind of them to send any word ahead. There'd been radio silence since responding to the check-in weeks ago. They'd requested assistance for the situation developing around the re-activated Outrider and its new Wardens, as well as guidance regarding their house-guest. Their only previous response was an automated message stating their inquiry was received. There was no hope of putting together any sort of grand welcome, but at least they didn't need to worry about the suite being in good standing. The base on a whole was in better shape since Capri got the maintenance crew moving. They'd kept working as she ranted and raved in her room. Mostly because Maxwell threatened to feed them to Capri if they were caught dawdling.

"I assumed they'd send Reggie or Vic," Maxwell said, now standing in Gregory's doorway, scrolling on his own tablet. "You know, a pushover like us."

"Might be someone new. Easily convinced this was an exciting opportunity." Gregory pulled up the directory, tapping through to Councilor Aldrich's listing. The first item that caught his interest was the title "Acquisitions" under his name. "Oh. He's a salesman."

"They're liquidating us?" Maxwell sounded hopeful.

"No, he mostly handles Non-Lenian materials." Gregory scanned the footnotes of recent deals highlighted on the Councilor's profile. "Sold an Empyrean Warp Drive to Mooneaters. Not sure what they'll do with that. Middleman'd a trade of Gear Grinders for half a swarm of stripped Comps. Poor trade, but not my business. His biggest deal was auctioning off a patchwork Guardian. Wonder who he stole that from initially."

"Ohhhh, he's here to liquidate them."

"Seems so." Gregory put the tablet down and turned to Maxwell. "How annoying do you think this will be?"

"Very." Maxwell tipped his head toward the Capri feed. "Think he'll have any interest in her?"

"Do people buy people these days? Feels gauche."

"What if he somehow gets the Collective gear off those kids? Then bundled her in as a team leader for the highest bidder. Or maybe a trainer."

"No one would go for that," Gregory scoffed.

"I'm trying to keep your pet alive."

"She's not–" Gregory stopped himself from shouting. "She's struggling. Her entire identity was stolen from her. By a teenager."

"And to think it was all for nothing," Maxwell replied. "She doesn't know her order is already long dead."

"Yes. That." The true conversation he was avoiding. The one he fully intended to send up the chain to this Councilor Aldrich as it would likely result in another act of violence from Capri. Gregory stood and stretched. "We should probably get food prepared."

* * *

They fell into a brief tiff over the tone of the lighting while waiting for Councilor Aldrich's transport ship to dock. Maxwell was insisting Gregory wanted to make him look sickly.

"You know that warm lighting makes me look like basic gold," he huffed.

"We can't rob the Councilor of your buttery highlights." Gregory rolled his eyes. "You know I don't care about the lighting enough to mess with it."

Maxwell scrunched his nose as he nudged the dial. "Well, if only all of us were lucky enough to be made emerald."

"If only."

The maintenance crew, aggressively buffed at the last minute so their navy blue shone, lifted trays of finger foods as the doors smoothly pulled open. Their shorter stature put the goods within easy reach. The Councilor's polished violet body gleamed in the now cool light of the walkway. Lenians were typically broad chested, but this Councilor was even more so. Gregory was unsurprised to see he'd opted for adornments. Lines of spikes ran across both shoulders and down the length of his arms. One on the front, one on the back, and one down the middle. Another set started at his waist and trailed down to his feet, the same configuration of a line on the front and back, with the final strip down the outside. There was a spiral pattern covering his chest. Gregory wasn't familiar with that modification's function. Gregory traced a thin line from the spiral over to the Councilor's right arm that traveled down to the side of his hand. A shiny patch laid on the side of Aldrich's pointer finger. He suspected this was a trigger of some kind. Must be a newer trend. They were behind on news from home out here. Aldrich also carried a satchel with him, made of a rough plastic fiber that withstood the spikes. He appeared unbothered by the slight scratching sound their contact made as he moved.

The Councilor glanced over his shoulder, eyeing Capri's escape pod joined to the scouting ship on the far side of the bay. "A unique design."

"A product of our guest's madness," Maxwell said with a smile. He, thankfully, omitted the few dozen idle hours both engineers spent on the project recently. There'd been nothing better to do without another Capri scheme to enact.

"For sale?"

"You'll have to ask her. If you can get a full sentence out of her."

Councilor Aldrich plucked a freshly burnt piece of sourdough bread from the tray and scooped a bite of the oily dressing they enjoyed from Earth.

The pair watched him pop the entire piece in his mouth. He gave the tray an approving glance as he continued through the base. He paid no mind to the wall sections in need of buffing or any of the doors seized open in the absence of new gears. Gregory couldn't remember which one of them was supposed to be crafting those—probably Maxwell, the oaf. The engineers stayed back, keeping the crew in front of them, allowing the Councilor to reach for more snacks as they came to the center of the base.

Councilor Aldrich gathered the remaining small bites on one tray, stepped inside the elevator car, and shut the grate to the rest of them. He happily chewed as the cage rattled and carried him up. The engineers shared a glance before climbing the stairs. Maxwell sent the crew off to fetch more snacks. The elevator stopped on their floor. The Councilor stepped out and headed for Gregory's workroom. He quietly cursed as he remembered leaving his system unlocked when they left to prepare the food. Once the Councilor was out of sight, he shoved his way around Maxwell to take the remaining stairs two at a time.

"Leave something lewd out?" Maxwell called after him, not feeling any need to pick up the pace.

Gregory dashed the last few floors, only halting steps away from the doorway to catch his breath. Allowing him to glide into the room. The Councilor idly swiped through designs on his workstation. Crumbs covered the console. He'd need to use precision tools to clean the seams later.

"These are interesting," Councilor Aldrich said without looking up. "What's your turnaround time?"

"Depends on the scaling."

"Full."

"Two days, maybe three for the more complicated designs or last-minute alterations."

"Impressive, being only the two of you."

"Maxwell is rather skilled at," he stumbled over the compliment as it left his mouth, "efficiency on the production line."

"Such kind words." Maxwell stood in the doorway, of course arriving in time to hear. "He flatters me."

Gregory glared as Maxwell made no effort to return him a compliment.

Councilor Aldrich tapped away, setting the now empty tray on top of the mechanism Gregory had been working on earlier. He gave no design more than a second or two of consideration before swiping to the next. His face showed no clear indication of which, if any, of the creations impressed him. Aldrich scrolled long enough to find Gregory's birds. This batch received a raise of an eyebrow. The selection was rather extensive. For all the failings of the planet they were stuck monitoring, there was a wonderful array of avian life that Gregory found fascinating. Given the amount of free time they'd enjoyed until recently, he'd perfected several models.

The Councilor expanded schematics up from the table. A red-tailed hawk, a raven, and a blue jay fluttered and stretched. He added Gregory's favorite version of field sparrows; a non-anatomical, overly round adaptation that Gregory had made for his own entertainment. They'd been designed for annoying Maxwell, engineered to burst when batted away and cover the victim in whatever material was stuffed inside. Councilor Aldrich watched the birds as the engineers watched him. He finally broke his eyes away from the table. "What exactly do these do?"

"Nothing," Maxwell answered automatically.

"Design studies," Gregory attempted to cover for himself, as Maxwell was being extremely unreliable. "A crafting exercise from when we first arrived."

Councilor Aldrich watched the birds hop about, gave a small laugh, and left the workroom. Gregory expected him to head for Maxwell's workshop, disturb his belongings next, but the Councilor stepped into the elevator and crawled upward again. For the entire one floor he needed to reach Capri's room.

As they climbed to the next floor, the Councilor observed the Comps pacing outside her welded doorway. They'd been charging themselves off the escape pod in turns to maintain a watch. Gregory supposed that even without the Pak, Capri's expert programming kept the Comps loyal to her.

Councilor Aldrich reached inside his bag and pulled out a small, foldable handheld to photograph the Comps. "People love vintage designs these days."

Gregory felt a little perturbed he'd not taken pictures of his birds.

The Councilor pointed to the welds. "I need those cut."

"She's not in any state," Maxwell began.

"We have communications established in our workshops," Gregory continued.

"You can mute the insults and obscenities."

"And she can't throw things at you."

The Councilor stood waiting. They stood waiting. He leaned on the welded door, intently checking messages on his handheld. Gregory tipped over the side railing, spied the maintenance crew near the bottom with their new arrangement of snacks. "Get your saws. We need this doorway opened immediately."

The crew set the trays on the steps and hurried off for their tools.

"Oh," the Councilor sighed, "is there no more finger foods?"

Maxwell gave a tight smile and started down the stairs for the abandoned trays. "Allow me."

* * *

As the crew cut the last weld, Gregory realized he and Maxwell had retreated to the other side of the floor. While the Councilor stood right in front of the door.

"She'll strangle him with that bag strap within a minute," Maxwell whispered.

"I know."

"How are we supposed to explain a dead Councilor?"

"I don't know."

The crew finished and retreated in a rush. The Comps stopped their pacing, their attention now also locked on the door. Councilor Aldrich grabbed the edge of her sliding door and pulled it aside. Other than the sound of metal grinding, nothing happened.

Gregory edged closer. The in-person view of the room was worse than the cameras. Food scraps and shredded clothing mixed with shards of tables and machinery. She'd been thorough in her destruction. Surprising, given how Capri seemed to take pride in her quarters previously. He risked taking a few steps closer to see around Councilor Aldrich and the workstation.

The cot was empty.

He'd been about to state that fact when the Councilor stepped inside the room. A scream came from the right, the corner they couldn't see from the hall, and a blur rushed Aldrich.

They disappeared on the other side of the doorway. The Councilor's bag flew off his shoulder and fell to the floor. *Well,* Gregory thought as he rushed in, *at least she can't strangle him that way.*

Aldrich was against the wall, both hands around Capri's neck to keep her away. Capri looked wild as she clawed at his arms. Aldrich was also fairly wide-eyed at the moment. Her hands pounded away on those spikes. Gregory could see she was only hurting herself. She kicked at his legs and shredded the bottom of her shoes. The Comps raced by him, their small blasters drawn. Gregory thought to grab one out of the air. They couldn't let her kill a Councilor. Not within the first hour of him arriving.

Aldrich shifted his right hand, losing inches to Capri as she lunged forward again, and ran his thumb along that smooth trigger set along his pointer finger. The spiral on Aldrich's chest bloomed with green light, the glow looped around and around until the light covered the entire pattern. The spiral pulsed, energy sparked across the center row of the Councilor's spikes, and a wall of force shot across the room. Throwing Capri into the corner she'd attacked from.

The engineers also fell from the impact. Static covered Gregory's vision, but he heard two thumps nearby, which he believed were the Comps falling. He sat up as his eyes cleared. Aldrich stood, now observing the unconscious Capri across the room, appearing rather pleased with himself.

Councilor Aldrich turned to them, smiling widely. "Neat little package I received as a gift from the Empyre. Mix of an EMP and concussive force. Allows you to fend off organic and nonorganic types."

"Do you, um, often deal with assailants?" Maxwell asked as the pair stepped inside her room.

"When people know what they have, they like to play hardball. Some play dirty." He scrutinized Capri. "Feral thing, isn't she?"

"Yes," both engineers answered. Gregory eyed the smears of blood across Aldrich's arms.

"Your report claims she's from the original exploration team. Has that been confirmed?"

"She prattles on about the Collective like someone who doesn't know they're a joke," Maxwell said.

"Some factions are rather sanctimonious, but being such they would have made a fuss over sending forces this way. Which I certainly would have heard about." Councilor Aldrich tapped Capri with a cautious foot to ensure she'd become incapacitated. "I'm willing to believe she's legitimate. That temperament could be an issue though."

"Capri has been generally hostile," Gregory answered before Maxwell could. "The loss of her Pak has escalated her violent tendencies as of late."

"Believe she can be reasoned with?" Aldrich leaned over and grabbed one of Capri's wrists, giving her arm a soft shake.

"Compromise is difficult, but not impossible."

"If you don't mind all the threats," Maxwell added.

When she didn't respond to the prodding, Aldrich dragged her over to the workstation. After a few tries he found a non-damaged fingerprint to press into the sensor. He draped her limp body onto the cot. Gregory was surprised he didn't drop her like the food tray, but the Councilor was actively estimating how much she was worth to him. No need to scuff her up more than she already was.

Her workstation came alive with the data she'd gathered about the team currently in possession of the Paks and Outrider. Once again, the Councilor flipped through files without saying a word. Clips from their few fights over the past weeks played along the top. Gregory tried to interject about mind control capabilities when the schematic for their Mock Pak appeared, but the Councilor wasn't listening and scrolled away.

Maxwell had been taking a stab at explaining the purpose of Pawns crafted to fall apart when Councilor Aldrich went still. Gregory was trying to figure out what about the footage from their dual monster fight was displeasing when the Councilor snapped back into action. He clapped and pointed at both of them. "Are those birds weaponized?"

"Not the active models," Gregory answered. "Though we could upload Pawn programming to make them more aggressive."

"Do that. Get some of the bigger ones on the production line and put in weapons where you can. I want to be on that planet as soon as possible."

"You're going to attack?" Maxwell asked. "With birds?"

"I want to see this team work in person." He hunched over the workstation, focused back to his scrolling, Aldrich was finished with the engineers now that he'd given orders.

While that hadn't been a direct answer to the question, they let the matter go and left.

Maxwell led them down the staircase to their floor. "We called for aid."

"Yes."

"A Councilor arrived to deal with the situation."

"Yes."

"We're again being made to send creations after those children."

"Yes."

"Those creations now being your damn birds."

Gregory smiled at that one. "Yes."

4

Hold on to Your Mugs

Mina thought she enjoyed the current song the band was playing. There was a lot going on, which left little mental room for picking out lyrics over the shouting crowd who already knew them. Steph had been very excited about them playing at the cafe. Mina tried learning their songs beforehand, but outside of teasers used on socials to announce a forthcoming EP, they had yet to release anything. Clips from other live shows did little to help her. One of those videos turned out to be them playing while the whole "disappearing mountain" situation kicked off and she'd fallen down a rabbit hole of watching different angles from people who'd been filming. At the time being inside Outrider felt dangerous, but turned out they'd been safer than anyone else in the area.

A poke in her side. Zane pointed to the stage before once again clapping along with the song. He'd taken up a spot along the back wall with her when he arrived, but they hadn't gotten the chance to talk yet.

No one used the group chat yesterday, outside of them trading funny videos. Steph insisted giving them the day wasn't the worst idea, as there was no active threat. Mina reluctantly agreed and worked on her Lockpuck. There were small tweaks she wanted to make after seeing the completed prototype. She'd also kissed Steph another time or two while waiting for parts to print. Both activities helped distract her.

34

She'd thought they'd talk this morning, at the latest on the drive over here for the show, but Zane had texted that he was running errands for his parents and would meet her there. His mom sending him to do runaround chores wasn't surprising, but him not bringing her along for the company was. Mina had watched his Pak's signal bounce around town without her, so at least he hadn't lied.

Mina feared that Capri's drive was going to be too much for him. For all of them. When Mina got to the cafe, the first time she'd felt unhappy to teleport, Sean and Steph were stationed at the front counter. Steph smiled and waved. Sean gave her a wave too before going back to his drinks, but she saw none of his usual flourishes. While Steph snuck away for part of the show, she bounced and sang along on Mina's other side, Sean remained up front in what must be a nearly empty room. Henrie and Emma stood on the ramp, bobbing their heads along with the songs. They'd come in from the balcony side right before the set started. Emma had spotted them, but Henrie wouldn't even glance their way and the pair made no effort to reach them.

It's normal to have alone time with your girlfriend, Mina thought. *Calm down.*

She gave a look to Steph, now jumping to what must be her favorite song, before glancing at Zane again. There hadn't been a chance for her to tell him about the kissing, and she wanted to do that in person. Zane caught her wandering attention and pointed to the stage, wiggling his shoulders to pull her back into the moment. She gave the tiniest wiggle in return, barely more than a shrug, simply happy to receive any kind of communication from him. He shimmied harder. She hitched her shoulders a little higher. His brow furrowed, and he aggressively shook in her direction. Mina laughed and retreated, backing herself into Steph on accident. She turned to apologize, but saw Steph was laughing at Zane too.

"What's got into him?" Steph asked.

Mina pointed down. "He wants me to dance, but my feet don't work."

"What?"

"I have two left feet. They don't move very well."

"You can't move your feet?" Steph turned Mina, making them face each other, and her hands grasping Mina's arms at the elbows. "Super easy. You find the beat and move on it."

"Move what and where?"

Steph gave an exasperated look to Zane over Mina's shoulder. "Okay. When I move one foot, you move the matching one. Got it?"

"Theoretically."

Steph shuffled her left foot back, Mina pushed her right foot forward. When Steph moved forward, Mina moved hers back again. They repeated the step with their other feet. After a few rotations, Steph slid her hands down Mina's arms until they were holding hands. As they continued the pattern, Steph pulled gently to twist them from side to side. They continued around in a circle. She caught sight of Emma filming them from the ramp. Far too soon, the song ended and Steph released her to cheer for the band. Mina retreated to her spot along the wall. Zane looked rather pleased, clapping toward her as the crowd carried on.

Maybe they would all be fine and she was panicking for nothing.

The lead singer smiled and waited for the crowd to calm down. "Thank you so much, Restoration Cafe! We are having a blast here with you today. We got a couple more songs for y–"

A shape buzzed over them from the higher floor. Mina thought someone had thrown a ball down, for an unknown reason, but the round thing swooped around the stage on tiny, furiously flapping wings. The small creature disappeared back into the level above.

The lead singer laughed and pointed up to the balcony, where the doors had been propped open because of the good weather. "Watch your heads! Looks like we got a bird in here."

There was a gasp as the bird reappeared. The way the stage lights glinted off the feathers felt wrong. Mina knew that shouldn't be happening. They all watched the little bird fly through the archway to the front room, where they heard more surprised yelps. A burst of nervous laughter came from the crowd.

The lead singer joined in. "Hopefully someone can catch–"

There was a bang similar to a large firecracker from the front. Shouts came from that direction. People near the archway began moving away from or toward the noise, including Emma and Henrie who were now working their way down the ramp.

Nek spun on Mina's watch. "Warden Sean was hit."

Mina saw Emma begin to shove her way through the crowd.

"Evil bird," came Sean's voice from the watch now, "blew up over the bar."

"I'm coming," Emma said.

"Bird bombs?" Steph asked. "Seriously?"

Mina saw each of their watches flash white, she hoped no one else caught that. Nek coiled into a tight ball. "Lenian creation confirmed."

"Nooooo." Steph stared longingly at the band.

Louder clamoring came from above them as more bomber birds flitted about the room. She watched three land on the rigging for the stage lighting, their tiny heads jerked side to side. Sean was out in the open at the bar. Maybe these tiny monsters couldn't pick them out in a crowd. Larger creations flew in near the ceiling and circled the performance area. Mina held little hope that the metallic hawk wouldn't spot them. And because she'd thought it, the hawk's eyes blazed a bright yellow before it screeched in her exact direction.

'Everything will be fine' was officially on her Do Not Say or Think List.

She grabbed for Zane and reclaimed one of Steph's hands. "We have to move. Now!"

They needed their suits, but couldn't activate the Paks while in the middle of everyone. There was a double door emergency exit on the side of the performance area. She pushed Steph in that direction. If they got outside, they could find somewhere secluded to suit up. People ahead of them slammed their way through the door, setting off the alarm through the entire cafe. The crowd surged toward the open exit. There was a second screech before claws dug into her outstretched arm holding Zane's shirt. She turned back to see her arm now sported several bleeding scratches and a retractable pair of feet returning to the hawk via chains.

The little ones were bombs and this one, she hoped it was only this one, included grapple feet. Capri had finally sent fresh trouble their way. They'd wondered when she might attack them directly now that she knew their names. Mina was shocked she'd held off this long, but thought it strange she hadn't seen any Pawns joining the fight yet.

Two small creations exploded while on the rigging, sending sparks over people's heads as the lighting popped next. The crowd scattered in different directions. Either out the side door, toward the front, or up to the balcony exit. She saw a Lenian bird dive over Emma and Henrie's heads. The creation hit the wall and exploded there. Broken plaster flew and dust fogged the air on that side of the room. Emma and Henrie kept pushing for the archway. They'd get Sean and hopefully get out of here, too.

Steph pulled them toward the emergency exit, but stopped as a bomber bird popped directly overhead. Bits of metal rained down around them, peppering Mina's newly acquired wounds with painful shards. Her hand slipped from Zane's shirt. She turned back, surprised that Zane had disappeared from her side. She spotted him with a grapple foot latched onto his shoulder, he was being reeled in by the hawk. Or more so, held in place, given the strain he was showing. In the midst of the tug of war the hawk's other foot shot out towards Zane's side, right where his Pak remained hidden.

Capri wasn't only after her own Pak. Mina hunched over her watch, hoping the general chaos would keep people from noticing her. "Watch your Paks, the hawks are grabby."

Aid incoming! Scrolled across the watch face from Comp2876.

"No," she hissed at the watch. "Stay put for now." If Capri was out to steal, Mina wanted to avoid putting Comps on the ground. No need to give her more to use against them. Mina lunged back toward Zane, but both Steph and the crowd pulled her farther away.

"Why?" Henrie came through the watch. "We could use–"

Screeching in the front room cut her off. Sounds of broken glass overtook her words, but Henrie didn't try repeating herself.

Mina tugged Steph toward Zane, but the crowd filled in between them and pushed the two girls closer to the exit door. She fought against the tide of people while watching him pull both claws off himself. The chained feet retracted to the hawk, which then screeched and dove for him.

"Zane!" she shouted.

He flung himself toward the ramp at the last second. The hawk crashed into the wall and fell to the floor. The crowd kept pulling her away as they all scrambled for the door. She let go of Steph in her efforts to get back to him.

"Get outside!" he yelled. Zane jumped over the low wall behind him. His voice came through the watch as he started up the ramp. "I'll find you out there."

Mina felt a swell of pride at seeing her friend so comfortable in such a tight spot. As Steph grabbed her hand again Mina tried to relocate Emma and Henrie, but they'd disappeared into the other room. She watched a bomber bird explode in the archway and a Lenian raven screeched as it flew across the portion of the front room Mina could see.

Steph pushed harder toward the emergency exit. Mina saw the glow of Steph's Pak inside the pocket she'd stashed it in. They were all desperate to get their suits on. As they reached the door, a screech pulled her attention. The hawk was back in the air, eyes flashing as it set about finding them again. They spilled out into the alleyway. The crowd carried them toward the rear of the cafe. Mina pulled Steph under the staircase and balcony supports. Everyone else ran on into the street or down the sidewalk, wanting farther away from the birds. She could see more circled high above. They pressed as far back into the space as they could.

"Nek, do we seem clear?" Mina asked.

They remained a tight ball on the watch. "As clear as possible."

Mina and Steph activated their suits. As their teal and purple bands rolled out, they each materialized their preferred weapons–dual blasters and a charged saber.

The pair ran out into the thinning crowd. Steph started for the emergency exit, but Mina stayed put. She wanted to find Zane first. A crash came from the staircase behind them as her best friend tumbled down the last steps, a Lenian blue jay repeatedly pecking at his head. She felt uneasy about how much red had soaked through his shirt.

A program running on Mina's heads-up display targeted the bird, making for an easy shot to put the tiny monster down. The Lenian creation briefly sputtered on the ground between them. She grabbed his arm and whispered, "Are you okay?"

He took a large breath in to steady himself. "I want my suit."

Steph gave a small wave to the alcove. He caught the meaning and slipped by them.

Mina examined the bird again. She'd assumed they'd used colored metal on these newer designs, but that was wrong, at least for this blue jay. The fragments at her feet were the standard shining Lenian metal painted to match a real blue jay's coloring. Which made even less sense.

Zane's Pak activation came across her system. He rejoined them and their trio headed for the cafe. The thinning crowd moved around them. Several stumbled to a stop at seeing Wardens charging down the alley. Mina sidestepped a woman being pulled away by another woman and heard a faint "I wanna see" as they reentered Restoration.

The performance area was nearly empty, but there were sounds of a struggle still coming from the front. People were shouting for others to duck and watch out, followed by what sounded like chairs being thrown across the room. She couldn't tell if a person had done that to fend off a bird or if the birds themselves were tossing the place. Steph immediately sent a saber bolt toward the circling bomber birds near the ceiling above them, slicing three clean in half. As well as leaving a burn mark from the combo of her bolt energy and their small explosives.

Steph cringed. "Oops."

Mina shrugged as she targeted the hawk, whose yellow eyes were on her again. "Mitch will think the mark adds character."

The hawk's head peeled back as it dove, revealing a very familiar Pawn blaster. Seemed unfair that the hawk had two things. The Lenian creation shot on her as she jumped to the side and shot back wildly, her targeting thrown off by the sudden movement. Steph swung as the small monster neared, clipping a wing and sending the bird spinning. The hawk avoided crashing, instead landing on the stage and continuing to fire at them. Zane's mace flew through the air and smashed into the creation. The firing ceased as the crushed body became pinned to an amp.

"Why birds?" Zane asked while recalling the mace to his hand. Bits of Lenian metal broke and scattered as his weapon returned to him.

"Maybe Capri discovered Hitchcock?" Steph suggested.

A batch of bomber birds fluttered in from the higher level. Mina popped two out of the air. Steph scattered the rest of the flock with another charged bolt, but also burned art along the wall.

Mina scrunched up her shoulders. "That one Mitch might get mad about."

Zane took a batting stance and knocked a bomber away, making it explode high in the air. He caught a larger piece as the debris fell. "Next question. Why did she have them painted?"

"That's what I was wondering!" Mina was glad someone else noticed. She headed for the front room, but stopped when she caught movement beside the stage, fearing the hawk was somehow continuing its crusade against them. Instead she found the band huddled behind their gear crates. She lowered her blasters, not wanting to scare them any further. "Oh, hello."

The drummer waved, the rest continued to stare. The bass guitarist was blinking hard at the dormant hawk stuck in their ruined amp. She hoped the band could afford to replace that.

Mina picked off a bomber bird coming in on her side. "Sorry about your show. We, uh, heard you were good."

"Th-thanks," the singer replied.

"If you want to run, you should be good now."

Their group dashed for the emergency exit, Steph gave a small wave as they went. Zane also found people stowed away in the storage room. They all bolted for the door and left the Wardens alone in the performance area. Which they immediately left for the front room, the remaining Lenian birds close behind.

While the front was originally near empty when the attack started, a scattering of the people who'd run that way were still crouched beneath tables. The normally meticulous drink bar was in ruins. Perched over the door, the raven opened its beak and let out an ear-splitting screech. A window pane cracked, turning into a giant spider web suspended within the frame. From behind the bar came a flying caramel drizzle bottle that clipped the raven and stopped the aggravating sound. The raven took off for a new place to perch.

Mina stepped around the bar and found her other teammates pressed into the corner. Emma looked scratched up the same as Mina, as well as sporting a chunk of braids harshly cut shorter than the rest. One creation must have clipped them during a dive. Henrie had a series of marks that matched Zane's pecking. Sean was in the roughest shape. There was a gash down his front. That first bomber bird must have blown nearly on top of him. They were all splattered with a mix of different drink ingredients, garnishes, and tiny bits of broken mugs.

"No Comps?" Henrie asked, her judgment clear.

"Not now. Please." Mina needed the critique to wait for later. Because she was busy shooting birds and making sure they all got to later.

Steph and Zane helped the last few civilians out from under tables and got them going for the door. The raven landed on a trashcan in the corner and aimed for them, but Mina put a series of shots into the monster. The body fell into the bag below. Once outside people dove into cars and left, rapidly emptying the parking lot. No one wanted to stick around for more avian chaos.

She eyed Sean's bleeding chest again. "Be honest. How bad is that?"

"Looks worse than it is, promise," he said while grimacing. "Meds will have me buttoned up in no time."

"Don't move, dummy." Emma went to shove her cousin out of habit, but held off as he winced in pain. Her attention turned to the ground, where three severed lengths of braided hair were scattered at her feet. Her hand instantly found the matching cut braids on her head. "These were new."

"Could get a small batch of a fun color," Henrie said. "Wouldn't even take too long to put in."

Emma smiled. "Sounds like a date."

Sean groaned, "These two flirting has been worse than the bleeding."

Mina watched the last person decide to leap through a broken out window rather than get to the door. Steph sent a bolt toward the performance area to scatter the small flock that were gathered in the archway. Three popped from the hit and took the rest as a chain reaction. Plaster rained down as more of the archway crumbled. She feared what this place would look like by the end of their fight. Zane pinned a blue jay to the wall with prongs off his mace. This was their weirdest fight yet.

"We're clear. Sean, suit up for the healing help, but stay down if you need to. We can handle the birds," Mina said.

"No way." Sean pulled on a shelf to help get to his feet. "I want revenge for my bar."

The three of them activated their suits. Emma wasted little time by jumping over the counter and landing a kick on a low-flying bomber bird as it went by.

Henrie helped Sean the rest of the way up. "Shouldn't be too hard, since they're coming for us anyway. Like a shooting gallery."

Sean pointed out to the parking lot. "I think Mina is going to count that as saying easy."

Outside, the air had taken on that familiar wavy appearance. The force of the Lenian teleport pushed the few remaining cars farther away in the lot. A figure came into shape in the center, one Mina quickly determined was not Capri. Too short. Too wide as well. They were solidly built. Well, maybe. Hard to be sure, because Mina thought they could be wearing armor. Purple armor. Everywhere. They also carried a messenger bag slung over their shoulder. Maybe this was a door-to-door salesman knight. The remaining Lenian creations flew past them to circle around the new arrival, who appeared to be patiently waiting for them instead of making their own attack.

"Lenian," Henrie said as she hopped over the counter.

"Hold on," Mina called after her. "Give us two seconds to plan something."

"Do what you want," Henrie called back as she headed for one of the broken windows. "I'm going to actually get something done around here."

5

Taking Inventory

Aldrich set his pack on the ground. No need to jostle his belongings around more than necessary. He pulled his handheld and recorder out. With these he could dictate and document as he observed and, with luck, negotiate a deal. The spherical recorder hovered above his hand until he locked it into position over his left shoulder.

Rather unfortunate that the flying creations hadn't retrieved even one Pak. That was the main reason he'd let them fuss about for so long unattended, hoping the Wardens had been sufficiently surprised. Dealings going forward would have been so much simpler if he'd gotten his hands on one. He'd planned on threatening them with returning the Pak to Capri to make them more agreeable to his other offers. Aldrich was certain no one wanted that mad relic with one of those in hand again. Once they'd all activated, he threw that proposal in the trash and redirected to hoping these makeshift Wardens could be bought. He'd brought in enough deals this year, these last two decades for sure, that the Higher Committee would swing him the funds to satisfy this lot. From his small observations of the region, their idea of wealth would come in far below the expectations of some of his other clients. All the same, a shame to pay for what could have been free.

On his expedited voyage in, Aldrich had chastised himself for not digging the Collective ship up a hundred years ago when a scout first pinged the anomaly, but he hadn't held the sway he did now. He'd been too new to the battlefield that was galactic arms dealing. There had been no way of knowing if the thing would even power on after sitting dormant and buried for four hundred years. It was a gamble, but nonetheless he marked the planet for observation and prepared a presentation for the day it became worthwhile to mine the area. The meddling humans had saved him a large sum in recovery costs. He'd keep that in consideration, were they willing to make a deal.

A Warden stepped through a broken windowpane. The rose pink stripe along their suit glinted in the sunlight. He'd spent a short time committing their names, faces, and unique coloring to memory. Personal touches often won you favor. Pink meant this one was Henrie, the one who'd taken Capri's Pak. His research estimated she wouldn't be the best to reason with. That aside, while she was approaching rather authoritatively, she wasn't the leader here.

He tilted toward the recorder as he watched her rapid approach. "Suits appear to be in rather pristine condition. No sign of dematerializing because of faulty Suitor Protocols. Also no sign of wear from overly long activation or delayed repairs."

The rest of the team were jogging to catch up. Blue-Mina, the leader he wanted to see, trailed behind Henrie. Silver-Emma flanked her other side. Green-Zane and Purple-Steph walked on either side of Orange-Sean, who stumbled a little as they struggled to keep up. Aldrich recalled the injury he'd observed the first bird inflict, a nasty hit indeed. Only a few inches higher and the Warden would've been incapacitated and…he was getting distracted by 'what ifs' again. Aldrich needed to focus on the deal at hand.

That injury did make him wonder if the suits were self-sanitizing or required special care. He'd never come across cleaning instructions in his years of acquisitions. There must be someone on his contact list he could ask.

Several of the approaching Wardens held weapons. He'd earmarked footage of them in use during previous altercations, but held off making comments. He'd wanted to be onsite to confirm their craftsmanship. Plenty of colleagues in the past were hoodwinked over "Collective crafted goods" to find their lots were nothing more than bits and bobs thrown together from refuse piles. Any faction worth the time of day possessed a small number of Fabricators, the smart ones sold usage of the system to melt down anyone's scrap into new goods. They could all make items that imitated the originals. Collective materials—those alloys which crafted the Guardians, the suits, and their ship—could not be mimicked. They remained proprietary even in this day and age, and the supply grew increasingly scarce ever since the demolition of the Collective homeworlds. Traditionally crafted pieces were heavily guarded, but his colleagues were always on the hunt for a faction desperate enough to make a trade.

If this deal went poorly–badly enough that the ship came down again–he could make his investment back several times over with the material goods alone. Aldrich forced himself to stop running the numbers because Henrie was closing in fast.

Emma's Pak glowed, releasing particulate material that formed into a pair of gauntlets around her hands. She shook them once and Aldrich saw sliding mechanisms set themselves into place along her knuckles.

"Weapon load-out protocols confirmed in good standing. Team has crafted individual armaments. Need to compare these with the known catalog and update listing details." Anything exceptionally unique was dollars he could add to his take.

Henrie never released a weapon, but activated enhancements to pick up speed on her final approach. She launched herself a good few feet off the ground; he believed going for a cranial attack. Aldrich pushed his bag further away as he dodged to the left.

"Boosting is fully functional. Wonderful bonus."

"Get off our planet, Lenian." Henrie kicked out, aiming for his left thigh.

Aldrich caught her ankle and lifted the leg higher to inspect the boots. They integrated seamlessly with the suit. Genuine. For some unknown reason, when the internal materials started to wear from long activation, the boots were the first pieces to go. Many factions with active Paks were walking around in whatever footwear they could make best appear to blend with the Warden suits. "Personal assessment has confirmed the Paks are in grand condition."

"Who are you talking to?" Henrie jumped off her one foot, aiming a kick at his stomach.

Aldrich tossed her aside before the hit could land, sending the Warden to the ground. "Not you. Do mind the bag."

Mina stepped between them, her blasters aimed at his face. "What do you want?"

"A moment of your time." Aldrich bent his head to get a better view of the blasters. The casing was curved, smooth, and tapered down to the muzzle. Not the blocky utilitarian model that came during the war, because of the shorter Fabrication time. Or the "whatever is on hand" they typically pieced together these days. If the team made their own hand weapons, he couldn't be sure they hadn't tweaked these designs as well. "At first glance, blasters appear to be original. Note, compare known models used by Collective. Traditionalist factions will pay extra for Pre-Division. Especially if authentic. Little less for replication."

"What?" Mina lowered the blasters from his face.

"Oh, don't mind me. Notes for myself. Now, my understanding is you are the team leader."

"Y-yeah." She straightened her shoulders and tried to appear taller. "Yes. I am."

"Fantastic. I was hoping we could discuss—"

"Shoot him, Mina!" Henrie yelled as she made another run for Aldrich.

"No names!" Mina yelled back.

He turned enough to aim his chest toward Henrie and flicked the trigger along his finger. Releasing a small Disruption burst that pushed Henrie away and put a crackle of electricity in the air. The Pink Warden hit the ground rolling this time. Her system wouldn't short out from the hit, but he'd bought himself a brief window to get a word in.

Emma went for her, but looked back at Mina. "What are you doing?"

Aldrich turned back to the Warden leader, her blasters once again aimed at his face. "Might we step off somewhere private, Warden Mi–Blue?"

He figured it best to acknowledge her dislike of acknowledging their actual names. Using their coloring wasn't especially creative, but he personally preferred it to the call signs some of the other factions insisted on going by.

"I'm not going anywhere with you. Get off our planet."

If she wouldn't leave willingly, he'd have to get her alone by other means. He gave a small tap on the handheld to reset the birds to their Pawn programming. As the screeching started above, Aldrich tabbed over to his information graphics. "Might I show you some data?"

"I…um…what?" Mina became distracted by Zane and Sean being forced to separate as a pair of the smaller birds swooped between them and detonated. She spun back to Aldrich, changing her aim to the handheld. "Drop that. Now!"

He held his hands up, letting her see the screen. "The engineers made intriguing little creations this time, didn't they?"

"So you work for Capri too."

"No. She is a squatter that is being dealt with. I must say I find you impre…" He stopped because the Warden leader wasn't listening. Aldrich was not about to waste flattery on an inattentive audience.

Mina moved one blaster off him to shoot a set of birds keeping Emma and Henrie on the ground. Steph crossed over, helping them get on their feet. He observed Zane swing and release prongs from his mace into the air to fend off one of the larger birds. An unusual tactic. Aldrich was waiting to see what trick Sean pulled with his batons when the handheld exploded next to his face. The Warden leader had pulled her trigger while he'd been distracted. Destroying his presentation.

"Off. Our. Planet," she demanded again. One blaster remained trained on him as she continued to send shots at the flock with the other. Multitasking appeared to be a small skill of hers.

Aldrich might have come on a little too strong with this plan, but he was not one to give up on a deal so easily. He dropped the fragment of handheld to the ground, trying to avoid getting broken pieces in his bag, and smiled. "A simple discussion is all I–"

A gauntlet that glinted silver smashed into his jaw from the right, a second hit coming shortly after as the fist caught up. Emma landed another blow to his chest while he was bent over. She'd done him a favor with that second hit, knocking him back upright. Aldrich triggered a full Disruption. The wide pulse pushed the three Wardens away, notably sending Henrie to the ground for the third time. Her frustration with that fact was audible as she fell away. The move would lose him favor, but would momentarily shut them down and give him time to reassess.

The attack also pushed his bag away. Aldrich scolded himself for thinking that leaving his goods on the ground was a sound idea. Thankfully, a dazzling transport vehicle stopped the bag from flying too far. The vehicle's side appeared dented from force damage, but he believed it easily fixable. He set his bag on the front of the vehicle and tipped toward the recorder. "Research planetary transportation methods. Mark any suitable for other worlds. Plenty of eccentrics want something unique to go around in these days."

His eyes fell on the wheels which looked far too fragile. He tipped his head to the right, speaking for the first time to the comms sitting in that ear. "Engineers, research modifications for this wheel structure. They don't appear as if they could handle the rougher terrain of the wider universe."

"Will do," answered Maxwell.

The transport he was admiring rocked. The metal of the front door split in half. One side fell to the ground as the rest swung open on its hinges. Aldrich turned to see Steph brandishing a classic saber with the added bolt charges. "Note, Purple's weapon of choice will be kept as part of my finder's fee."

"Do you know we're fighting you?" Steph asked.

"You're performing adequately," Aldrich answered. "Might I ask, how fast is your charge time?"

"This fast." Steph gave the saber one spin around her fist, on the next spin she hurled a bolt toward the transport.

Aldrich watched the nose of the transport be sliced away, his bag miraculously untouched. He regretted losing the transport, but his pack was much more precious. Zane was helping the fallen to their feet. Sean twisted his batons to unleash a pair of blades and closed in. Aldrich stepped away from the transport to protect his belongings. Sean moved to remain facing him, but Aldrich noticed he wavered in keeping the weapons held at the ready. "Are the suit's medical functionalities activated?"

"I don't know wha–"

"Given that you're standing upright, I'm assuming yes. Can you tell me the level of numbing agent you have selected? Simple pain management or full dissociation? Those are the most common, from my research."

"I told you," Henrie shouted, "these suits could–"

"Please, not right now," the Warden leader cut her off. Mina was shaking her head clear from the Disruption wave.

Aldrich continued on with his conversation with Sean. "If you ask me, the truly bizarre ones are those that disable the feature entirely. What is their stupid mantra again? Pain is memory. Or something like that."

The remaining flock, now a pitiful few, held Mina's attention. Being a distance away, Aldrich counted the shots verse hits. The ratio spoke well of the targeting system. Steph also refocused on sending bolts toward the birds. The bounce-back would retrieve most of the creations. He hoped Gregory could get them back in working order quickly. Aldrich intended to send the survivors out as gifts for his eventual highest bidders.

He glanced over the Warden team, trying to determine if there was anything further he needed on this assessment. While this first attempt at negotiation was unsuccessful, his mental checklist remained rather well met. There'd be time for a follow up with the Warden leader, once he found a way to get her alone. Talk some reason into her.

Aldrich watched Zane and Sean cautiously move in on him with their mace and batons. He attempted to picture their faces behind those helmets, but became distracted by an extra detail for the initial package and tipped toward the recorder again. "No faction crest or markings on helmets. Clean surface ready for customization, if desired."

He'd offer having the engineers install any detailing the buyer wanted, for a small additional fee.

"I kind of miss Capri's insults," Sean said.

Zane nodded as they closed in. "At least she paid attention to us."

Aldrich realized he'd let himself get boxed in while assessing the helmets. Sean swung both batons high on Aldrich's left, while Zane went low with the mace on his right. The mace hit his lower leg, knocking him down to a knee. The batons hit his arm near the shoulder. The blades on the batons snagged on his spikes and the sudden pull brought his other leg down. Henrie appeared between the two and threw a knee into his face. His vision spun as he fell backward. Aldrich heard the loud smack of the recorder hitting pavement as it held position with him. No doubt the casing would be scuffed. If not cracked. That aggravated him. He could take a longer buff than usual tonight and be fine, but the recorders were delicate. His data could become corrupted.

Without moving from his prone position, he triggered another Disruption. The force pushed the surrounding Wardens away and gave him plenty of room to sit up. The other three were fighting the remaining flock. Emma had talons clawed into her shoulder, but had wrapped the chain around her spiked gauntlet and was pulling a hawk closer. He could see the charm in her weaponry choice and would highlight that in the pitch. Aldrich put a hand over the recorder and deactivated the device. He stood, stunned Wardens at his feet, and tilted toward the comms in his right ear. "Pickup, same mark."

"That's, um, that's all?" Gregory asked.

"You do," Maxwell said, "have a small upper hand right now."

"Pickup," Aldrich repeated as he stepped over to his bag and stuffed his recorder inside. He briefly considered leaving one of the offer packets he'd put together, but decided against it. They weren't in a receptive mood.

"Teleport incoming," Gregory said.

Aldrich casually walked to his needed location, watching the Wardens fight the last few birds. He could tell from the jerk of their heads when the Wardens got an alert for the teleport. Far delayed, from his estimation, but they wouldn't have the same level of frequency detection available on their ship. Easily updatable. He would have the engineers work up the expanded sensor arrays for those who didn't mind mixing their tech. For the purists, he would offer them schematics for a smaller fee.

The warmth of the teleport wrapped around him. The Warden team regrouped to watch him leave. Emma was holding Henrie back. How darling. A quick flash and he was gone, turning his mind to the bidding war he was about to ignite across the stars.

6

One Big Happy Spaceship

Mina watched as the destroyed Lenian birds disappeared from around the parking lot. One day she would figure out how they did that. For now, she was happy the fight was over and that Nek was moving them to Outrider. The pecking had been getting old, even with the suits protecting them. Trading blows with a MegaPawn felt dangerous, circling a parking lot with a blue jay was nothing more than embarrassing. Why did the new guy change from the status quo? Did they run out of Pawns? That would be a blessing. Or were the birds his specialty? Along with the appraisal talk and that blast move he kept using.

Her entire system had briefly gone offline. Once her head stopped spinning from the initial hit, the eeriness quickly took over. When you were used to programs running on the edges of your vision, it was unsettling to see nothing but tinted sky through your visor. She'd even become acutely aware that the tiny whir from the fan circulating air through her helmet was absent. Mina shook herself as they all landed on Outrider. A familiar and welcoming electrical hum surrounded her.

Comp2876 was waiting for them. *All Wardens to medbay! Please!*

As the team shuffled into the bay and dropped their suits, Mina realized she shouldn't discount the birds. They'd done a number on all of them. Her entire team spread across the room with Comp controlled Meds coming to mend them. Comp2876 floated down the main aisle, checking the seriousness of all their injuries. Nek hovered over Sean's bed. They insisted he'd be fine, but the Med was taking its time patching his chest.

Zane required a large amount of attention, his torso filled with small bandages covering the liquid stitches the Med had applied. He'd taken the bed next to her, but they still hadn't spoken much. Nobody had. She found it hard to start a conversation. Something was telling her that everyone, mainly Henrie, was mad at her for how the fight went. Even Steph, who sat on the bed across from Mina, could only muster a weak smile when they'd first come in. Henrie's mending was finished rather quickly, but she sat twisting the thin bed sheet into bunches on either side of herself. All the while alternating between glaring at the floor and Mina. She mentally begged someone else to talk first, but couldn't catch anyone's eye.

"I've never felt like such an object," Sean huffed from his bed.

"Must be nice," Steph said.

A sliver of the tension eased out of the room. Mina certainly breathed a little easier.

"Do you know who that was, Nek?" Zane asked.

Nek shifted from side to side on the panel. "Nothing in our records. Lenians live longer than many others because of their natural design, but five hundred years is beyond them."

"I think he was some kind of assessor," Mina said. "He was specing us."

"Is that why you wouldn't shoot?" Henrie asked. "He got you talking shop?"

"What? No. I mean." Mina's Med finished bandaging her arm and backed away, leaving her feeling exposed. "I mean, I did think keeping him talking would get us some intel."

"He show you something on that tablet? Offer you a new robot to play with?"

"No! He didn't show me anything. And I shot that tablet, if you didn't notice."

Henrie stood from her bed. "After he sicced the birds on us again."

"Hey." Steph slid off her bed. "I don't think you're being fair. We do need information."

Henrie threw up her hands. "Sure. Fine. Whatever. How about you explain why you called off the Comps?"

Zane shifted so he could partially see Henrie, but his Med kept him sitting. "Maybe we wait to cool off a bit before going over this."

"No! I want to know now. 2876 was coming, but you called them off." Henrie jabbed a finger at her, Mina swore she could feel it stab her shoulder from across the room. "You care about them more than us."

"Henrie," Emma sighed. Mina got the impression this wasn't the first time she'd heard that accusation.

Mina wanted to leave, to physically retreat from this conversation. Lock herself in her workshop and…do nothing but prove Henrie right. She dug her fingers into the edge of the bed, holding herself in place. "I do not! How can you say that?"

"We were getting literally bombed out there. Half of this," Henrie pointed to all their different damage, "wouldn't have happened if you'd let them come down."

"The birds were going for Paks. I said so!" Mina looked to the others for backup. They must have heard her. Or they must have realized the same thing. "I mean, look! You four all have marks on your sides. They wanted the Paks. Calling Comps in would only give them something else to steal."

"We can make more."

"They aren't disposable! They aren't toys you play with until they break and then toss aside." Mina was now on her feet, her small bit of fear of the other girl vanished as she crossed the room. "I am begging you to try thinking something through for once. Capri strapped a box to your back and sent you out. Look at the trouble that caused us. What do you think she could do with a bunch of Comps we carelessly let her have?"

She'd almost come within arm's reach of Henrie, but Emma appeared at the last second and firmly kept Mina away. Emma didn't look too pleased to be there, given the glare she sent both of them. "Drop it."

Her order wasn't enough, Mina and Henrie started yelling around her. Henrie pushed in against Emma's back, trying to get into Mina's face. Emma kept her solid stance between them. Mina wasn't even sure what either of them were saying. Wasn't sure if her thoughts were coming out coherently, but she was tired of being endlessly picked at. Constantly critiqued for every decision she made. This was her team, robots and all. Henrie agreed to that weeks ago. She wasn't picking Comps over them, she was looking out for their entire team. Something Henrie couldn't understand because she was bent on being an army of one against any problem. This was exactly why she'd wanted more control over who joined.

"Enough!" Emma shoved Mina away and pointed at Zane. "You wanna come get yours so I can take care of mine?"

Hands grabbed her arms, Zane pulled her away to stand between their beds. He shifted to move her behind him. Mina couldn't tell if that was to protect her from Henrie or Henrie from her. Probably the former. Sean's Med released him. He sat up, but seemed too stunned to say anything. Steph stood at the end of her bed, also quiet. Emma was talking softly to Henrie, who now sounded like she was hyperventilating. She was trying to get Henrie to sit on the bed, but the other girl wasn't cooperating.

"I was right," Henrie said.

Mina sucked in a breath, wanting to ask what exactly she meant by that, but Zane's hand on her arm tightened and she let the question go.

Luckily, Henrie continued on by herself. "I said more would come."

"We have a new player in town, that's true," Emma said.

Steph took a cautious step closer to the other two girls. "He's got one good trick up his sleeve, but seems more like office management than a bad guy. I mean, did you see that bag?"

Emma gave her a small smile for the assist. "I'm going to use it to break whatever is on his chest the next time I see him."

Sean spoke up, "The birds weren't great. But," he tipped sideways enough to see Mina, "I get why you didn't have Comps come. And we did have that guy on the ropes for a moment."

"For the birds," Nek spread across their panel, "Comps are analyzing the footage to track their flight patterns. They will have a patch for the targeting system by morning, if not sooner. Your systems will be better equipped if they come around again. I am also checking for any references we might have on the weapon the Lenian utilized. Their modifications are typically decorative, or they used to be. This one was very unusual."

"See?" Emma focused back on Henrie. "We are figuring this out. One step at a time. How about you straighten that blanket for me?"

Henrie's breathing remained rather uneven, but she listened to Emma and turned to straighten out the wrinkles. She pushed out a long breath as she ran her hand along the top. After another repetition, Mina realized she was timing her breaths to the motions. Probably a technique she'd learned from therapy to help with her panic attacks and nightmares; neither of which Henrie had admitted to having. She always shut down and closed the rest of them off. Small luck that she'd at least told Emma about this trick. So much of Henrie felt off limits because of how she reacted. Which made it hard for Mina to feel as if Henrie was fully part of the team.

So far, Henrie had only spent one night on Outrider and she didn't make it the entire way through. Most of her concern was because of the strict curfew her mom set. Henrie feared oversleeping and missing the morning check-in. They'd finally convinced her with a movie marathon. They'd all set alarms to ensure Henrie was home on time. A Comp was assigned sentry duty in her room. In the chance a late-night visit happened and a mayday hologram could save the day. Everything went well during the marathon. They'd all shuffled off to their rooms a bit after one in the morning. Henrie woke up screaming around three. Emma physically held her down until they could make her remember she was safe on Outrider. Mina had suggested resurrecting the blanket fort, trying to be supportive, but Henrie ignored the offer and insisted on returning home. The following morning, Emma let her lead training and no one mentioned anything. Mina thought the extra responsibility would give Henrie a way to burn off those more intense emotions and get her comfortable enough with them to open up more, but neither happened.

"Make sure you get that top corner," Emma softly coached Henrie through another round of breathing. Henrie followed the request.

Steph cleared her throat and bent to see Mina. "So, um, the Lenian guy.

You said he was specing us?"

Mina kept herself quiet, unsure if her talking would be enough to set Henrie off again. "He talked about my blaster like it was a collector's item."

Steph nodded. "He asked me about my saber's charge time."

"He inspected my boots," Henrie added as she pushed out another breath. "I think he was taking notes."

Sean moved to lean on the wall behind him. "He asked me about the suits' medical stuff."

Henrie's head jerked his way. "What'd he ask?"

Emma turned toward her cousin. What Henrie couldn't see, but Mina could, was the quick gesture she made telling him to drop it.

Sean shifted again slightly. "Only if it was functional."

"Why would he be interested in that?" Henrie's wide eyes shot to Emma. "I told you it was a problem."

"He could have been going off a checklist," Zane offered.

"The suits mess with you! That stuff messes with you."

Mina felt her argument spinning up in her head, she pressed into Zane's back, but another arm squeeze from him stopped her from speaking up. She found it aggravating that she was the one having to stay silent. The group went over the programming together after Henrie joined. Nek had also shown Henrie how to turn the medicinal aspect off, but she hadn't. They'd compared the suits' medical aid to Earth medications. The level they were at, the minimum setting by the way, was basically high-end ibuprofen and only triggered when a certain level of damage got through the suit. Henrie knew all this, but these panic attacks got her stuck in a loop. Going around and around about the same worries and paranoias. Which caused Mina to rehash the same argument with her over and over as she couldn't understand the girl's inability to remember the simplest of facts.

She now realized why Zane made her stay quiet. Arguing didn't mix well with a panic attack. Henrie was working at a bit of a disadvantage. Mina knew Henrie was still reeling from everything Capri had put her through in those few days of controlling her body. She surmised that Henrie was also wary about specifically Nek and Mina because she didn't want anyone else having any sort of control over her. All Mina wanted to do was prove that she wasn't the bad guy here, neither was Nek. But Henrie seemed determined to keep them cast in those roles. Mina continuing to argue with Henrie only proved her point.

Emma reached inside Henrie's pocket and pulled out the Pak, pressing it into Henrie's hand. "Everything in here protects us."

"He said–"

"How others abuse it," Emma looked sorry to cut her off, "is not on us. They aren't us."

"I need to go home."

"Okay. I suggest we make a pit stop at the rooms to get cleaned up. Your mom will be mad if I bring you home with caramel in your hair."

That got a small laugh out of Henrie as she made a beeline for the exit. Emma wasn't far behind her, but stopped in the door to look back at Mina. "You went a little far with this one."

"She said that–" Mina tried to get around Zane, but he kept her boxed in.

"Later." Emma left to catch up with Henrie.

"I'll be here," Sean called after the two of them. He laid down on his bed and turned toward the wall.

"Hey, Sean." Mina was surprised when Zane let her step around him. She supposed the threat of a physical fight had walked out the door. "You know I care about you, right?"

He didn't turn around. "Absolutely I do."

"You know that–"

"Mina, I promise you're not the one I'm mad at. I'm just a little beat, literally and figuratively."

"Sure. As long as you…yeah, okay."

That kept the people upset with her at two. Emma couldn't really believe Mina didn't care about them. She couldn't. She would say so. What she was doing was siding with her girlfriend. Her trauma riddled girlfriend. Who Mina had yelled at and brought up part of that very trauma to while trying to win an argument. Was she sure she wasn't the bad guy? Mina sat herself down on a bed, the mixture of rising guilt and residual anger making her feel nauseous.

As if in response to her emotions, Zane crouched over the bin next to his bed and gave two hard coughs. Mina was on her feet with a hand on his back within seconds. He didn't have hair long enough to need held, but she wanted to give any type of support she could. She wanted to do at least one thing right by him today. When he heaved again, a bandage on his back bloomed red as the wound reopened.

"We need the Med," she whispered over her shoulder to Comp2876.

Task confirmed! 2876 tucked itself into the Med.

She let Zane catch his breath before helping him to the bed. A quick check over confirmed that only the one cut reopened, which was good. Mina fetched an empty bin to prop at the end of the bed and gave the used one to a different Comp for cleaning. Zane hunched over as the Med got to work on his back.

He sighed over the bin. "And just like that, the Days Without Stress Related Vomiting counter flips to zero."

"This was my fault. I shouldn't have gone off on her."

"Things need to be said, good and bad."

"Don't be nice to me. You threw up so hard you split stitches."

"That's one order I can't follow, my dear captain."

"Well, dang." Mina let out a shaky breath. This felt so good, Zane and her talking again. As nonsensical as it was, she'd needed this. She felt the urge to ask him the same "are you mad" question, but held off as not wanting to jeopardize her lifeline now that it had returned to her. Her next thought was to tell him about the kissing Steph thing, but this felt like an even more inappropriate time for that conversation given everything that had happened. Especially with Steph standing right next to them. She'd moved to the end of his bed as Mina got him comfortable.

Nek rolled along the panel across from them. "I believe Wardens Sean and Zane would benefit from some extra rest here in the medbay."

"You are most certainly right." Mina checked around the bed. "Oh, you need water. Let me grab that."

Comp2876 popped out of the Med, the new bandage now firmly in place.

Task accepted!

"No, really, I can…" She let it go as 2876 disappeared into a tunnel. "Okay, so 2876 will bring you that. I will get out of your hair."

Before she got away, Zane snatched one of her hands and gave it a squeeze. "Everything will work out. You gotta have faith in that."

She squeezed his hand in return and lied. "I do. You two get some rest. We can talk later."

He smiled and gingerly laid himself back on the bed. The lights dimmed as she headed for the door. Mina assumed Nek was behind the change until she saw Steph at the control panel. She hadn't realized she'd stepped away during her small chat with Zane. Steph took her hand as they headed down the hall. Mina let her lead, unaware of where they were heading. Following Steph down random hallways felt good for the time being. When she finally took stock of their location, she found they'd wandered down a corridor dedicated to storage. There was a rhythmic hum in the distance that told her they were circling around to Fabrication. They could have easily gone on walking in silent circles around the ship. Except.

Mina spoke slowly, "I have to ask."

Steph stopped them in the middle of the hallway. She took Mina's other hand, forcing them to face each other. "I did initially think we could have used the Comps. I–"

"If they–"

Steph held up a finger. "Wait, please."

"Sorry."

"It's all good." She shook their joined hands. "I didn't think about the possibility of Comps getting back to Capri and I appreciate you sharing your viewpoint. We got out of there alive. The boys are on the mend. That goes to show the Comps aren't absolutely necessary every fight."

There was a long enough pause that Mina risked speaking. "But."

"No but. But negates everything you said before it." Steph gave her hands another shake. "And. And I think that conversation with Henrie wasn't handled as well as it could have been."

"She said I didn't care! She makes it sound like I'm fine with everyone getting hurt. She has it out for me. You see that, right? Every training, I get called out way more than all of you."

"I didn't say she was in the right either. I think both sides had high emotions battling each other. I believe Henrie feels very defensive right now. Her fight or flight is still in overdrive and that causes her to lash out. I believe you are very protective of this ship and this team. Any of us questioning that would receive a large response from you, not just Henrie."

"You're using therapy on me, aren't you?"

"I feel you are catching on."

"Do you think we can work this out?"

"I think we're on the way, but she needs more time. Healing isn't linear." Steph kept hold of one of Mina's hands as they started walking again. "Now, the next thing I feel is that we need to not think about Warden things for a bit."

"Easier said than done."

"Usually true, but I have an idea. I bet I know every dance number from High School Musical."

Mina let herself once again enjoy being pulled along by a cute girl. "And we prove this by?"

"Playing the movie. I dance when they dance. You watch and confirm if I mess up."

"What brought this to mind?"

"A second ago when you said 'work this out' and the song popped into my head."

"Fair enough."

Steph slowed as they came to Fabrication's large main entrance. "No. Wait. I thought I was going to the movie room this whole time." She looked down the hallway they'd come from. "Were we supposed to take a left back there?"

Mina hit her armband and pulled up the Outrider map. "Zane swears the walls don't move, but I don't believe him."

7

Getting up to Speed

Capri felt like her head was floating an extra foot above her shoulders as she sat up on her cot. A marked improvement from the hefty weight it'd been whenever she'd last woken up. They'd removed something in the mix used to gas her at night, or backed something off. Her mouth felt full of fuzz, so whatever mood regulator they used was still there. The Pak would have filtered everything out automatically, but not having it was the reason she was in here.

She pushed herself to her feet. Her palms stung as she did so. They were wrapped in gauze, as well as a good portion of her arms. On her fingers she could see the ends of small, angry, red cuts. Capri had done something again. Inspecting the room uncovered no new broken items. The space actually appeared cleaner. Pushing against the haze that filled her brain, she tried remembering what caused these newest injuries.

A ringing filled her right ear, she shook it away and additionally broke loose the edge of a memory. Moreso, the memory of a sound. Metal chewing through metal. Capri turned to the door, shut now, but it had moved. She was certain that for the first time in weeks the door had moved. More pieces filled in as she leaned heavily on the workstation. She had stood to the side, watching the sparks fly around the edges. When the door finally shifted, she pounced on what she'd expected to be an engineer, but someone else caught her. They'd called in a Councilor to deal with her. They were done with her antics.

Her hands spiked with pain as she remembered clawing at that arm. Her chest ached with the flash of whatever they'd used on her next. She peeked inside her shirt to see new bruising across her torso. A shifting tenderness told her the damage stretched up her neck as well. Her suit would have–

"Stop it," Capri hissed.

The last two weeks Capri's mind had been little more than a constant cycle of all the things the suit could have been doing for her. Seems she'd finally run out of steam for her pity party. With her fractionally clearer head, she wanted something new to stew over. Not get stuck in her same loop. She knew where her Pak was, on that stupid girl down on the planet. Henrie. Probably making a mess in her Guardian while prancing around in that ridiculous new three-headed form she'd selected.

Capri pressed her hand on the workstation sensor. It took longer than normal to verify her print, but eventually the board came to life. Her files on the teens were open, thrown about the table by someone who held no sense of order or decency. She pulled files along with heavy fingers and reorganized her work. Underneath the mess, she found notifications regarding recent additions to the joint folders the engineers had added her to.

She hit the Dumb folder and saw a handful of new clips featuring those horrible, fake Wardens. Capri opened the first and watched from an onboard camera as something dove into a male from the team. He wasn't wearing his suit and it took her rewatching the attack to realize this was Orange. The clips following that featured the rest ducking and hiding, Green fell down a set of stairs at one point. That clip was her favorite. Eventually she gathered the chaos was from Gregory's birds chasing them around. What could have convinced him to send his pets to the planet? Or, more accurately, who?

The same person who'd bruised her and messed with her things, no doubt. She expected the Councilor was up in the suite. Capri could send a message, but that was too easy to ignore. She was also too far away to yell for them, but could bang on the door and get someone else's attention. Her Comps should be nearby, they'd pester one of the engineers on her behalf. Pushing off the workstation, her legs wobbled slightly as she moved forward. After two steps Capri discovered that her equilibrium wasn't fully functional yet and she careened toward the wall. She overcorrected to avoid that collision, which only resulted in her falling into the door instead. Gears squeaked and moved above her. The door slid an inch open.

They hadn't locked her in after the Councilor came through. She'd assumed they had installed a latch or something on their side. Yet there she stood, after a ridiculous amount of effort to push the door wide enough to get her face through, looking out at the rest of her floor. A view quickly blocked by the Comps coming into her eyeline.

Hello there.

Please, let us assist.

Small pincers wrapped around the door's edge. The Comps shoved the door open the remainder of the way with ease. Her vision crossed briefly, giving her four Comps instead of two. She willed her eyes to refocus and solidified the pair of Comps before lurching toward the railing.

Capri stumbled more than walked, tipping her top half over the side. A pincer grabbed the back of her shirt, pulling her away from danger. She turned enough to see the Comp holding her upright. "Thanks."

Glad to assist.

She held onto the railing as she moved around to the elevator. The car was gone. The Councilor had pulled it into the suite. Below, the engineers were quietly working in their rooms. They were either focused, fighting, or trying not to draw attention. Capri looked up to the suite hatch and decided it was time she properly introduced herself to their new guest.

Her Comps attempted to steer her wavering steps toward the elevator call buttons, but she didn't want to give the Councilor a heads up she was coming. She stumbled to the back of her floor, finding the false panel that opened to the service stairway along that end of the tower. There were only two flights of stairs between her and the suite, but the steps were aggravatingly tall. The effort of repeatedly lifting her legs higher than what felt necessary was frustrating, but the Comps kept support on her back and she pulled hard on the railing to keep her momentum going forward. Her injured hands stung from the work. On the landing she took a brief rest while propped up by the cool metal of the railing. Capri's eyes fluttered shut for what she thought was only a moment. Her head felt clearer, fully on her shoulders now.

"How long was I out?" she asked the Comps.

Twenty-three minutes, both screens answered.

No one apparently noticed her room being vacant in that time. Or they were searching everywhere, but here, for her. Using Comps to lift herself up, Capri got to her feet and trudged up the next flight of stairs. She took another rest on the landing outside the suite door, but stayed on her feet. That climb further cleared her head, but her limbs felt loose in their sockets. Capri was glad for any type of improvement.

She knew the suite door opened inward from seeing the engineers use it when they came to check on her during her last recovery period. A fact she was thankful for because the damned thing was heavy. Getting inside the suite required throwing her entire body at the door. She couldn't imagine having to pull it open. The Comps could have taken care of it, they'd tried but she shoved them off. She wanted to do at least one part of this venture on her own.

On the other side, she found additional resistance caused by a pile of fabric bunched up along the wall. The bundle must have been right next to the panel. She picked up the coil, getting briefly lost in the softness, and realized this was the length usually wrapped around the staircase railing. As she slipped the yards through her hands, Capri found random sections snagged and frayed from being yanked off whatever once attached it to the banister.

Capri kept the coil with her as she moved further into the suite, finding other pieces of fabric and coverings ripped and strewn about the place. One of the velveteen loungers was torn with a strangely precise line of punctures. Stuffing spilled out from the holes.

"I liked this one," she grumbled.

An angry curse came from nearby. She turned to see the Councilor standing not all that far away with his back to her as he hunched over the bigger lounger. Along his arms and legs were spikes, and caught on many of those discreetly sharp ridges were bits of fluff. Even her semi-drugged mind could line up those spikes with the damage to her lounger. She crept up on him slowly, the railing fabric clutched in one hand, and pulled a large piece of fuzz off his shoulder. Capri blurted out a laugh before she could stop herself.

The Councilor spun on his heels, glaring. Stuffing and snags of fabric also covered his front row of spikes. The hidden barbs were his doom in the suite. He couldn't be the one originally in mind when building this base. She snorted and covered her mouth in shock at herself. Capri came here to be intimidating. She needed to pull herself together.

He looked her over. "I see you're awake. Can't say if you're more agreeable, though."

After a long exhale, during which she hiccuped a few more laughs, Capri spoke. "I think the suite is ahead of me in being disagreeable with you."

"The space was meant to—no, that doesn't matter." He pulled a piece of fluff off his arm and shook it into the air. "Times change. As do people."

Capri watched the bit get caught in a current of air and resettle slightly farther up his arm. "Certainly. You need somewhere that matches your… fuzzy aura."

"Was there a point to you being here?"

She straightened her shoulders. A Comp pushed against her back to keep her upright. "Seeing as how I am the de facto leader as of late. I wanted to know who was in my base."

"I am Councilor Aldrich, and this base was never yours. Lenians don't observe squatters' rights."

"I've done a fair bit of—"

"Damage. Amassed a hefty amount of paperwork for me to complete. And wasted an ungodly amount of resources with little to show for it. Actually. You're at a personal deficit, are you not?" He pointedly glanced to the space where her Pak should have sat.

"If this outpost hadn't been left in such horrible standing, perhaps I could have accomplished more."

"Not my department." He flicked a scrap of fabric at her.

Capri tightened a length of the fabric wrap between her hands. She lunged at his outstretched right hand, coiling the piece around it multiple times before he could react. While stepping around him, she pulled that arm along with her and pinned it against his chest. Covering up that strange spiral modification felt like a good idea.

"Unhand me!" Aldrich yelled.

The Comps caught his other arm as he took a swing at her. While he struggled against them, she hooked two loops over his eyes. The Comps wrangled his left arm behind his back, which she tied down quickly. Then finished by twisting the remaining fabric into a knot, securing him in the improvised restraints. The amount of exertion had her huffing by the end, along with seeing a faint double of him an inch to the left, but she'd done it. No Pak required. Her and the Comps could still get a task done.

Capri hoped she didn't throw up as she wobbled toward the ruined lounger. "Not so tough when you can't get your little light show off."

Aldrich strained his arms, the fabric pulled tight and ripped slightly where it rubbed his spikes. This wouldn't be the longest lasting restraint she'd ever made, but it'd done in a pinch. Capri was more after sending a message. He'd break out soon enough, but there'd be more bits stuck to him, which she also counted as a win.

How far her standards had fallen.

He twisted more while she flopped onto the lounger to catch her breath. The Councilor was growing agitated and snapped out, "You are an obsolete maniac."

"I've been called worse." Usually by the thoughts in her own head. Although not so much in the last two weeks. She'd been too delirious to form a full thought, much less a self-deprecating insult. The realization that none of those ghosts spoke up as her head cleared left her uncomfortable now.

Aldrich raised one of his shoulders up and down in a rapid motion, she thought he might be trying to saw his way through the fabric. "You don't even know how pointless you are."

That felt like a rather direct insult, but she didn't understand the context. "I am far from–"

"Do you know that your precious Collective is dead?" He fell on the other lounger, immediately using the extra friction of the seat to rub against. "The factions left are nothing you would recognize."

Capri stiffened, more alert as ice shot through her veins. "What do you mean?"

"From what I recall, your quaint little expedition was about the last standard operation the Collective sponsored. Umph. Get off!" He threw his back into the chaise, tearing the fabric of the seat more than breaking his binds. "High thread count bull–"

"The Collective is gone?" She wasn't sure if she was asking more to herself or to keep him focused.

"They imploded. Turned to infighting. Someone tried for a, mmmph, mutiny too close to headquarters and failed. Or succeeded, depending on the faction you ask." Aldrich wiggled until he fell from the couch to the floor. "Damn it all."

"There was a plan. They were going to bring others on board in turns."

Aldrich rubbed his head against the lounger, rolling the fabric there and uncovering his eyes to glare at her. "And how well did that go for you? Not well, from what the engineers tell me." He sat himself up and stopped trying to break free. "Their homeworlds were destroyed. They nearly took the planets they once patrolled with them. Records say the main war was a marvelous spectacle to watch. From a distance."

"Liar. The Collective is–"

"I suppose I should take some of that back. There is a 'Collective'." He wiggled his head to put quotes around the word. "A scattering actually. Those claiming they're carrying on the heavy-handed direction your leaders desired. And some softer folk wanting to reclaim the name. Suppose they'd get along with that group down on Earth. I should see about digging up a contact for one of them."

"Liar!" Capri shot to her feet, but the move was too sudden. Her head spun and she fell hard into the seat.

"It's history. Though I suppose that does mean there is a lie or two in there. Neither one of us would know, either way."

"If there is anything of the Collective left, I will return to them a hero. They will know I was one of the first to join–"

Aldrich laughed. He laughed at her while restrained in that frilly fabric. "You think, with the millions of lives being lost in their pitiful war, that an expedition out to an unknown region going dark held anyone's attention?"

"I was chosen to–"

"Chosen! If you were so integral, why didn't they keep you nearby? Why not beg you to come to their aid when their revolution went sideways? Or send someone to retrieve their lost savior?"

Her fingers found the edge of a hole and dug in. "You don't kn–"

"And neither do you. Relic. Five hundred years. I don't think that's fully hit you yet. We've been here for a hundred without anyone else even considering moving this direction. Do you know why? Either they've forgotten or they don't care. From what I've seen, it's mostly the former. And even if they did remember where you were, none of them possessed the time or resources in all these centuries to exhume your team. You're honestly lucky I bothered earmarking this for observation."

"You?" Capri looked to the destroyed suite around them, the cush and tattered drapings made even less sense.

He understood her confusion. "Tastes change. The job changes you. I was the only one who saw potential here. No one wanted to spend the coin required to dig up a wrecked ship, but no one blinked at putting lower class plebs onsite. 'Ensure the local populace does not obtain' was the reasoning I put on the report. There are enough humanoid beings running around out there. Why let more join?"

Aldrich twisted again; a long pull ripped the arm behind his back free. "No one paid much attention to the squabbles of those white-knuckling Paks for a long time. They continue to mostly fight themselves, you know. Only I saw the bigger picture. I started making deals with the ones turning their sights to grander things. I figured I'd eventually come across some nostalgic sap willing to pay for the trip, but no one knew about your expedition. Good thing I'm a patient man. Letting them burn up more of their precious resources has only raised the demand for this hidden stockpile. I knew one day they'd give any price I named for Outrider's coordinates alone, simply for the chance of anything useful."

He unwrapped himself from the fabric, setting the coil beside him and rubbing one of the few areas that was undamaged. "And wouldn't you know it? I hit the jackpot. A full set of functional Paks and Guardians. With a fully operational ship to tow everything home in. Extra bonus, I didn't have to dig anything up. I love cutting costs."

"So you don't even want any of it? You're just going to tell someone else where to find them?"

"Acquiring the treasure trove that is Outrider and selling it piece by piece would be more lucrative in the long run. So I'm willing to put some effort in on that front while alone here. But if someone offers the right price, I'm not against letting them do the legwork. Especially given the additional resources I'm finding to export off this planet." Aldrich looked around the shambles of the suite's sitting room. "I think I left my handheld upstairs, but if you're truly done being obnoxious there are a few questions I had about–"

"This is nothing but a deal to you." Capri's vision blurred on the edges again, but not from the drugs this time.

Aldrich pushed himself up onto the couch, tearing more fabric as he did. "Everything is a deal. At this point, I usually ask what the other person wants, but you don't have anything left to trade."

Her eyes snapped up, ready to prove what she could give him right now. Maybe this time shove that fabric right down his throat while the Comps laid him out with blaster shots. She noticed his thumb press the side of his finger and electricity sparked down his spikes, a warning of what hit her before. Capri was only now getting back to herself. She didn't want to be thrown under again. Instead, she stood and went for the elevator. The Comps stayed close on either side of her.

"Leaving so soon?" he called after her.

Paranoia screamed that she was turning her back on an enemy, even with the Comps providing cover, but the engineers could have killed her days ago without her knowing. She expected they would have preferred the easy route. Efficiency.

"If you can manage to play nice," he said as she pulled the grate closed, "I do have some options for you too."

Her grip tightened on the elevator controls, but she didn't respond. This Councilor wouldn't kill her either then, not yet anyway. A couple of hits from that weapon in his chest would have done it. Odds were he was waiting to hear if any buyer held interest in a living artifact to put on display.

It was unfair that as soon as she regained control she was made to feel so disconnected from her own body. Not all of her was in the elevator as it lowered from the suite and into the tower proper. Most of her mind was elsewhere, lost in time with everything else she'd held dear. Everything she'd killed for. Everyone she'd killed, directly or not.

When the car stopped, she surprisingly found herself on the engineer's floor and not her own. She opened the grate, but stalled halfway through.

Gregory came to the doorway of his workshop. "How, um, how are you doing, Capri?"

"He made you send your birds down." She'd never asked about the birds, often forgot about them until one flew by, but she knew from her small observations that they weren't intended as weapons.

His face twisted, a sad pride in him now. "He did."

"He was the one who got you stuck here. Maybe not personally you, but he arranged this mission."

Gregory shot a glance at the suite hatch. "I didn't know that."

She walked into his workshop and sat on the stool Maxwell sometimes used as they went over designs. He wasn't far behind her, returning to his seat. There were new birds in production on his small forges around the room. Capri watched a tiny tapping arm create one of the swirling patterns he enjoyed so much. "I killed my team for a cause that ultimately failed. Anyone that meant something to me is so long gone their names are forgotten. Along with mine."

"Seems so."

Capri was painfully awake, slammed back into her body as reality caught up with her. Decisions she'd made, like calling her team cowards when they didn't immediately agree with her that day. Arguments had gone too far.

She hadn't meant to hurt Caro that badly, but no one believed her. Blood on her hands. Jarden, Ali, and Camden had tried to hold her off, but she'd knocked them down one by one. None of them were supposed to die though. Between the suits and the Comps, she would have fixed everything once Outrider was under her control. But Nek set that EMP to keep her from taking the ship. Then Rin finally caught up to her, ending her rampage with that stasis pod. She could hear Rin on the other side of that glass as the pod kicked on, screaming and asking her why. Why had she done all this? Another screaming voice pulled Capri's guilt forward in time, all the way to Henrie. Who she'd trapped on another planet and tortured under the guise of proving a point. And she was shocked that the Pak started to fail on her.

Gregory didn't press about what happened in the suite. Maybe he already knew. Her chest tightened as tears welled up in her eyes, but she wouldn't let them fall. She didn't deserve that release. He resumed working on his sheet metal and drew out the next pattern, letting her watch him work in silence.

8

Death Ray: For Display Only

Mina thought she might actually get away with spending the entire day being a lump. A plan that was going rather well while bundled up in her bed on Outrider, doomscrolling through different social apps. No one arrived for training. No one asked about meeting up. By noon she felt certain she'd seen the entire internet. For a short while she texted with Steph, who was planetside and returning to the cafe. Steph told her they were taking the day to clean and board up the many broken windows while Mitch and Sam got an estimate together for the damage. Sean wasn't there with her. No one blamed him for wanting to lie low, but he also wasn't the only employee missing. Carter's mom showed up to tell Mitch her son wouldn't be coming back. According to Steph the others were trying to act upset about the news while secretly high-fiving. The last message she'd received said people were showing up and trying to order drinks, so Mina expected Steph would be busy for the next few hours murdering people.

She didn't know how someone could hear about a Warden fight happening inside a building and seriously expect that business to be up and running the next day. Mina realized she should have checked in with everyone this morning to see how their parents had taken the news about the cafe being attacked. She opened her text chat with Zane and stalled out upon seeing the series of links to funny videos she knew he hadn't watched because he always marked them with a reaction when he had. There would be no crying about him being done with her. Not for a third time today, at least. She instead rolled over and reopened one of the mindless match three games she'd downloaded.

There was a knock on her door.

"Zane?" she called out, sitting up from her pile of pillows.

"Sorry," came Sean's voice, "Just me."

Mina hadn't expected him up here today. She figured he was at home, curled up in bed the same way she was. That wasn't Sean though, was it? The showman must go on. She adjusted her messy bun to the top of her head. "Come in."

Sean cracked open the door and peeked around the edge. "How are you feeling?"

"Like I should have asked you that first."

He stepped further into her room. "Little tight in the chest, but otherwise not too bad. I only woke up about twenty minutes ago though."

"Did your parents freak out?" The Meds got him well on the way to being healed, but he'd gone home with plenty of bruises.

"Didn't tell them about the full extent of my damage. Just that I got shaken up and wanted to stay away from the cafe for a day or two."

"Steph said people are trying to order stuff."

"Which means Sam and Mitch will have the tent up soon."

"Extra reason to not be there."

"Exactly." Sean sat on the corner of her bed. "Have you talked to Zane?"

Mina frowned and backed into the headboard. "No. Him and Henrie must be off talking about how much they hate me."

Sean shifted to sit cross-legged. "Henrie is dealing with a lot of stuff. Which, being honest, I don't really know how to help with. Emma seems to, but she hasn't talked to me about it. As for Zane, he's just working through all the stuff we learned."

"Sure." Mina fussed with the blanket, smoothing out her surrounding area. "I'd feel better if he could say that to me."

"I know. I actually came up to–"

Mina's phone ringing cut Sean off. She typically kept it silent, but wanted to know when any notification came in. For whenever Zane might start talking to her again. She snatched the phone from under a pillow. Mina's hope vanished as she saw the name. Her mother was calling.

"No, thank you." Mina hit the decline button and dropped the phone.

"Who was it?"

"My mom. She'll leave a passive aggressive voicemail about the Expo. How it's bad optics for them to not have their daughter there." Mina was honestly surprised her mom was the one calling. Their irksome assistant Mel had left the previous messages.

"Do they make you work the Expo?"

"Not directly. They want me there for appearances. They do the same routine for every company they work for. Certain investors want the whole happy family dynamic mixed in with their researchers. Prove that you don't have to pick one or the other. So when needed, they pretend to pay attention to me." Mina wouldn't mention how much she used to impatiently wait for these days. How much she used to lean into the fantasy, allowing herself to believe those days were her normal experience. She hated to think it, but she wouldn't have to explain anything to Zane. Because he already knew. It'd taken a lot for her to open up about that to him. The idea of doing that again with everyone else felt exhausting.

"Maybe we should go. For appearances."

"My parents are–"

"Totally evil. For sure. We won't stick by them, but we'll go to the Expo and walk around. Maybe talk to people, if you can. They'll see you and back off. We don't want them paying attention to you, so we throw this little bone to tide them over."

That was a good point. Once the Expo was over, they'd be on to their next project. With luck, they'd soon be out of town and she could breathe easier. She only needed to wait them out. No different from any other time before. While Hephaestus Labs was not her favorite place, if she could confirm they'd be there the rest of the day, that would give them a solid window for getting inside the home lab.

"Are you up for a little superheroing afterward?" she asked.

"House heist?" He'd followed her train of thought. Or maybe Sean had come here with that already in mind.

"House heist. You'd only need to check files. Hold stuff for Spud to scan." She'd spent some time recalibrating her favorite tiny recon Comp. Allowing Spud to scan, upload, and analyse even faster.

"I'm your man."

Mina flipped the covers away. "Let me shower quick and I'll be ready to go."

"Sure thing. I'll wait for you in the movie room."

She did her five minute shower routine, not wanting to keep Sean waiting for long. Mina purposely pulled pieces out of her bun to let them hang around her face, knowing this "unkempt" look would annoy them. Her parents expected a business casual kind of appearance from her on these occasions. Mina pulled on a pair of leggings and a random t-shirt she'd left there that weren't visibly dirty. They'd take what she gave them.

As she neared the movie room, she heard Nek speaking to Sean. "...sure you are ready for a mission?"

"I'd go more crazy sitting at home. The Meds fixed me up good, Nek. I promise. And today is more about recon and stealth." He smiled at Mina as she came into the room. "Any chance we can Mission Impossible into the office?"

"Sadly, the ceilings aren't high enough," she answered.

Nek rolled closer to Mina on their panel. "I've created a new waypoint for the Labs. There is a clearing not far inside the Park's treeline. You can land there and appear to come from a side parking lot."

"That sounds great. Thank you, Nek."

He held out his armband to her. "Race you!"

Mina smiled as she jumped to activate her teleport before Sean could. They both shimmered and disappeared from Outrider. She tried to push herself faster, but knew realistically it was out of her control. The two of them reformed in an empty clearing, Sean's teleport cleared away half a second before hers did.

He threw his arms into the air and gave a loud cheer before wincing. "Might have whooped too hard there."

"You okay?"

"Yeah, just stings a little."

"Let me buy you something inside, as a thank you."

"I would whoop again, but I have learned my lesson."

"Smart."

They kept up a rambling bit of small talk up as they walked toward the building. There was a well-kept path connecting this clearing to the employee backlot, making Mina assume people came out this way often. There weren't any signs of this being a secret smoking section, but maybe the more normal interns needed a spot to sneak off and scream. Mina was aware Sean was keeping her away from any sort of serious topic and she appreciated it. Spending these few minutes not churning over the list of questions and unknowns in her head was nice.

The bronze and robotic Hephaestus hammered away as they neared. She wondered if the arm got tired on days like today. Who did the upkeep on him? Surely researchers like her parents would think that beneath them. Probably some poor intern got assigned to climb up and check his inner workings after the event was over.

There were extra guards manning the front desk, ensuring everyone coming in was scanned and signed up for whatever bogus newsletter the lab was running. With a bit of 'could we interest you in doing a survey in exchange for a discount at the boba stand?' thrown in. This was a big day for generating lists of new test dummies and focus group candidates.

Mina attempted to steer them away, but was cut off by a guard she'd missed and their glowing tablet. She matched their empty smile and pressed her thumb on the scanner. Sean did the same and they were let by. As they took a left toward the first batch of display rooms, Mina said, "We have about four minutes before Mel tracks us down and insists I go talk to my parents."

He hooked an arm through hers as they neared the first display. "I'll make sure she can't steal you."

The sudden physical contact threw Mina, but she got herself to relax fairly quickly. Truthfully, the sensation wasn't all that bad. The contact grounded her, kept her focus on Sean. She checked over the offerings in the display room, a lot of the basic robotics they showed every year. They always boasted better fluidity in their movements and precise articulation. There was always a batch of kids pressed against the window wanting to see the robot do a flip.

Sean held her in place as the humanoid robot prepared for that very trick. He whispered to her, "This was always my favorite."

She tried willing the machine to fall, but it stuck the landing and the small crowd clapped. Sean joined in happily. They moved on to the next room, which was more of the same. Easy to entertain, and distract, the masses. Mina glanced over and saw the grin on Sean's face as an automated arm folded perfect origami animals in under a minute. She felt guilty for being so jaded. Her own feelings shouldn't ruin Sean's bit of enjoyment.

She tugged on his arm to get his attention as she pointed to the robotic arm. "The program is based around lasers and math."

"Magic," he said, as if he were correcting her.

"So what they do is–" she was stopped by his hand covering her mouth.

"You're great, and super smart, and I think it's awesome that you know how this stuff works. But can this all be magic for today?"

She nodded against his hand. When he pulled it away, she said, "I've never figured out how they got the movements so fast, though."

He wiggled his fingers through the air. "Magic."

The next room at first appeared empty as they walked behind the crowd. Until Mina spotted the intern standing in the far corner. They were finishing up loading ten pound weights into a crate, Mina estimated the box could hold around two dozen of the weights inside. There was some kind of lining along their arms, but they were too far back for Mina to get a great view. After taking a deep breath, the intern lifted the crate and walked stiffly across the room. The intern looked rather strained by the movement, but Mina had the sense it wasn't the weights causing them stress. When they turned to set the box down, she realized what she'd seen on their arms were pieces of a Lenian exoskeleton strapped along their backside. Thin bars of Lenian metal also ran across the intern's back and legs, apparently offering additional strength to the wearer. Pieces of metal stretched and bent as the intern straightened up, as if it was reacting to how they moved. They watched the intern take slow, deliberate steps across the room to another crate and stack of weights. Given the careful way the intern moved, Mina imagined there must have been a hell of a warning given about damaging any of their new technology.

"They're using it," Sean hissed.

"Of course they are."

They'd known Hephaestus was scooping up Lenian and Comp parts any time a fight broke out between the Wardens and Lenian creations. Mina hadn't been sure what the plans for the scavenged pieces were, but she certainly hadn't expected to see them trying to repackage the stuff only weeks after they'd gotten their hands on the material.

Hanging from the whiteboards inside the room were overly simplified information graphics about what people were seeing. Mina gave them a quick scan to find that Hephaestus Labs was passing off their stolen alien tech as a new highly pliable, yet fiercely strong, metal alloy that showed great promise for physical labor needs. Coming soon, upon further testing. Patent pending, of course. They were going to strap people into Pawn parts and sell it as nothing more than a back brace.

"Bet those weights are foam," muttered a man off to their left. "All for show."

The woman next to him playfully pushed on his arm to shush him. "Even if it is, don't ruin the fun."

Mina realized they were Zane's parents. He wasn't right next to them, or else she would have seen him immediately. She popped up on her toes and stretched to see over to the next display, thinking he might have gone ahead. Standing along the wall behind them, holding his phone up to take a video, was her best friend. His jacket covered most of the bandages, and his bit of visible bruising wasn't too horrible. Most were heading toward that green-yellow color of being healed. Zane noticed her inside his video.

He stopped recording and appeared to relax a little. Mina headed for him, pulling Sean along by their still hooked arms.

Sean realized who they were heading toward and waved. "Oh, hey man. Didn't know you were out here."

Zane kept his eyes on Mina. "It was my parents' idea. They insisted. I thought you'd be avoiding your parents."

So he went where he expected her not to be? No. He didn't invite her because he wanted to keep her away from them. That one. Maybe. Hopefully. She tightened her grip on Sean's arm. "Sean thought if I showed my face quick they'd leave me alone. And if we can confirm they'll be here all day, we could do the house heist."

Zane frowned, but nodded. "Alright. One quick question, is that something we need to stop?"

He pointed behind them to the intern, now carrying those same boxes to the other corner of the room. As they shifted their grip the Lenian metal moved to match, expanding over their hand to give them more purchase and stretching to keep their back straight. The intern dropped the box outside of the designated area and reached for a phone on the wall.

"I don't know ho–" A hand grabbing her shoulder cut her off. Mina turned to find a smirking Mel behind her. "Took you longer than I thought."

"I have actual responsibilities today," Mel said, leaning into her British accent. She tended to do that when she wanted to be seen as 'more than an assistant'. Blunt acrylic nails dug into Mina's shoulder. "And chasing you around is not one of them. With me, now."

"Oh, right away," Sean parroted her accent. "Lead us on then, gov."

Mel didn't acknowledge Sean or Zane as she stalked down the main hallway. She led them through the bay of elevators and into the cafeteria. They'd stashed the normal tables and chairs away for the Expo. Instead the space was filled with sets of couches and armchairs to create more intimate talking spaces. Tucked away in one corner was a small stage where throughout the weekend researchers would take questions and talk about their current projects. This is where her parents would be for the duration of the Expo, no project demonstrations for them. Not for the public anyway.

They'd take private meetings up in their office with those precious few they deemed worthy.

Mina surprised herself by not only keeping hold of Sean but also hooking her other arm with Zane as they neared her parents. A group of people were gathered around the pair as they held court from a couch. Her mother appeared bored, while her father did better at keeping up his fake enthusiasm for the shareholders. Mel pointed for her to stand beside her mother, took the time to glare at Zane, and then disappeared off to another task.

"Pardon my sudden change of topic everyone," her mom said as she wrapped an arm around Mina, pulling her away from the guys. They let her arms go but didn't move away. Mina caught her mother giving her outfit and injuries a quick appraisal before plastering on a wide grin for the group. Her mother became more far animated than they'd seen on the short walk over. "You remember our daughter, Mina."

There was a muttering of hellos her way. Mina didn't remember a single one of their names or faces, but she nodded to play along with the charade. She wanted to pull away from her mother's touch. The last time this happened, they'd done an experiment on her. Somehow, her mother sensed that and kept her arm stiff to hold her in place.

Her dad scooted himself forward on the couch to see her better. "Yes, she's usually a fly on the wall here, but it's been a rather exciting summer for the city. Lots of activity."

One shareholder spoke up. "Oh, I'm sure. I heard about the latest attack as we flew in. Hurst is having an interesting time indeed."

"We were there, at the cafe." Mina watched their eyes flicker down to the bandage along her arm. Others were now taking in the beaten up shape of her and the guys. The last thing she needed was her parents asking questions, but this was an easy cover. She saw several people, her father included, ramping up to inquire further, but she cut them off. "We missed the Wardens, though. Honestly, we miss most of the big crazy stuff."

"Too busy doing her prep work. She'll be a senior this coming school year," her mom said to get them back on script, giving an appropriately sized squeeze to her side. "All advanced classes, of course. We've kept her in a standard school so she's close to those her own age, but we have an arrangement with the local university to keep her properly stimulated." She gave a well-rehearsed smile to Zane and Sean, as if she was friendly with either of them. There was zero chance she even knew who Sean was. "Socializing with peers is crucial. Mina's emotional well-being is of the utmost importance to us."

Mina tried not to laugh as there was another round of muttered agreement. A different shareholder leaned toward her. "What are your college plans?"

Taking Outrider further out into space was the first thing that came to mind. Mina stuck on a smile and gave a canned answer. "Hephaestus has a stellar scholarship program with the state university. One of the best engineering programs in the county. I'll study there and build up experience by working in the labs right here."

That was her line since they first moved here three years ago. There was always a product to sell.

"We can't wait to have her on board," her dad said. "We'll be rearranging the office to fit her desk in soon enough."

More polite laughing and nodding. The family that engineered together, stayed together. Her stomach turned. Mina peeled herself away from her mother's grip. "The kitchens are still cooking, right? Sean's never had the stir fry and forgot to eat lunch before coming out."

"Sure thing, dear." Her mother slipped back into position on the couch, back to her refined and coolly bored demeanor.

Her father put out a hand to catch her attention before she turned away. "Take out the chicken when you get home. We'll see you for supper."

Mina gave a wider smile for the sake of the crowd, this one a little more genuine. "Sure thing."

Her father had gone out of his way to ensure people heard him making dinner plans. A thing they never did. Their version of cooking was pouring takeout onto plates rather than eating from the containers. Which meant they had no intention of being home by dinner. Giving them plenty of time for the house heist.

Zane hooked her arm and pulled her toward the food lines. "Glad that's over with."

Sean kept pace on her other side. "Not sure if this is news, but I think your parents are psychopaths."

"Yeah," Mina sighed.

They weaved around other conversations to reach the row of ordering windows along the back wall. Mina pulled them toward the line for the stir fry. As the food was genuinely good, and she was the one that hadn't eaten yet. Zane normally would have bugged her about eating hours ago.

He bent closer to her ear. "Don't overeat now to make up for anything. That'll just make you sick."

So he'd caught on to her; that felt nice. A sliver of normalcy in these very odd times. They shuffled forward in the line and placed their orders. Mina paid for Sean as she'd promised. Once they had their dishes in hand, Mina looked for somewhere to eat that was out of sight from her parents. Someone calling her name pulled her attention toward the closed off side hallway. The intern posted there waved her over and tapped in a code on the door as they neared, pulling one side open for them. Mina didn't expect nonemployees were supposed to be allowed in, but she'd once talked this particular intern through a panic attack induced by her parents. They stayed away from her parent's projects now, but the two of them would share a quick conversation when Mina was in the building.

"You sure you don't want to go back and schmooze?" they asked as the trio passed by.

"They probably already forgot I was here," Mina answered.

They stepped into a tight hallway where all the missing tables and chairs were being stored. Others were scattered through the stacks, hiding away for their own precious minutes of rest and food.

The three of them found a big enough spot on the floor for them to sit side by side. Mina and Zane took up their usual grumbling about how unfortunately delicious the food was. Their knees pressed tightly together in their little alcove, Mina felt comforted by the pressure of him there. Sean sat on Zane's other side and dug in, enjoying his meal without conflict.

"Do your parents know where you are?" Mina asked Zane between bites.

"Texted them that I'd found you. They won't be expecting me home until later."

"If you, um, want to stay with them, Sean and I can do the next part."

"Absolutely not. I'm all in for a house heist."

Sean gave a small woot, and then nearly choked on a piece of pepper. "Glad to have you along, agent."

Zane nudged her knee with his own. "Sorry I wasn't here earlier."

She nudged him back. "It's fine. You're here now."

Sean slapped Zane's other leg. "Yeah, now we've got brains, brawns, and pizzazz."

"What does pizzazz do on a stealth mission?" she asked.

"Look really, really cool."

"Even if no one can see it?" Zane asked.

Sean wiped away a fake tear from his eye. "That's the burden of being pizzazz."

Once done, they dumped their trash and headed out the door on the other end of the hall. Which put them at the opposite end of the walking loop around the main floor. More display windows ran the length. Innocent faces gawked, baffled by technology they couldn't truly understand. People would write everything off as practically magic, same as Sean had. She wondered what else the Labs were trying to slip by public notice. A new fear of finding Comp parts in one of these rooms shot to the front of her mind.

The thought rooted her to the ground as the guys continued for the side exit. "Hey Zane, how much of the Expo did you see?"

He scanned the displays nearby. "Um, most of them. We started down this side first, actually."

"Was there anything else, uh," she looked around at the large amount of people milling about, "worth taking a video of?"

He considered something for a long moment, but then sighed and headed up the row of displays. "You'd see it online eventually."

She felt her stomach tighten as they came to a display room that wasn't filled with technology, but posters and graphics. Which was a confusing sight, as Hephaestus rarely gave space to anything that was still so early in development. Then Mina took in the large banner spread across the whiteboard, **Who are the Wardens?**

In the middle of the room stood a cardboard cutout of their Silver Warden, someone had caught a clean shot of her with gauntleted fists up and ready. Next to the cutout was a poster board listing off all their guesses and estimations of Silver's build, fighting skills, and character. Blown up pictures of her Drake hung along the walls. A TV on a stand played shaky footage of their very first time fighting against MegaPawns before jumping to a more recent clip from Restoration's parking lot. Taped directly to the display room's window was an official Hephaestus Labs press release stating they were proudly aiding local authorities in identifying the mysterious Wardens and determining their true intentions here in Hurst.

The nerve Hephaestus had to be questioning the Wardens' intentions.

"Hey," Sean huffed as he read the infographic, "no one gets to call her aggressive."

"Sean, shush," Mina said out of reflex. Saying 'her' wasn't the same as using a name, but from what she was reading they hadn't pinned a gender on Silver for certain and that was fine by Mina. Better to leave them guessing on as much as possible.

Zane pulled on her arm. "All the Wardens have one."

Sure enough, the next five rooms featured one of them. She moved from window to window, barely paying mind to the crowd around her. Zane gave apologies in her wake. Each showcased the Labs' work in determining their true identities, she took small comfort in the fact that most aspects were largely guesses. Each also featured blown up Guardian images that Mina was sure came from her mother. The Pink Warden room was currently playing footage of the Cerberus Guardian coming into shape, whoever had used their telephoto lens to focus on that had thankfully missed the fight going on in the crater below between Capri, Henrie, and Mina. Blue's room did state that Hephaestus believed they were the team leader. Mina felt a small swell of pride over that fact. The final room was dedicated to Capri and the Lenians. A cutout of her all black suit stood next to one of a MegaPawn, a risky move given that they were using some of those parts on the other side of the floor. The casing the MegaPawns wore covered most of the hardware they were utilizing now. Along the wall were pictures of Henrie's smoke-formed suit. You couldn't see the girl inside the swirling mass, but Mina didn't love that they had pictures at all. The silver lining being that they hadn't connected that mysterious figure to the Pink Warden arriving.

Zane eventually pulled both her and Sean away from the rooms. They stood across from Purple's room as more people stopped to gawk and gossip. He laughed as a guy half his size walked by trying to convince a girl, who must be his date, that he could be the Green Warden. "I mean, we did know they were looking."

"Not this publicly though," Mina said.

"This is probably the first time Hephaestus has ever willingly helped local authorities," Sean said.

Mina almost brought up the defense contracts the Labs held, but let it go. That was a different mess for a different day. "Was this everything?"

"Yeah," Zane answered.

"No Comp parts out anywhere?"

"None on display."

"Okay. Alright." That didn't mean they weren't somewhere in the building, along with the rest of their Lenian stash, but there were too many people around and too much extra security on patrol. There'd be no way she'd get upstairs unnoticed, much less the three of them. Mina pushed herself off the wall and headed for the side exit. A tiny voice in her head, that sounded like Henrie, chided her for caring more about the robots, but she shoved that agitation away. The accusation still upset her, but she couldn't focus on that right now. She needed all of her attention on the next task at hand, stealing from her parents.

9

Operation: Evil Parents

Mina stood in the doorway of her parents' office rechecking the camera angles via her armband for the fourth time since arriving at the house. Zane and Sean waited on either side of the door. Spud paced back and forth behind her head. Nek rippled on all their armbands. She nudged the camera behind her father's desk another fraction of an inch.

None of them wore their suits. Mina tried making a case for them on their way in, mainly using the helmets to provide them with anonymity. The guys thought that was excessive and talked her down. Sean pointed out that Wardens breaking in for seemingly no reason would raise suspicions, but if they were caught in plain clothes, it was simply Mina gaining a rebellious streak.

"We have to go in, Mina," Zane said quietly.

"Do you want one of us to go first?" Sean asked.

"No," she answered far too quickly for her voice to sound calm. "I'll go. I can, um, I can do it."

Zane stood close behind her. "They won't know we're here. You made sure of that."

"Yes."

"Your Lockpucks work perfectly, as to be expected."

"The Comps did the hard part." Spud gave a little whir of appreciation next to her head.

"And if by some chance they get on to us, you're not alone. They won't punish you for going in there."

"Lab Regulations." She knew only Zane would get the reference. The handy little booklet that contained all the rules they'd made her memorize growing up regarding this room. The primary rule being "no little girls", supported with overly specific examples of what might happen to a silly little girl who wandered in alone. Mina showed her copy to Zane, intending it as a joke. Thinking he'd enjoy the spectacle of the strange children's book her parents put together, but he hadn't laughed.

"You are literally a superhero," Sean whispered from her other side. "It is our duty to kick your evil parents' asses."

"Right. Right. You're right." She nudged the closest camera farther toward the wall.

Zane put a hand on her back. "Five more seconds and then I'm pushing you in."

Mina sucked in a breath and stepped into the lab. Nothing happened, as she'd been repeatedly told would be the case. Nek had done a careful sweep of the entire house days ago. Her parents had installed cameras on the entryways and a home security system, but a teleport into Mina's room bypassed those cameras and she had the codes for the house if needed. Altering the camera feeds in the lab was all that had been required. Her parents were unusually confident no one would dig around their personal office. They probably figured no one else was smart enough to understand what was inside.

She stepped along the wall toward her father's desk, watching her feeds to ensure she was unseen. Zane slipped in and headed the other direction, towards the cabinets where her mother stashed physical copies. Sean came in next, following Zane toward the cabinets. They'd have more to dig through on that side. Spud bobbed between the two guys, ready to scan anything they found worthwhile. She ducked as she rounded his desk, pressing tight against the side. Tighter than she needed, but the panicked part of her brain was telling her to get out of this room. An image of electrical burns, featured on page six of the booklet, remained seared into her memory. Once behind the desk, she crouched next to her father's computer tower and poked her head over the top to check on the guys.

Zane pulled the first Lockpuck out of his pocket. The large metal cabinet looked similar to something you could pick up from any office supply store. Mina knew her parents had re-engineered the handles; they were secretly fingerprint locked. They wouldn't budge no matter how hard you tugged. If you tried to pry with ordinary lock picks on the keyhole, a silent alarm went off on their devices. Same with the file cabinets Sean would sift through. Zane pressed the adhesive side to the cabinet. They all watched the top spin left, right, left–like a padlock–as the programming worked on the system inside. The spinning was purely for flare. She couldn't stand the idea of building something that only did a mundane task without any showmanship. Small lights blinked on around the edge to show the progress. When the lights completed their loop, the puck flashed blue once. Zane grabbed the handle and pulled; the door swung open quietly. Rows of binders filled the shelves inside, catalogs of all of their completed projects.

"She's thorough," Zane said.

"Focus on anything more recent. Anything we could leak or put a stop to," Mina said. "She would have filled it from the top down, so start from the bottom right."

Sean and her both attached their Lockpucks as Zane started digging. While Sean's only needed a couple seconds, Mina's churned through a bit more protection. He was pulling the first drawer open before her Lockpuck was halfway completed. The files were project ideas in different stages of progress, research and notes loosely organized until enough was compiled for a presentation. Mina knew they rarely threw out a research project, simply shelved it for later if the topic fell short of expectations.

"Same for you Sean," Mina called over. "Anything looking close to being in production would be best. Those might be, um, she would do–"

"Alphabetical," Sean supplied. "The files have extra tabs next to the names. Paused. Outsourced. Sold. Active. There we go." He pulled out a slim folder and started flipping through pages.

"Yeah. Yeah, that makes sense." Mina tapped on her armband and started a timer, deciding on the spot that they'd spend fifteen minutes digging around. The drive between Hephaestus Labs and the house took about twenty minutes. If something failed and her parents were alerted to the doors opening, they'd have a small buffer to get out.

Her Lockpuck flashed. The monitor jumped to life as the password auto-filled and his desktop opened to her. Files were in neat rows, but filled a good portion of the screen. His organization was based more on interest. He kept items holding his focus near the center, where he'd naturally be looking when the screen unlocked. Lesser items would be off to the sides. She feared finding one with her name, and where on the screen it would land.

Nek spun on her armband display. "Copying files now."

"Make sure to only touch stuff on this system. Anything connected to Hephaestus they may see you touching."

"Yes, will do."

She didn't need to give Nek directions. Of course Nek knew what they were doing. Mina was the nervous one. Instead of watching her timer run, she decided to click through files while Nek worked in the background.

Dead center was a folder titled UTAH. Mina tried to remember if they'd ever done a stint in that state, but nothing came to mind. The folder held only a scattering of PDFs. The first she opened was sketches of a velociraptor type creature. The next was the skeletal structure of the same creature, with some sort of mechanism woven through the bones. Or maybe they were meant to replace the bones. There were various versions sketched out. She didn't know why her father held any interest in building a dinosaur, outside of an easy profit. Maybe this was a daydream of an idea, a brainteaser project to get his mind going in the mornings.

She closed out of that and scanned the files around that one. One titled RECOLLECTIONS turned out to be the box she'd stolen. There was a video file saved, one she could tell from the thumbnail was when they'd tested it on her. Judging by the dates on everything, that project stalled even before she'd stolen it. She opened the most recent addition anyway, a screenshot simply named EMAIL. The only sentence in the body of the original message was, *What are you doing about your daughter?* Her father's response was below that, *The missing prototype was deemed a dead end prior to its disappearance. Will inquire with Mina on its whereabouts after Expo has concluded.*

Mina felt a rush of embarrassment as she closed the file. So they knew about her first break-in. Mel and that guard's reports must have been enough for them to investigate. That hadn't been a perfect plan. The date on the email was the day after she'd stolen the box and they hadn't questioned her at all. The Expo did keep them rather busy though.

"Oh." Zane let out a groan.

She poked her head around the screen to see him a little paler than he was before. "Something bad?"

"No, well, I don't think so. I just sort of forgot about the anatomy part of what your parents do." He tipped the binder that Spud was scanning a page from, surgery pictures of something being implanted.

"Animal or person?"

"Both."

Plenty of the work they helped develop held legitimate medical applications. It's what they built their own name on before Hephaestus called with a lucrative deal to get them here. That said, you didn't need a secret lair if all your work was for the greater good. There would be consent forms in all of those binders, and it stood to reason that some were forgeries. They'd scan everything and verify back on Outrider. Her stomach turned a little as she settled back behind the monitor. She moved on to a folder titled KUDZU.

Nek flashed on her armband, cutting off her timer. "Warden Mina, stop."

"Are they here?" She glanced toward the hallway, waiting to hear the front door opening.

"No, they aren't. Don't look into that folder. For now."

She glanced over the general contents. Seemed the same arrangement as the others. Scanned images of sketches at the top, PDFs of more fully realized schematics, an additional file full of pictures, and two videos. They all featured a man, one who looked rather average in build from what she could see in the thumbnails. Mina opened the sketches.

Nek spun on the desktop screen, blocking the images. "Please, Warden Mina. Come back to Outrider."

Their worry was only making her certain she needed to see this immediately. "Nek, please move."

They shrunk into a corner. Behind them were rough sketches of a male human body. She hated to admit her dad wasn't horrible with his digital drawings. The first model sported a sort of exoskeleton of machinery, what they'd seen the intern wearing earlier at the Expo. This was probably where they started from. The next sketch was more anatomical, showing the Lenian machinery aligning with bones. When she scrolled down again, the alien hardware replaced the bones. Why would they do that? Unless there was something maybe deteriorating the organic material? Or were they hoping to use the Lenian scraps to create higher end artificial implants? She didn't know much about the anatomical end of things. The next version was of the same male model with less machinery on the outside, but she could see wires and such looping about. The replacements still needed power. This project didn't make sense.

Below that was a new male model, this one had more details in the face. As if her father had used a direct reference when he'd drawn it. Mina looked back at the main folder and squinted at the man in the thumbnail images, it could be him. These last sketches also revealed that the man pictured was wearing prosthetics because these models were missing their left hand and the left leg ended at a stump just below the knee. Sketches of MegaPawn limbs were drawn in place of the missing appendages, making them into prosthetics. What would be the point in that? She rattled her brain for benefits to the new artificial limbs. Enhanced strength and durability was all she could come up with. The pieces didn't look human in the slightest, but perhaps certain customers didn't mind. Or her parents planned to dress these items up somehow.

Mina clicked the pictures folder. Inside were photographs from the real life man in the sketches taken from every angle, with and without his normal prosthetics. She wondered if her dad did those drawings on the fly. The next batch showed MegaPawn pieces being held up alongside the missing limbs, she noted measurements being taken in several. They'd gotten lucky to come across larger components, usually the Lenian bounce-back grabbed those bits. The Pawn parts weren't re-engineered practically at all. From what she could tell, they were trying to find existing pieces that fit the man instead of adjusting the parts. Probably because they couldn't. Too afraid to break their stolen goods. There were pictures showing the man being fitted into a new socket that included some small piece of Lenian material in the end to attack to the larger pieces.

Mina called out to the guys, "They're using Pawn scraps for more than that exoskeleton."

"What else?" Zane asked. She could hear him flipping through more pages.

"Looks like artificial limbs. Can't imagine those will be cheap." Mina scrolled further down to see the limbs being attached to the sockets, which appeared like an easy process. There were a few action shots of the man moving around. One of him giving a thumbs up to the camera.

The location changed to somewhere with more room, the man was shown in a runner's starting position. One clear shot showed the man mid-stride, MegaPawn foot out in front of him. There were several rows of blurry shots after that, Mina had a hard time picking the man out in them from how much he appeared to be moving. The most she could tell was that he was reaching for the Lenian limbs. At some point he fell over while still pulling at a wire wrapped around his bicep. Mina went back up to the installation, confirming there hadn't been anything that high on his arm before. She scrolled down to the blurred shots to see they ended only another row down. The man laid unconscious, how they'd done that she wasn't sure, and his reason for panic was clear.

That wire wasn't going around his arm, but pierced through it. The length snaked up from the metal skeleton-like hand, dug into the skin just above the socket, and reappeared higher up on his bicep. The end was turned back toward the man's arm, like it planned to go in again. His leg was in no better shape. Rods had shifted up from the MegaPawn shin to better secure itself to the human thigh above.

"What did they do to him?" Mina asked.

Several times now Mina had watched up close as Pawns twisted and bent their hardware in ways that should have been impossible. When they were doing so to graft themselves together into MegaPawns the process was almost mesmerizing. Seeing that same feature attempting to bond with a human body was horrifying. The file name made sense now, kudzu. An invasive vine species that overtook whatever landscape it was planted on. Notoriously known for choking out the other plant life around it. The Lenian material wasn't only trying to secure itself to the human's form, but assert itself as the dominant structure.

Zane snapped a binder shut. "Mina."

The pictures continued on, they'd documented every inch of the morphed Lenian parts. While showing no sign of actually helping the poor man they'd harmed. Outside of stopping his bleeding, but she imagined that was more because the blood was covering up what they wanted to see. Mina went for the videos. The first was the original file of the man in the lab being measured and the Lenian limbs being attached. Their first warning that this was dangerous should have been when the Pawn parts extended toward the pieces on the sockets to form connections. He took a timid walk around the room, getting accustomed to the new prosthetic. They'd had him pick up a couple objects from a table without issue before he'd given the thumbs up she'd seen before. The intern's slow movements at the Expo made more sense now, that didn't appear to trigger the Lenian material's expansion.

The second video was in the new location. The man hopped foot to foot, she noticed him give a curious look down to the Lenian foot before someone offscreen got his attention. Mina reached for the volume and unmuted the video, her mother could be heard explaining how their first test would be the man running a simple lap. The camera panned slightly and she caught the edge of her father with his tablet and stylus in hand. Whoever was holding the camera snapped back to the man as he took his starting position. Her mom counted down from three and he took off in a sprint. The man made it one step on the Lenian foot, but Mina thought she saw him wince. By the time the artificial limb came down a second time, the man was already reaching for his wrist.

"Something's moving in there!" the man shouted as he tried to pull the socket off.

"Mina," Zane called over again.

The man took a step back on the Lenian foot and cried out. He turned and Mina saw the first rod had punctured through the back of his thigh. That's when he'd fallen, his frantic pulls at the Lenian hand continuing the whole way down.

"Help me!" he begged from the floor.

"Hold." Her father's voice was stern. Daring anyone else in the room to take a step forward.

Mina and the cameraman watched that length of wire come through the man's arm as he screamed for someone to help him. Eventually one of her parents gave a signal offscreen and a masked intern ran forward to inject something into the man's other arm. He fell unconscious and the Pawn parts settled as he did. With a shaking hand Mina scrubbed through the next bit of the video, not needing to hear her parents' cold observations. Hoping to see the man actually being helped. The most she saw was two seconds of a stretcher coming in before the video ended.

"They just watched." Mina went limp to the floor. "All they did was watch."

Nek spoke to the others across the room. "You all need to return to Outrider. Immediately."

Doors and drawers shut from their side of the lab, which sounded farther away than she knew it to be. They were moving towards the door; they were getting out of here. She didn't want to be left alone in the lab. Mina pulled the Lockpuck off the tower and crawled around the desk on her hands and knees. Zane was crouched in the doorway, hand held out to her. He pulled her the last stretch out and they fell into the hallway.

She didn't initiate physical contact much, but on this occasion she buried her face into him. "Th-there was no...no reason."

Zane tightened his grip around her. "You're okay. It's okay."

"N-no it's not. They're horrible." She thought to that first file, whatever that thing was with the machinery woven directly through it. "They want to make monsters."

"It's all the rage," Sean said from next to them.

Zane loosened his hold slightly. "Let's listen to Nek and get out of here."

She nodded into his chest. Letting herself get pulled up to her feet. Mina clung to Zane because she didn't want to touch the walls. Hated that she had to step on the floor. She no longer wanted anything to do with this house that they sparingly shared.

Mina forced herself to let go of Zane once they were in her room. She pulled a suitcase from her closet and threw clothes inside. A portion of her wardrobe, and all of her toiletries, were already on Outrider, but she would no longer be coming here for anything. Mina pulled out her stash of duffle and tote bags, usually reserved for hauling hardware, and arranged most of them across the bed without a word. The last few she hung directly from Zane and Sean's arms. They stood for her, waiting as she filled each with more clothing and items from around her room. She stripped her bed and shoved everything into her hamper. The bed set wasn't a necessity, but it was hers.

A normal person could look around and tell that someone had left with no intention of returning. What would her parents see? She'd probably get a text asking if she was spending the weekend at Zane's again.

Once she finished raiding her things, Nek brought them to Outrider. The guys deposited the bags in her room. Sean had to get home; his mom was under the impression he'd gone out for a movie and quick bite with friends. Mina thanked him before he teleported away. Zane began unpacking clothes without her asking. Comp2876 arrived with a stack of hangers dangling from its extended pincer arms. They began filling up her closet and dresser quietly.

Mina pulled a shirt from a tote bag and jumped as Spud buzzed into the air from underneath. She must have trapped the little robot in her frenzied packing. "My bad, Spud. Sorry about that."

Spud turned to 2876, who promptly displayed an *All okay!* on Spud's behalf.

Zane didn't press about what exactly was in the video she'd watched, and

Mina had no intention of telling him. Not with all the horrible discoveries they were tackling from Capri's hard drive. She regretted that Nek, and potentially the entire swarm, had seen it already. Along with any other horrible thing they'd filed away. Zane and Sean certainly saw plenty of horrid things in those binders and folders. Mina knew digging through all that data was a task ahead of her, but she forced herself to keep her mind on the one at hand. Which was currently dumping all of her unmatched socks into a drawer and arranging them into stacks.

Zane shook his head at her. "It takes two minutes to pair up socks."

"Just to pull them apart again when I put them on. Makes no sense."

Once free of hangers, Comp2876 called another Comp to help take her hamper away. Mina expected they'd have her few dirty clothes and bed set cleaned, folded, and returned before the end of the day. She saved enough space in the closet for the extra comforter and sheets. Not long ago she'd worried they'd never use these rooms; now the space was filling up rather fast. Lucky that she'd previously set up the workshop, which had taken several trips. There was for sure something she'd left behind, but she would happily buy a new whatever it was–or make it in Fab–before going back to that house.

Zane's dad eventually texted, asking if he'd be home for dinner. Neither of them had realized that much time had gone by. He demanded she go with him and she tried to insist she wasn't hungry. As well as having no desire to be near that house again so soon. After a nod of agreement, Zane called his mom and begged for them to go out to eat. He'd weaponized her parents, saying Mina was dying for the barbecue place over on Pine, but her parents would never go there. Mina could hear his mother huff from where she was standing. When he cracked a huge smile at her, she knew she'd be eating a pile of brisket and burnt ends. Her stomach growled at the realization.

Far sooner than expected, she found herself back on Earth. Zane and her appeared at the waypoint Nek had created behind his shed and then acted as if they'd come from her house. His mother gave her a squeeze when they came through the door, muttering about how the Expo wasn't all that interesting this year. They all headed out and ordered far too much deliciously slow cooked meats. His parents carried the conversation for most of the evening and Mina was happy to listen. Her life revolved around vengeful aliens and evil parents. Hearing about their office dilemmas gave her a pleasant reprieve from the chaos. She was more than happy to help his dad plot a prank against a colleague while munching on a cornbread muffin. There'd been a moment where she'd become overwhelmed with appreciation for her surrogate family and excused herself to the restroom, but Zane—as always—covered for her.

At their house, he went through the motions of walking her through the yard the same as he always did. With a heavy to-go container in hand, Mina realized that the vast majority of food up on Outrider was snacks. Peeking over to her parent's house, her stomach twisted at the sight of it, she saw no lights were on.

"Maybe we should go raid the kitchen," she said.

"No, we'll do a grocery run. You're not going inside that house." He checked toward his own home, saw they were in the clear, and pulled her toward the shed. "Just to say it once. All of your family lives on this side of the fence now."

"I know." She gave him the quickest of hugs before waving him off. "Talk to you later?"

"I gotta catch up on our chat, but yeah."

Despite the few pounds of food in her stomach right then, Mina felt lighter. She smiled as he headed for his backdoor and she called for a teleport. Dropping in on Outrider took away the light feeling, the overly full stomach making itself known again. Mina grumbled and headed for her room, eager to fall into her now only bed.

Nek's waves appeared along the panel beside her. "Did you have a good meal with Warden Zane?"

"Yes. Too good. I might be in a food coma for the rest of the night."

They were silent as Mina popped into the kitchen to put her leftovers away, only speaking up as she headed for the private quarters. "I'm sorry for what you witnessed today."

"I'm sorry you had to see it too. And I'm sorry I didn't listen to you. You tried to stop me."

"Yes, but," their waves tightened slightly, "you have to look at the uncomfortable things. At the hard things. Even if they hurt you."

"That's true." That was certainly something they were all learning from Capri's hard drive. "That man. I think we need to find out who he is."

"I have Comps working to identify him already."

"Great. Thank you." Should have known Nek would already be on top of things. "I guess I should ask. Is there anything else horrible I need to know about?"

"We're still organizing everything."

Which wasn't a direct answer, but she didn't feel any desire to push the issue. "Just let me know, mmmm, tomorrow. Let me know tomorrow."

"Will do, Warden Mina." Nek faded out as Mina arrived at her room.

She'd known going into that lab would bring her no good news, but she hadn't expected to find them being so senselessly cruel. They were serving no purpose other than satisfying their own twisted curiosity. Acknowledging that they were operating under the *knew that you could, didn't ask if you should* mentality made that bespoke monster make more sense.

Mina fell onto her bed. Full and exhausted, she could have easily called it for the day. Then Zane started responding to her stack of links. She'd missed updates from Steph during their whole outing. Sean was also in the group chat, telling the others what they'd seen at the Expo. Her team was inching their way back together. There was a peace that came over her as she squirmed under her blanket and caught up on the different conversations happening. She was safe here. She was home.

10

This Baby Can Fit so Many Teens with Attitude Inside

"It doesn't change the fact that you are trying to sell us goods you aren't in possession of," stated the pinch-faced Empyrean once again. Getri was always a needler, constantly leaning in so you could hear the ticking of him, but he represented one of the largest Empyrean regimes so Aldrich was forced to deal with him far more than he would like.

Aldrich wanted to knock his gears loose, but instead held his grin as wide as ever and shook a finger toward the troublesome square within the wall of potential buyers. He preferred having them in group calls early on, let them know how many interested parties there were. "Easily rectified. These are primitive beings, after all. They're skittish, but give me a little more time and I'll have them brought around to reason."

Or dead in the street. He wasn't picky. They'd broken his recorder and scuffed him up significantly. Then that madwoman tied him up in fabric not much thicker than tulle. This planet needed to show better results than trick birds and transport vehicles. He wanted to keep the ship operational, purely for the hauling capacity, but this deal was quickly leaning towards rubble and fire. That was for him to sort out, not for prospective buyers to worry about.

"What about the Sinnetian?" Getri pressed. "You've not mentioned them yet."

"They've only allied with this group for a short time. Surely their allegiance will be more to their vessel. A simple conversation will see to that."

Or another body. Again, he didn't really care. Though getting the ship back would be far more difficult without the Sinnetian alive.

"And the supposed survivor from the original team?" Malia, a Warden-type called out. He didn't deal with many of the gentler peacekeeper types, but her troop had made enough progress in their region to entertain for at least one call.

He'd been weighing options for what to do with that relic when she'd infiltrated the suite. Aldrich had originally considered bidding her off to someone interested in her historical knowledge. Perhaps set her up with an academic that would put her on a shelf, but he didn't feel she deserved that sort of kindness anymore. Giving her over to someone still carrying on the fight she seemed desperate for was briefly an option. Another kindness he could have extended, let her die in glory like the mad ones always want, but not after her stunt. Now she'd twiddle her thumbs in this tower and watch him take everything she couldn't. Then he'd leave her to rot, alone on this dusty planet.

Aldrich fixed his face into an appropriate frown. "Sadly, assessment of her mental state was not favorable. I fear the long stasis had unexpected side effects. She was deteriorating before I arrived. She had to be put down. As a mercy."

Several looked notably disappointed with the news. Those who'd lowered their helmets anyway. The factions thought another piece of their pitiful history was lost to them.

"I gave her fire and glory, I assure you." Maybe he'd set the tower on fire on his way out. Depending on how she continued to behave.

Mos, a Solstice Monk bored with the Warden questioning, growled and half-shouted, "And how long are we expected to let you hold our money with these empty promises?"

A small deposit for entry into a high stakes deal like this was standard, nothing to get so moody about. Especially with the teaser footage he'd provided, for free, with the invitation. Aldrich shifted back to a small grin, hoping to come across as good natured. "I find it humorous that I am the one telling you that patience is a virtue. I have plenty to show for proof of goods."

He switched his feed to the highlight reel he'd made of the Warden team in action. Aldrich ripped footage from the human news channels, utilizing their clueless rambling to build tension, before showing the long distance footage the engineers snagged of Outrider. More news clips of chaos in the streets and shaky footage of the Wardens making their appearances. The video ended with the footage from the first fight showing the Lenian creation surrounded by five Guardians, then cut to two seconds of the sixth Guardian's fire breath weapon before cutting to black.

While the reel played, and they couldn't see him, Aldrich relaxed his rigid stance. Dropping his shoulders and staring off at the wall while different clients huffed and grumbled. He would have loved to sit during this meeting, but the only chair in the office was yet another cloth covered disaster waiting to happen. Earlier, Aldrich grazed the edge of the seat with a spike and gouged the thing. Being practically alone on a distant base offered a great opportunity to slip the new modification on and adjust, but he'd forgotten the decor he'd mandated at the time of building this outpost. Foolish to think that Plush Decadence was a trend that would stand the test of time.

"Are we buying retooled propaganda footage?" Mos asked.

"I have no interest in funding a passion project," Getri added.

"The one with antlers is interesting," someone else threw out.

Aldrich straightened up and put himself back on screen. "I assure you, this is all new footage pulled from either planetary sources or our own personal surveillance."

"I believe that it's real." A figure sporting a black helmet with yellow stars sprayed across the side bent toward their feed. Aris, a leader from one of the more destructive factions. "What I don't understand is why we should pay you for Collective property."

His smile shifted up in watts. "We all understand the concept of a finder's fee, yes? I'm even offering to deliver everything right to your door."

"For a sizable price."

"Compared to what it'd cost you to venture out and find this planet for yourself, I'm saving you money."

Several more called out questions. Some asked about the coordinates, some about his exact plan, and some were already getting distracted by other goods the planet could provide. They were talking over each other. Aldrich knew they'd be fighting soon, driving the interest and price up without him having to do anything at all. He let them go until he heard his subordinate planted in the wall of voices ask about how old the footage was, putting them back on track.

He muted everyone with a press of a button. "Everything you've seen is from the last few weeks of their time. I have the planet's metrics in the informational packet with the Lenian conversions. You'll have to convert them to your personal systems of measurement from there. I want to remind everyone that you are the first to have eyes on this very exciting development. But I hear your concern of only having footage. You want something tangible. A task I have my engineers working on."

Aldrich went to open another clip, but the file jumped away from his finger. It looped around the screen as he attempted to press it again. He watched the file drag itself back and forth across the screen. Though she was floors below, Aldrich swore he could hear Capri laughing. Aldrich caught the video with a quick jab and finally opened the short clip he'd taken earlier that day of Capri's Comps patrolling the hallways. He threw it into the feed to play before she could bother him anymore. Potential buyers shifted in their frames, interest regained at the sight of such pristine Comps.

A message appeared from one of the nameless Sunderfolk. **What good are two Comps?**

"This new team is a little crafty with their assistive tech." He'd hovered a finger over his next video. Ready to strike before she could. A good call, as the file had twitched in place right as he'd opened it. Aldrich moved a shorter reel he'd compiled of Comps being used on the ground during Warden altercations into the feed. Their archived Pawn footage had much to offer showcasing the swarm moving about the city streets and clearing out targets.

Malia raised a hand on screen, Aldrich unmuted her. "You said your engineers are working on something?"

"Our estimations show that the team is utilizing a full swarm, something not seen for centuries." He eyed the Collective and Warden factions among the group. "I believe they can stand to lose a few. Something I could then pass on to those truly interested."

"How do you expect to wrangle Comps away from their Wardens?" Aris asked.

"You must allow me a secret or two in these early days." He gave a wink to the screen, caught a few eyes rolling at the gesture.

Aldrich had provided the engineers an invasive bit of coding bartered off a Sunderfolk several deals back. A simple program made for infiltrating nearby electronics to display their *End is Nigh* messaging for effect. He'd requested the engineers strengthen the functionality to break through a Comp's protections and bring them into Lenian control. His control, specifically. Testing would require the use of Capri's personal pets. He feared they'd be too cowardly to follow through. If the coding failed, there was a backup plan of Pawns with large nets. Which was a rather unsophisticated answer, so Aldrich wanted to keep it close to the chest for now.

Multiple icons across his desktop began moving. They swirled around into new locations, he watched a few blink out of existence. He didn't panic as there were backups for everything, but the process was annoying. A rogue file headed for the call feed, he caught it with a heavy press of his finger and pulled it away. The video opened and played for him alone. Aldrich watched himself squirm like a fool in Capri's fabric restraints.

Chicken, popped up as a message from her room below.

He tapped out a quick message to the engineers. **Deal with her. Now.**

On the call, Aris flicked a finger into the air, Aldrich unmuted him. "How do you plan to get Comps on the ground? They didn't appear to use any in the most recent fight."

"A small contingent of Pawns and the new avian models should pull their attention nicely." Small was an appropriate word. He'd be sending almost all they had on hand and whatever was being finished on the production line as they spoke. The bases' standby supply of Pawns had been nearly depleted due to their previous fights. The Earth team surprised Aldrich by not utilizing Comps during their first interaction. Put those grapple hooks nearly to waste.

Aldrich spared a glance to open the camera feed in Capri's room. She stood behind the workstation, he could just make out the copy of his desktop she'd somehow hacked into laid out before her. Gregory stood in her doorway, talking far too calmly for Aldrich's liking. Though whatever he was saying was keeping Capri distracted.

Another hand went up. Aldrich unmuted everyone, tired of having to hunt them out on his controls. "I'm glancing through your packet right now. The last dated appearance of the Guardians was days ago, and there was notable damage done. Do you have confirmation of their repairs?"

He'd send his ever helpful shill extra credits for the well timed question. "Sadly, no. We have a plan in place to draw those out as well. Which will also reconfirm the ship's capabilities for repairs and demo the Guardian's abilities in real time."

Aldrich backed away from the wall of buyers and switched his feed to the Pawn waiting near the window of his office that faced the telepad. He opened the window to push the Pawn outside, letting his audience take in the creation coming together.

The engineers had done a number on this one. Upon his request, they'd pulled from the prehistoric era of the planet. Something called a tyrannosaurus rex. The model had been the first in the templates folder, but Aldrich assumed it was number one for a reason. The beast would tower over any of the Guardians. The claws, when tested for functionality before moving on, dug grooves into the telepad floor. Three rows of spinning saw blades ran down the back and tapered off along the thick tail, tearing into anything that tried to take a bite from behind. The head currently sat propped up on the ground as the jaw was pieced together, razor teeth being set into place as they all watched.

This time while off camera, Aldrich held his grin because of his personal interest in seeing the creation at work. He'd been moved off the creative track early on in his career, better suited in more analytical areas, but enjoyed getting the chance to flex different skills. The Pawn did one full circle of the telepad before Aldrich called it inside and returned the feed to himself.

"As you can see, we have a rather good fight lined up for you."

Noriko, a more rigid Collective faction leader, spoke up. "And what does it have for ranged attacks?"

"A personal touch of my own." He relocated the creation schematics on his desktop and dropped them into his feed. Revealing the oversized Disruption charge set inside the throat. He'd found it impressive that the engineers could craft a functional replica so quickly. The throat section was working its way through the production line as they spoke. Aldrich would keep them on once they began developing this planet for other ventures. Even if they were an odd pair.

Aris sat back. "You're going to break the Guardians and then expect us to buy them at top price?"

"If the ship can repair them once, surely it can do so again," Aldrich laughed. When he heard others laughing with him, he was glad to have unmuted them all. The small chuckle filled the call. "You'd insist it's all fake if I didn't test them properly."

Aris shook his head, flashing those yellow stars along his helmet. "You don't know what you are up against."

"I can promise you, I do." Aldrich hunted for his next diagram, but found it missing. That must have been one Capri deleted. He gave her room a glance while he reached for his new handheld. Both her and Gregory were gone, but he didn't have time to hunt for them elsewhere in the tower. There was a chance she was committing physical harm to one of the engineers or crew. All fine by him, as long as she was bothering someone else. Aldrich swiped over his copy of the new Pawn design for the call to see. These were built to deliver the virus, once they got it working. The changes also made the Pawns incredibly agile, if they required the nets. "These will give the Comps quite the challenge."

"Prove it," one of the other screens huffed. Aldrich didn't catch who'd said it, he would have cut them from the call otherwise.

"A demonstration is imminent." He gave a glance to the stack of progress bars tracking the multitude of jobs in production. The engineers had stated concerns about overstressing the systems, but Aldrich was certain everything would hold fine. Long enough to get his projects together anyway. He needed results for this gluttonous crowd sooner rather than later. "A small bit more patience."

"I think proof of goods is a reasonable request," Getri spoke up again. That maddening ticking coming through in full force.

"Can you not prove your little virus is functional?" asked someone else he didn't get eyes on.

All of his willpower was spent focusing on keeping his salesman smile plastered on. "Let me check with my engineers on the status of our Pawn production. I'll get back to you within the next hour."

There were gruffs and scowls. Aris was shaking his stupid starred helmet again. Aldrich was losing them. The idiots were so jaded by the state of every once Collective sector they couldn't let themselves believe in the treasure trove he'd found. He would show them and then ramp up his asking price for all the trouble.

Aldrich clapped his hands to pull their shifting attention back. "Wonderful! Yes. I will confirm our available numbers and arrange another demonstration for you. You'll hear from me soon."

With the press of a button, the screens blinked off across his wall. Now alone, Aldrich fell into the chair and swiveled himself side to side. The fabric shredded beneath him as he moved.

"Well, shit."

Aldrich tried calling the engineers, but neither answered. He checked the tower's cameras via his handheld and found the pair standing in the dining room doorway. They jumped to the sides as a chair went flying between them, Capri was tossing the dining room. It'd been a mistake to open her door. He'd been planning on setting up a viewing station in the dining room to watch the next fight while he ate. Another plan thrown off course by that relic's mad behavior.

Her programming abilities would have been a wonderful addition to his Comp virus plan, if she wasn't so damn annoying. She could have gained a new job, a new mission. Could have still gotten a win over those new Wardens. Capri had instead gone out of her way to pester him, for zero personal gain, and made her exclusion from his work a necessity. He'd lied earlier when telling the buyers about her being put down. If she caused him much more aggravation, he'd make that statement true.

11

Never Split the Party

Steph and Sean were assigned to the back drink counter upon their arrival. This was good for them as Sean was still somewhat on the mend and Steph was happy to have the lighter load. If Mina and Zane didn't come in, she wanted to steal as much phone time as possible today to keep Mina chatting. All Sean told them was that the house heist turned up rather disturbing experiments being done by Mina's parents and refused to go into further detail. Steph hadn't ventured into any files yet. Zane informed the group Mina was not to return to that house and privately told the others he'd appreciate any help distracting Mina from obsessing over their findings. At least for a day or two, if they could. Given the heavy amount of not fun information they'd been taking in, Steph felt they all needed extra time not thinking about serious things. She'd love for everyone to sit at the back counter and talk about nothing.

Too bad there was a new bad guy, who apparently wanted to sell them for parts, hiding somewhere on Mars. There was only a certain level of detachment they could safely allow themselves right now. Maybe that would work out well for Mina, focus on the alien bad guy and not her own parents being evil.

"You think Emma will stop in today?" Sean asked as they relieved Sam of soloing the back. As the cafe reopened so quickly after the attack, people were filtering through to see the damage in person before workers started on repairs.

"We are her favorite dealer," Sam commented as they headed for the ramp.

"You'd probably be a better guess on that than me," Steph said. "Aren't you two usually pretty in sync?"

Sean only gave half a shrug before a customer stole his attention. Steph pinned the moment in her mind as something to circle back to. The group chat remained rather quiet yesterday until the heist went down, which she'd let go as everyone needed the processing time, but this morning their usual hellos returned. She didn't expect any of them would be too far behind her and Sean, even if he didn't seem too sure of that fact.

Sean took up his rightful position as barista and she started cleaning off tables, though most were empty of patrons. People were milling about more than they ever did. There was a lot of "A Warden stood right here!" going on in and around the building. She was fascinated by how casual most were about the entire event. In only a month, people had become used to random attacks throughout the city. That was how life was now in Hurst. There hadn't even been a lull of people staying home after their last appearance.

Steph knew people becoming used to chaos and minor tragedies wasn't a good thing. She wondered how rapidly people on Collective planets became desensitized to constant battles back in Capri's day. Did they bother rebuilding when a Guardian could smash through at any moment? Or maybe they wore it as a badge of honor. Plaques outside rubble that boasted *This building has been destroyed (blank) times in pursuit of justice!* with a little hook and numbered sheets to change as needed. People probably traded their near-death experiences like stories of bad dates.

The edges of her superhero story kept getting more grim. A rather downer of a thought, but it stuck with her. Another nagging question she'd kept chasing the day before; what were they doing now? Capri's hard drive shed a lot of light on how they'd all gotten there. The history lesson wasn't great, but those crimes were all in the rather distant past. Maybe not so much for Capri and Nek, but still. What did that all mean for them now? They didn't know where the Collective stood today. Were they fully evil? Or were they marching forward in their overly militarized, foul deeds for good reasons mentality?

She could only discover that storyline by sticking around, staying on the team. She wanted everyone else to stick on as well. Being a Warden became harder by the day, but Steph believed their team could figure this problem out.

Steph caught Sean looking a little sour behind the counter and decided someone else was needing a bit of distraction. Leave the heavy talk for later. She slid up to Sean as a customer stepped away and left him free. "So I know too much has happened in the last three days, but."

He pointed a chocolate drizzle container at her as a threat. "You can't stop on but like that. It's illegal."

She leaned in closer. "I kissed Mina."

Sean squeezed the container in excitement, sending a ribbon of chocolate across the counter. He continued to cheer as he moved to clean up his mess. "Holy shit, what?! Just like that?"

"Just like that. Well, kind of." Steph grabbed her own rag and wiped down the other end of the ribbon. "It was right after the hard drive info dump. She was getting worked up thinking we'd all quit on her. And, I don't know, even her upset rambling is kind of cute. So I kissed her and said 'I'm good here'. Or something like that. I can't remember what I said exactly."

"Miss Diaz. Forgetting a line? You got it bad."

"Maybe. Sorta. Oh god, I don't know. At school I thought she only kept up a conversation with me to be civil. A way to survive having me as a table partner, you know? Then she started coming around here, but I wasn't sure if that was her or Zane's idea. Then this stuff," she gestured between the pockets their Paks hid in, "got in the way."

"Well, it's good to know that even with all the other stuff," he also gestured between the Paks, "going on, you two finally got that sorted."

"Finally? What do you mean?" Steph hadn't known how the kiss would go until she was doing it, but Sean made it sound like they'd been a sure thing. "What do you know?"

"Oh, nothing. Don't mind me." Sean smiled and retreated as Steph got closer. He brandished the chocolate drizzle as a weapon to keep her away.

Sam appeared at the top of the ramp and stopped before heading inside the office. "You two okay?"

Steph glanced over her shoulder. "He's withholding information from me."

Sean tipped around her to see Sam. "She kissed Mina."

Sam's bemused face tightened slightly. "Everybody is kissing these days."

"Wait," Emma appeared from behind Sam, "You and Mina did what?"

Sam's face fully fell, and they moved into the office without another word. Emma didn't seem to notice being blown off, but Steph marked it. They'd thought Sam would eventually come around and lighten up on Henrie, but her and Emma dating threw a wrench in that forgiveness plan. Crushes were stubborn things.

"Just, sort of, you know, kissed or whatever." As Steph stumbled over her words, she realized Emma was standing there alone. Unusual to see her without Henrie these days, but maybe that was for the best with how Sam was acting. Since they were in the clear now, she waved to either side of Emma. "Where's Henrie?"

"Oh! Big day. Her mom is letting her drive again. Only here and then home in two hours, but it's something." Emma slid onto a stool. "Now about this kissing."

Sean held out a hand. "Hold. I spy a Zane and Mina on the balcony."

"Does Zane know yet?" Emma hissed out in a whisper. "I want to see his face if he doesn't."

Steph spun toward the windows. Sure enough, Zane's tall blonde frame was politely weaving through the crowd. She shifted her eyes slightly lower to spot Mina and, sure enough, she followed in his gentle giant wake. Mina appeared a little tired, understandable if she hadn't slept well the night before. Her work tablet was clenched tightly in her hands, so he'd made her compromise about stepping away from the workshop this morning. That was something Steph should have thought of. Zane knew Mina's habits better than anyone. Now that she and Mina were…something more than friends, she'd need to study up.

The pair made their way inside and joined the others at the counter. Mina gave her a quick smile before her attention went to the tablet. Steph guessed she was working on the Comp horn project again, which had turned into more of an impossible puzzle game for Mina.

"Usual drinks?" Sean asked, smoothie ingredients already filling a cup.

"Yes, please," Zane answered and nudged Mina toward the nearest table.

Emma was cutting her eyes between Steph and Zane, clearly waiting for some kind of reaction. She was only picking up the same thing Steph had; he didn't know yet. Which was fine. Mina should be the one to tell him. Yesterday had been rather heavy and hectic, easy to see how it hadn't come up.

Steph gave Emma a quick signal to keep quiet before starting on Mina's drink. Emma held her hands up in silent defeat and stepped away to join Zane and Mina at their table. She watched Emma lean over Mina's shoulder and start pointing at pieces. Mina would give a quick explanation of what the part did as she shifted components around. Any minute Henrie would come up the ramp and Steph would get exactly what she wanted out of today.

Nek sprung up on their armbands. "Lenian Pawns detected at three different locations in the surrounding area."

She was coming to understand Mina's DON'T SAY EASY rule. Thankfully, the Lenians weren't within visual range of the cafe as no one nearby was panicking. Steph caught movement behind her, Sam leaving the office. They didn't give the group any notice, but Steph waited until they disappeared down the ramp before pointing the others toward the vacant room. Their group shuffled in, Sean awkwardly getting the door closed behind them. This closet-sized office was not meant to hold five people.

Steph worried shifting into their suits would make it feel further cramped, but Mina sprung hers as soon as the door snapped shut. The rest followed her lead. They looked ridiculous squished into the small space. Sean and Emma clinked the sides of their helmets. Without another word, Nek lifted them out of the office.

Her feet hit solid ground a second later, and an alleyway took shape around her. Zane landed to her left. He gave a quick scan around the alley, expecting to see Mina drop in too. Steph couldn't hold that against him, as she'd been hoping for the same. If there were three different areas being attacked, that left only two of them to cover each location. Nek must have made the call to split them up.

There was nothing immediately around, but a shriek cut through the air above them soon enough. Her head snapped up to catch a small flock of birds flying over the alley with a pair of Pawns close behind them. They ran after the Lenian creations. She was unsure how they'd get their attention when one bird circled and cried out again. The rest redirected, now aiming right for her and Zane.

He unloaded his mace, and she did the same for her saber. With a small twist of her wrist, she set a charge and waited for the diving hawk to enter her range.

"Looks like they were heading for the cafe," Sean said over their team channel.

"I don't know how many more explosions that building can take," she said and freed her bolt up into the air. Her hit cut the hawk cleanly in half, but also snapped a cable line running across the street.

Zane took a batting stance and swung for the Pawn coming in low, releasing a set of spikes. The Pawn darted out of the way, only one spike sunk into its casing. He used his backswing to try knocking the thing down, but it narrowly avoided that hit too. "Let's do what we can to keep these away from anyone."

"We'll do the same here," Emma called out via the comms.

Steph watched the Pawn bank straight up into the air to avoid colliding with a wall and hover there. She felt these were moving faster and they looked slimmer than usual. Not to mention that the Pawn had yet to open fire on them like they usually did. Last time the Lenians changed the Pawns, it hadn't been a good thing for them.

Comps ready! came across Steph's display, a message she knew everyone could see.

The team went a little silent, waiting to hear Mina make her call. She'd made a good point about not needlessly offering up Comps the other day, but Steph didn't like that they were so physically divided right now. A quick check of her system told her they were several blocks apart. Sean and Emma were ahead of them, while Mina and Henrie were behind. Putting those two girls together might not have been a great idea.

"You're putting us at risk here," Henrie snapped across the chat. Steph expected she hadn't meant for that to go out to everyone.

Zane turned in their direction. "Hey! We need–"

"Comps," Mina cut him off. "She's right, we need Comps on this one. Let's be smart though. Only two per Warden for now."

On the way!

A bomber bird dropped between her and Zane before detonating, knocking them away from each other. The small ones were the most annoying, but at least they took themselves out with their one hit. Another tried to get in close, but Steph cut the bird away and sent the explosive into the street. The city would have to fix the pothole she'd created, but things could have been worse.

Two bright points of light appeared on either side of Zane. Steph realized she also had two around her. Comps materialized, small blasters at the ready, on either side of her. The previously damaged Pawn was closing in on her now. She sent a bolt directly at it, but the Pawn jerked to the side and only lost a sliver of casing as it continued forward. Her Comps laid out shots, but the one on her left stopped shooting to dodge the Pawn careening by. It hadn't shot back the entire time, simply made a dive attack. Before she could send another bolt after it, one of the blue jays flew in low and sunk talons into her hip, digging at the top of her Pak. As if those tiny claws could break that section of the suit away. Her system told her minor scratches were happening, but nothing worrisome.

Steph slapped the bird away with her hand. "Interesting plan."

Zane caught the blue jay on the spiked end of his mace. He shook off the bits into a dumpster. "New guy is already resorting to straight up thievery."

The other Pawn pushed in, the sides opened to release two long pincer arms. Steph expected those might do a little more damage than the birds.

She charged up a bolt, but dots of pain pierced her back as she was yanked from behind. Another hawk had grappled her and was attempting to reel her back. Her bolt flew way off target, scorching up the side of the brick building on their left.

Add one to the destruction tally, she thought.

To her surprise, the Pawn didn't redirect to attack her but kept straight on for the Comps, who were busy putting an end to the hawk holding her. There was an odd yellow glow from within the Pawn, she'd never noticed that during their previous fights.

Steph broke the chain holding her to the hawk, letting the hook fall on its own as she leapt forward saber first. Her cut ran deep into the center of the Pawn, which still attempted to extend its pincer arm toward the nearest Comp. She charged a bolt while stuck inside the Pawn and let it loose. Pieces blasted out either side of the casing before the shell clattered to the ground.

"This is another weird one," she said to the group.

No one responded. From the general grunts coming across, she expected everyone was just as tightly focused in. She saw Zane swinging to keep the other Pawn at bay. The Pawn's new agility remained surprising. His Comps were low at his sides, aiming up at the birds circling above.

"You're right," he huffed as he caught one of the bomber birds on a swing and flung the broken Lenian creation into the wall she'd previously damaged. The building looked commercial. She hoped it was anyway. Something with weird hours that wouldn't be open right now. Something not likely to have many people inside.

"Swing high," she called out as she ducked below his arms. Steph jabbed out with her saber, expecting the Pawn to fly up and right into Zane's readied mace. Instead, the Pawn shifted quickly to the side and shot past them, toward her Comps still in a firefight with the hawk. That yellow glow grew and crackled around the Pawn. She didn't have enough time to yell a warning, but sent a charge after the Pawn. Steph hadn't reacted quickly enough as the Pawn beat her bolt and smashed directly into a Comp. That yellow energy burst and rippled across the little red robot. Her bolt caught up a second later and sliced the Pawn in two. The attacked Comp stopped firing on the Lenian bird, that yellow glow remained around it now.

"Comp3186 compromised," Nek said in their ears. Steph hoped that was only to them.

Problem! popped up on her display from Comp2876.

"Don't like that," Zane said. He smashed their final bomber bird to the ground at their feet. Neither reacted to the bits of asphalt flying around them.

Steph watched the damaged Comp turn on the other, who'd broken the hawk's wing and sent it to the ground. Again, she had no time to call out before one Comp collided with the other. That same yellow energy bursting out and surrounding the pair.

"Comp7429 compromised," Nek called out.

The two Comps righted themselves before crashing into a storefront window. When they turned toward them, Steph could read a message blinking across their screens, *Property of Councilor Aldrich.*

"Nek, you have to get them back," Zane said.

"It's a virus. All I can do right now is keep it off the framework at large."

Steph spoke off of the team channel, "Mina is going to freak out."

"Nek, pull these two back. Now!" Zane shouted as the infected Comps flew their way. Before Nek could do anything, his Comps broke off in different directions. The compromised pair split up after them. They fell into a dizzying dogfight above their heads, Steph kept losing track of which Comps were the infected ones. Zane held his mace ready, but hesitated taking a swing at their helpers too. An infected Comp landed a shot on its target and used the two seconds of stalled movement to close in and spread that sickly yellow glow. The three bad Comps made quick work of the final one, as Steph and Zane stood helplessly below. The set took off down the street, toward Mina and Henrie, ignoring the Wardens standing in the alley.

"Get the Comps out of here!" Mina screamed across the channel.

Zane and Steph ran after their Comps. She hoped they caught the infected set before they reached any others. Steph charged a bolt on her saber, afraid she'd be using it on their own robots soon.

12

The World is Your Rage Room

Emma had been desperately waiting for someone to bring up the Mina and Steph thing in front of Zane when the alert for the Lenian attack came in. She'd stalled long enough to steal a drink from Mina's iced coffee before following the others into the office, where she'd attempted to fit herself on top of the desk to make room for everyone. Thankfully, they suited up and teleported out quickly. Henrie's suit activation came across the system right as she'd materialized on the sidewalk a few blocks up from Restoration. Sean appeared next to her, as she somewhat expected by now, and she waited for signs of Henrie's teleport next, but nothing came.

"Just you and me," Sean said as he charged out into the street. "Don't act so disappointed."

Emma started after him. "What is that supposed–"

"Something going on?" a voice called out behind her. An old man stood in the doorway of an antique shop.

"Just a standard neighborhood sweep," Sean answered.

"Nothing to see here," she added and waved for the man to go inside.

Instead, the man stepped further out and pointed up to the sky. "Well, I can tell you those ain't standard."

They both caught the sunlight glinting off a group of birds and Pawns overhead. Emma spotted one of those ravens leading the pack. She was going to nevermore the shit out of it. The bird must have felt her challenge as it twisted around and redirected the group directly for them.

"Looks like they were heading for the cafe," Sean said to the team.

"I don't know how many more explosions that building can take," Steph said.

Zane came through a moment later. "Let's do what we can to keep these away from anyone."

"We'll do the same here," Emma called out as she moved herself further into the street. Her gauntlets loaded out over her fists. Sean was busy waving off other pedestrians in the area. She kept herself squared up as the first bomber bird swooped out of the air over her. With a quick uppercut, she knocked the Lenian creation back into the air, and it popped without any damage done.

"Ah, come on!" the old man hollered.

Emma spared him a look to see he was now staring at his shop window, which had shattered from the small shockwave. Okay, so some minor damage. The guy had to know that could have been worse. All she yelled at him was, "Go hide!"

That was enough to make the old man disappear inside. The glass fell out of his door as it closed behind him. Sean reappeared at her side with his batons drawn. He'd cleared everyone else out of their immediate area.

Comps ready! popped on her display.

She almost let out a "YES!", given that neither of them had much for ranged attacks, but held herself back since this turned into an argument before. A quick check on everyone told her Zane and Steph were behind them; they could probably handle themselves if need be. Mina and Henrie were even farther away. Henrie had yet to pick out any sort of weapon. Emma begged her every day to grab something. Anything. But getting a weapon customized required asking Nek or Mina for assistance, and Henrie was being immensely stubborn about going to them for anything.

"You're putting us at risk here," Henrie snapped across the chat.

"Not now, please," Emma whispered to herself. Those two getting into another argument while alone wouldn't be good for anyone. In a pinch, she could clear those blocks in no time with the suit on. Maybe the Lenian pests would chase her.

Zane came loud across their channel. "Hey! We need–"

"Comps," Mina cut him off. "She's right, we need Comps on this one. Let's be smart though. Only two per Warden for now."

On the way!

Sean speared a blue jay as it dove for him and chucked the dead creation to the ground. Emma jumped on the hood of a parked car, walked her way up to the roof, and shouted to get the attention of a Pawn hovering high above.

"I think we need to talk about unnecessary property damage," Sean said.

"I don't know what you mean."

Two spots of light appeared on either side of her. Sean had a matching pair that quickly formed into Comps. The raven let out a pulsing shriek as it swooped low on the street. The glass in the car under her burst, along with the cars to either side. This time around her ears were saved by the suit automatically blocking most of the sound. Her display glitched a little; the raven must have been doing a very minor sort of electrical attack, but everything stayed functional. She didn't want to be stuck in a dead suit again. During their last fight it had felt so heavy before everything booted back up.

The Pawn she'd taunted flew directly toward her, pincer arms stretching out ahead of itself. She jumped at the Pawn as it closed in, smashing a fist directly into its center. No boost necessary, gravity was helping her enough. She followed through all the way to the ground. Its pincer arms stretched out on either side of her, but didn't try making an attack. Sean came in with a quick stab to put an end to the Pawn.

He pointed toward the car behind her. She turned to see her jump had left a sizable dent in the roof. Sort of a minor issue when you considered what the raven did to the windows, but she saw his point. "Maybe I could be a little more mindful. But really, who doesn't expect a little collateral damage when saving the day?"

"And just like that the Evil Collective begins again." His Comps turned to shoot at the raven making a pass. He chucked a baton and stuck the bird through its metal chest, ending the shriek. Sean recalled the baton, with the Lenian bird still attached, and used the bulk of the dead robot to knock a bomber bird off course.

"Woah, hey now." She nearly dropped her guard from the mental stun he'd landed, barely reacting in time to block the incoming second Pawn and its grabby little arms. Her Comps moved farther out to the sides to fire shots without her in the way. "I didn't say let's brainwash children and take over a few planets while we're at it."

"I'm just saying you can get a little reckless sometimes."

There was a yellow glow emanating from the Pawn as Emma hooked an arm and snapped it from the socket connected to the body. "Why is this turning into a performance review?"

"Because you avoided me yesterday when I wanted to talk about all the Collective stuff." Sean ducked as his Comps took out a pair of bomber birds.

"Henrie needed–"

"Yeah, I know. Henrie needed you to talk her down." Sean grunted as a blue jay smashed into his side, fierce but tiny talons digging at his Pak. He beat it off with a baton. "Ever think I might have needed a chat too?"

"It's not like you're going anywhere." Emma used a boost to fully shove the persistent Pawn away. "You love all this."

"I do." He ran after the blue jay hobbling away on the ground. "I need this. And it's bad."

Emma watched him consider his baton before choosing instead to lift his boot and stomp on the Lenian bird. There was an unnecessarily realistic chirp that came from the thing as it shattered to pieces. His targeting system must have warned him about the bomber bird closing in as Sean knocked it away with a baton without looking. Sending the Lenian creation straight into a car across the street.

She gave a small laugh. "What was that about unnecessary property damage?"

Sean spun around to her. For a second she thought he might throw a fist her way. Over the team channel, she heard Steph say something about things being weird. She immediately regretted the thought; Sean was the last person who would ever turn on her. Emma did wonder what his face was doing right then. You could love someone and want to punch them at the same time.

Sean lunged toward her. "Silver, watch out!"

She'd been so focused on Sean that she'd missed her own system warning of the Pawn closing in again. Her Comps closed ranks to defend her back. The Pawn burst with that yellow glow as it collided with both Comps. Followed by the set crashing into her. Their tangled group fell to the ground as messages about compromised Comps blipped on her display. Emma shook off the alerts, more concerned with the firefight happening on top of her. In the scramble, the Comps each put a bolt into her at close range. The hits burned, but her suit kept her protected.

The Pawn pulled away, and the Comps followed. She expected they'd have it torn apart soon, but they stopped firing. As the Pawn turned for Sean, so did the Comps. Emma caught *Property of Councilor Aldrich* across their screens.

"Ummm, what?" she asked from her position on the ground.

"Comps3987 and 4128 compromised," Nek said in their ears. "I'm trying to–"

"Nek, you have to get them back," Zane said over the channel.

"It's a virus," they answered. "All I can do right now is keep it off the framework at large."

"Nek, pull these two back. Now!" Zane shouted as Emma watched her Comps shoot off toward Sean.

The Pawn wasn't far behind, but Emma got to her feet in time to catch that one before it got by. She activated the adhesion on the boots and dug in with her fingers on the Pawn's casing. Metal groaned as it fought against her. Sean took off running, his Comps staying close beside him, but the others were closing in fast. Emma dared to release one hand in order to set her gauntlet's knuckles and double punch the infectious Pawn through the back. Which would have been an awesome move to brag about, if the next thing she saw hadn't been Sean getting pinned down with Comp fire.

His pair returned shots as the infected ones closed in, not caring about the damage they received.

"Get the Comps out of here!" Mina screamed across the channel.

The infected pair glowed the same yellow as they struck the other two Comps. Sean's pair shook slightly before their screens shifted to the same *Property of Councilor Aldrich* message.

Nek was in their ears again, "I need to take–oh. Oh, no."

"Big oh no." Emma watched the four Comps take off up the street, heading toward Henrie and Mina's position. She dashed to Sean and got him standing. "What's the top speed that these can make us go?"

"Haven't gotten the chance to test that yet, but let's hope it's fast enough."

The road ahead looked clear. Emma hoped there'd been enough noise from the fighting to send everyone inside. She bolted toward Henrie's ping on her system. Anything in her way wasn't her concern anymore.

13

Fractured Framework

Comp2876 watched the waypoints for Wardens Mina and Henrie draw closer together. Things were strained amongst the team, but surely they could get through this altercation. All the same, 2876 offered Comp assistance, which Warden Mina thankfully took this time around. 2876 assigned two Comps to each Warden and sent itself as additional support for Wardens Mina and Henrie. Making the call that those two might require extra help.

As 2876 rematerialised in the fight, it witnessed Warden Henrie grab a bomber bird from mid-dive and throw it back into the air. The Lenian bird only went a short distance before exploding over her head. She didn't react to the surrounding fallout.

"Fab can have most things printed within an hour," Warden Mina said as she took shots on a Pawn farther above them. "And I can make modifications if you want something specialized."

"Fantastic," Warden Henrie sighed. She looked at the Comps now at her sides. "These should do fine for now."

"Comps aren't meant for…" Warden Mina let her own statement go as two blue jays plunged toward her. With little aid from her targeting system, Warden Mina knocked both out of the air before they touched her. She celebrated as the birds fell to the ground. "Hey, I got two at once!"

Comp2876 sent *Great job!* as it held its own against a Pawn. Which was strangely not returning fire.

Odd, 2876 noted to Nek.

Agreed, they replied.

Warden Henrie gave a grunt as a hawk's grappling feet latched onto her side and back. She twisted around to grab the chains and pull the hawk in closer. The bird screeched and resisted, but it was losing the battle to the suit.

Comp2876's system warned of an incoming attack. It lowered nearly to the street to avoid being assaulted by the heavily damaged Pawn. A pair of spindly arms reached out and snapped as it passed, a yellow pulse radiated off the entire machine. Warden Mina and her Comps followed the Pawn's path and sent bolt after bolt through its weakened casing. The Pawn strangely turned into the shots, aiming for Warden Mina, but scattered into parts along the street before reaching its target.

"Hey, um Pink," Warden Mina called out. "Watch your Comps."

"Oh my god," Warden Henrie huffed as she yanked the hawk within arm's reach. She grabbed a wing of the struggling bird and used a boost to break off most of the mechanism. "I promise not to let them get scratched, okay?"

Warden Mina was checking her system to locate the original Pawn she'd tagged. "No, I really think they are–"

The Lenian hawk shrieked from its fallen position and Warden Henrie gave a yell in response before smashing the creation with her boot. She turned back to Warden Mina. "Why did you let us use them if you're going to whine about it?"

Warden Mina raised her blasters toward Warden Henrie, who jumped back in surprise. Comp2876 spotted the Pawn coming in low from between a pair of cars parked on the street. The bolts Warden Mina sent hit the Pawn, but didn't knock it off course from colliding with one of Warden Henrie's Comps. That yellow pulse enveloped the Comp and remained as it righted itself and the Pawn careened toward Warden Mina.

Comp2995 compromised appeared on the framework. Notes of Comps from the other fights being compromised followed.

Property of Councilor Aldrich cut into their flow of prompts and commands. Nek instantly scrubbed the message. Another appeared and Nek pushed it away. The compromised Comp's pinpoints within the framework blinked and shifted to that yellow pulse. The intrusive command kept repeating as fast as Nek could clear them from the system.

Issue! Comp2876 alerted the framework, as redundant of a task as that was. 2876 watched Comp2995's screen flash to the same *Property of Councilor Aldrich* as it turned for the Comp on Warden Henrie's other side.

"Grab it!" Warden Mina commanded as 2995 shot across, while she kept the Pawn at bay from her own Comps.

Warden Henrie snatched Comp2995, but not before its front grazed the other Comp and that yellow pulse spread.

Property of Councilor Aldrich

Property of Councilor Aldrich

"Get the Comps out of here!" Warden Mina yelled as she put the second Pawn down, sending more bolts into the casing for good measure.

Nek pushed the *Return* command, Comp2876 rejected it. A feat of Secondary.

Assisting Wardens!

This virus is attacking the framework. It's taking most of my attention to hold it off. Return. Nek pushed the command a second time.

Comp2876 rejected the command again. A bomber and a blue jay swooped down on Warden Henrie, now unprotected. 2876 shot the blue jay, but missed the bomber due to pushing itself higher to avoid an attempted assault from the compromised Comps.

Property of Councilor Aldrich

More yellow pulses were closing in from the street ahead. The other lost Comps coming for them, with the other Wardens close behind. The infected pair went for Warden Mina's Comps. She raised her blasters but did not pull the triggers. Warden Henrie was knocked into a car from the bomber's explosion.

If this gains too many Comps, Nek said in their direct chat, *the entire framework will be lost.*

Problem!

Property of Councilor Aldrich

"2876, stay down here with me," Warden Mina called up. 2876 did as requested and commanded the other two to make a small formation with it near the street.

"Shoot them, Blue!" Warden Henrie ordered.

Warden Mina sent bolts toward the infected Comps, but went wide and didn't land a hit. The Comps as her sides knocked the infected pair off their path and saved themselves.

Property of Councilor Aldrich

"Nek, pull them back!" Warden Mina called out again.

"I'm unable to while stopping this virus," Nek answered. 2876 could tell they were strained.

Property of Councilor Aldrich

Yellow pulses closed in, heading straight for the trio of uninfected Comps. Comp2876 could see them now on the other end of the block they were fighting on. A saber bolt cut through the air and sliced a portion of casing from Comp3987. It lost speed as it recovered from the hit, but pushed forward with its pack.

A hawk dove onto Warden Henrie. A Comp broke rank to aid her, but 2876 halted the Comp and made it fire from a distance. Warden Mina dropped her blasters to tap away on her armband. Comp2876 saw she was attempting to set the teleport herself, but was being blocked by the infected Comps flooding the system. She couldn't get out the same way Nek couldn't get in.

Property of Councilor Aldrich

Property of Councilor Aldrich

A good Comp broke rank again as the hawk clawed at Warden Henrie, but was cut off by an infected Comp swooping in. They bounced along the street as a yellow blur.

Property of Councilor Aldrich

Cut section off! 2876 commanded Nek. Once selected for a ground task, Comps were relegated to their own channel for simplicity in sharing objectives and tasks. 2876 acted as their link to the framework, which is why the virus was bombarding the system. Nek could cut them and protect the rest.

"I can block this." Nek's presence flushed further into their squadron, attempting to replace 2876 as the link. Making themselves the barrier to the framework.

Property of Councilor Aldrich

Property of Councilor Aldrich

Dangerous here! Cut! 2876 pushed Nek away, keeping them out of the sector, as the compromised Comp4128 and 7429 plummeted toward it and the remaining Comp in good standing. They split in different directions and let the other two collide with the ground. Comp2876 attempted to send an apology for the damage, but only received the same message in return.

Property of Councilor Aldrich

2995 and 3186 closed in on the other Comp, pushing in from either side. It leaped into the air, right in the path of Comp3987. One more yellow pulse and Comp2876 was all alone. Surrounded by infected points on the framework.

"No! Stop," Warden Mina cried out, "Stop it. Please stop." She was attempting to push her teleport command through the system, but remained blocked.

Property of Councilor Aldrich

Warden Emma arrived to beat the hawk off of Warden Henrie. Warden Zane took a swing for a bomber bird and knocked it into a blue jay about to dive on Warden Sean. As Comp7429 shot off toward 2876, Warden Steph grabbed 7429 midair and pulled it toward her. Its blaster unloaded and shot her three times in the stomach before she let go.

"They aren't supposed to be able to do that," Warden Zane said.

"I can't get through." The vitals on Warden Mina spiked. "Nek, what do we do?"

Nek was heavy on the other side of 2876's hold. It felt them retreat on the framework. "I have to–"

For a brief moment there was silence, almost perfect silence. Only the static from the infected Comps remained. Nek cut them out for the sake of the rest of the swarm. Good.

Property of Councilor Aldrich

Property of Councilor Aldrich

Property of Councilor Aldrich

The message repeated over and over, jamming their now mini system with the noise. 2876 struggled to make a plan of attack while remaining low by Warden Mina. Who was now stabbing at her armband as her system undoubtedly cleared while 2876's cluttered.

"I can't see 2876 on the framework. Nek, what happened?" Felt strange to only hear her with auditory sensors, lacking the duplication across the comms.

Their tiny sector shimmered yellow around 2876. Wardens fell into a circle around it, weapons ready as infected Comps drew near. Noting their numbering designations became useless, their static kept decaying the log.

Property of Councilor Aldrich

Property of Councilor Aldrich

"2876 isn't infected!" Warden Mina cried. "We have to get them out now!"

"I can't anymore," Nek said this through their armbands, 2876 thought this might have been for its own benefit. "I'm sorry."

Warden Emma punched one Comp away, but a second landed a shot on her shoulder. "I'm now up to three friendly fires."

"Me too," Warden Steph said. Her saber held a charge, but she only stabbed it out at Comps attempting to get near.

"At least the birds are gone?" Warden Sean offered.

"If I get grappled again, that's on you," Warden Henrie shot back.

Property of Councilor Aldrich

Property of Councilor Aldrich

A set of shots landed on Warden Zane's lower legs. "I didn't really need to know what the Pawns feel like during our fights."

Comp2876 couldn't see vitals anymore, but that didn't matter. The Wardens were being hurt in the name of protecting it. That wasn't right. 2876 flew straight up into the air, away from the Wardens. The compromised

Comps wouldn't attack them anymore with it gone. 2876 would save the Wardens this time.

"Come back!" Warden Mina called. "We can't…"

2876 lost her words as it climbed higher.

Property of Councilor Aldrich

The yellow points of the infected Comps took chase after it. A bolt from Warden Steph shot up through the air and cut an infected Comp. One less enemy to outrun. The glimmering yellow crept closer.

Property of Councilor Aldrich

The virus grew stronger with each point collected. Nek was right to cut them off. Comp2876 feared with enough Comps they wouldn't require physical touch to spread the virus. If this batch took off for space and made it to Outrider, that could be the end of them.

Property of Councilor Aldrich

Forgive me. 2876 sent the message out, knowing none could see it. There was a shockingly small component, tucked away on a deck, that 2876 made an effort to never think about. Because it never enjoyed the idea of needing to use it. Certainly not since becoming Secondary and taking over direct care of the Wardens. Nek had set the piece off in Comps to stop Capri in the past. They now kept those Comp numbers on a list as a sort of penance that only Comp2876 knew about. It hated making that list longer, but knew Nek would understand.

They stopped pushing forward and fell into the airspace between the infected pack. 2876 reached for that dreaded component. A Comp jerked sideways and clipped 2876. Its processes froze, the self-destruct command not fully set. A yellow flash overtook its singular system.

Property of Councilor Aldrich
Property of Councilor Aldrich
Property of Councilor Aldrich
Property of Councilor Aldrich
Property of Councilor Aldrich

14

A Few Things Going On

Mina never looked away from her armband until Comp2876 left their protected spot between the Wardens. She'd tried calling 2876 back since she couldn't command it with the framework anymore. 2876 pushed higher and the infected Comps followed. The chase broke above the rooftops soon enough. Steph sent a bolt into the bunch, cutting one Comp in half. Mina felt part of her brain split off to track the halves as they fell. She'd repair it and Nek would fix the programming. They could fix this. Any second now, Nek would tell them they'd patched together a way to break the Comps from this virus.

Comp2876 stopped pushing higher, instead now falling into the group closing in. Mina felt confused about why it would willingly get closer until she remembered the self-destruct component. Her heart jumped into her throat as 2876 fell. An infected Comp clipped the edge of 2876. While Mina waited for an explosion, Comp2876 came to an abrupt halt below the pursuing group. Nothing happened for an excruciatingly long time, then their small forms all wavered and disappeared. Along with the bird and Pawn remnants around them.

"Nek, track them!" Mina pleaded, but she already knew the answer.

"I can't. I'm sorry." Nek sat low and muted in the corner of her heads-up display. "The Comps are gone."

132

"They were stolen," Sean said.

"We can get them back," Steph added.

"Good luck," Henrie said.

Emma jabbed an elbow in her side. "Hey."

There was a hand pulling on her arm, Zane was turning her around. "Blue, the fight is over. Let's go."

Mina tried pulling her arm away from him. "I have to find the parts."

The two halves of the destroyed Comp disappeared between two buildings farther up the street. Would only take a couple minutes to track them down. Steph's saber bolts ran pretty hot. There'd be a lot of melted casing and components to replace. Her mental catalog of Comp schematics compiled a list of the most likely affected.

Steph came up on her other side, putting another hand on her. "People are watching. We should go."

There were faces poking out of the surrounding buildings. People were inching out of doorways to take in the damage along the street. Sirens were closing in behind them. All the more reason she needed to find the Comp before anyone else did. She tried pulling away from both of them. "I need the parts."

"There's nothing worth saving from that Comp," Henrie said.

Her head snapped around to Henrie, glaring at the other girl through the helmet visor. "You don't know that!"

Arms wrapped around her sides, Zane pulled her several inches off the ground. "Nek, pull us up, please."

That was the first time Mina hated the feeling of their teleport. She screamed the entire way to Outrider and only stopped once Zane put her down on the landing pad. Mina immediately reached for her armband to set a teleport back. They were wasting her time. Someone else on the street might pick up part of her Comp now.

Her armband flashed white as Nek filled the screen. "I've locked down the teleport for the time being."

"Why?" She dropped her helmet. The air inside her suit was too warm. "I need down. Now!"

Zane dropped his helmet. He looked sad, but she expected that was more to do with her than the Comp they'd abandoned. "Nek is right, we should stay here."

Steph put a hand on her again. "If they send more of those contagious Pawns–"

"Stop it!" Mina shouted. She spun back to Nek's panel. "I am going back. Open the teleport. Now."

"Told you so," Henrie muttered.

One moment Mina had been looking at Nek and the next she was falling to the floor on top of Henrie. There'd been no thought about attacking Henrie, no plan or coordination in her punches. Her body had jumped into action on its own. She landed a couple hits due to catching Henrie so off guard, but the other girl quickly got her defenses up and threw Mina off. Giving an additional kick to Mina's stomach as she fell away.

"You're a goddamn psycho," Henrie yelled as she sat up. Her lower lip was bleeding, the worst of Mina's damage to her.

"You're a paranoid bitch," Mina shouted back as she lunged for Henrie again.

Arms looped around Mina's middle, pulling her away and up to her feet again. She glanced down to see Steph had been the one to grab her. Zane stepped in front of her, blocking her path to Henrie. He was staring the other girl down. His Pak glowed his bright green, like he might pull his mace out again. Emma stepped up to meet him, her gauntlets already reforming over her fists, while Henrie got back to her feet.

"Woah. Em, chill." Sean grabbed her shoulder, but she jerked her arm out of his hold.

"This really gonna be a problem?" Emma asked Zane.

"Ask your girlfriend," he answered.

"Ask your crazy best friend," Henrie snapped.

Zane and Steph both shouted back responses, talking over each other, but Mina couldn't pick out their words. Steph swapped places with Mina, putting more space between her and everyone else. Emma held her ground against Zane, but was now also holding Henrie back. Sean tried getting everyone to back down, but no one was listening to him.

Everything inside and outside of Mina jumbled into a roiling mass of noise. Fighting with Henrie wasn't what she wanted to be doing right now. Even if getting called crazy stirred up something dark and mean in the back of Mina's head. She wanted her robots back. She needed her robots back. Now. They needed to go, needed to stop wasting time, but everyone was too busy yelling at each other. Meanwhile someone else was getting their hands on her Comp. With her luck today, they'd be delivered straight to her parents. Who'd break the poor Comp open and turn it into some new and horrible monstrosity. Images of the man from the lab flashed through her mind.

A scream ripped out of her. Mina's head spun before everything went black. When she came around, she was sitting in the middle of the floor. Mina didn't know how long she'd been out, but she was breathing rather heavily. Her throat felt raw, like she might have kept screaming while blacked out. Zane and Steph were once again on either side of her. Steph's hands hovered over Mina's arm, as if she'd been ready to grab her. Emma and Sean were crouched by her feet, looking ready to grab her ankles.

Henrie stood away from them all, but somehow she was the first to realize Mina was aware of herself again. The girl held eye contact as she kept her voice level. "You're good. You're safe. Pull your legs up. Head between your knees."

Mina found she didn't mind this coaching and did as she was told. Her thoughts felt jagged and loud as she tucked forward and sucked in a long breath. She leaned heavily on her legs. Her messy bun was released, hair fell down around her. Even with her suit on, it felt as if lengths clung to her back in sweaty bunches. "Too. Hot."

"Oh, my bad." Steph picked her hair up and rolled it into a neater bun high off her neck. Fanning her for good measure.

Zane's large hand came to rest on her back. He curled up his fingers and stretched them out in time with her breathing, giving her a focus point.

"Guys, give her a little space," Henrie said.

She felt Emma, Sean, and Steph back away. Zane shifted a little, but kept his hand on her back. As Mina leveled herself out, she wished to sink through the floor. Now overly aware of the stares from her teammates and the pending embarrassment about whatever spectacle she'd made of herself.

"Is there a way to reprint the lost Comps?" Sean asked. "Copy their data or something?"

Nek answered from above Mina. "Replacement Comps are auto populated in Fabrication in the event they are destroyed or lost, but their numbering continues on from the last Comp to join the framework."

"The personality data," Mina heaved out her words as she breathed, "is stored locally. On their decks. Without them here. The Comp can't be the same."

Comp2876, along with the others, could very well be lost to them forever. Her chest seized tightly and Mina pulled in a long breath. She refocused on Zane's hand.

Steph whispered a small, "You're okay."

She caught Henrie's quiet voice from the other side of the room. "I gotta go. I pulled over so Nek could bring me to the fight. My car is in a random neighborhood. My mom is freaking out."

"Yeah, go," Emma said back. "We got her."

Zane, speaking up for the first time since Mina came back to her body, said, "You wanna maybe apologize before running away again?"

"Zane," Steph sighed.

Mina tipped her head up to see Henrie standing frozen, the cautious stature from before being taken over by her normal tense behavior. She appeared to be weighing her options for how to respond, but eventually shook her head and turned to Nek's panel instead. "Am I okay to leave?"

"Yes." Nek was practically a flat line. "You are clear."

Zane's hand pulled away from Mina's back as he stood. "Really?"

Mina sat up straight. She was afraid he was talking to Nek that way, but his stare remained locked on Henrie.

She stared right back at him. "You all are letting her dictate your lives. Why? Because she found the place? Big deal. She's not fit to lead."

Unfit for duty, echoed in Mina's head; stabbed into the bit of quiet she'd pieced together. That's what they deemed Capri when they'd run her off of Outrider. She'd seen 2876's log of the event. They'd take her Pak away. They'd kick her off the ship. She had nowhere else to go now. Henrie couldn't take this from her. Static built up around her little mental island of calm again.

Mina must have made a noise, because Steph reappeared by her side a second later. Giving her arm a light squeeze as she said, "You're good. Focus on me. Keep that breathing going."

Mina hung her head and focused on the pressure on her arm. Counted the fingertips she could feel as she breathed in. Counted them in reverse as she let the air out.

"Say you're sorry," Zane demanded.

"Come on, Henrie," Sean said. "Just…"

Mina looked up in time to see the last bit of Henrie disappearing in a teleport. The girl hadn't waited to hear what Sean was going to say. Zane shifted his glare to Emma, who initially only responded with a raised eyebrow.

"What do you want from me?" Emma finally snapped. "She's dealing with a lot of stuff."

"I do wonder who could relate to that?" Zane snapped back with an obvious gesture to Mina. He hadn't realized she'd straightened up.

"It's way different. Henrie is–"

"How long is that going to be the catch-all excuse for her?" Sean closed in on his cousin, who looked shocked at his questioning of her. "How much of her shit are you going to let slide? Or is this the Emma and Henrie Show now?"

"Hey, woah." Emma, for the first time that Mina ever witnessed, retreated from him. "Sean, if you want to talk–"

"I did want to talk! You," he shoved her, "blew me off for your girlfriend."

Emma regained her balance and lifted her hands to defend against another attack. "What has gotten into you today?"

"Oh, me? Are you actually wanting to check in on me now? Do you even care anymore?" He moved to close the gap on her.

Emma pushed him away. "What the hell, Sean? What are you doing? We're family."

"Oh! Do you remember that now? Had me fooled there these last couple weeks."

"Why the hell am I getting ganged up on right now?"

"Because you have made it very clear you'd rather keep your girlfriend happy than keep this team together. That'd you throw away your friendships here," he threw an arm out toward the rest of them, "and our relationship for the sake of Henrie. It's been like two weeks and I'm already sick of it."

"No, I just…" Emma dropped her fighting stance, she instead held her hands out to him. "I'm sorry. I'm so sorry, Sean. You're right. I've been an ass."

Sean lost some of that rage, his hands fell limp at his sides. "Yeah, you have."

"Let's go home. We'll talk at my place."

He turned to Zane. "You guys good?"

Zane glanced at Mina, slipping her a quick smile when he saw her paying attention, before nodding to him. "We got it here."

Emma tapped on her armband, but paused before sending them off. She only gave a brief glance to Zane before looking at Mina. "Once we're done, I'll get Henrie to apologize."

Mina wanted to wave her off and say everything was fine, mostly because she wanted to forget this entire event, but her arms weighed approximately fifty pounds each at the moment. Her body wasn't all with the program yet. She gave a loose nod before the cousins disappeared.

Steph let out a long sigh and ran one hand up Mina's arm. "How are we feeling now?"

Zane crouched down at her feet and gave her a quick scan. "She's moved on to being embarrassed."

Mina nodded again, sturdier this time. She also stretched out one leg to tap Zane with the toe of her boot.

"Glad you're back with us." Steph gave a quick glance over to Zane, before pressing a quick kiss onto the side of Mina's head.

Zane fell onto his butt. "What was that?!"

"Kissed," Mina blurted out. She wanted to be the one to tell him, nevermind that Steph technically beat her to it with the gesture. The spot on her temple buzzed from the contact. This was in no way the appropriate time, but it was the only crumb of normalcy she had. "The other day. After the hard drive."

"And then we all got a little distracted since then," Steph added.

Zane laid across the floor and pumped his fists into the air. "YES! FINALLY!"

"People keep saying finally."

"This is such a relief. I was struggling to play matchmaker with everything going on."

"Poor you." Mina poked his leg with her toe again.

Zane sat up, smiling widely. He glanced up to Nek, who'd been quietly churning along the wall, and his smile wavered. "We're kind of a mess again."

"I am keeping an eye on everyone." Their waves kicked up slightly. "I have faith you all will resolve this current issue."

That sentiment kept coming up, but Mina had yet to feel the same.

Steph looked around before catching herself and sighed. "I was waiting for 2876's exclamation point."

"I didn't want to cut them out," Nek said in a rush. "Comp2876 stopped me from investigating. The virus could have infected the entire ship. But I didn't want to do it."

"It's okay," Mina said. "This was a rough one."

"We'll get them all back," Steph said. "Capri will want to use them, right? We'll steal them back."

"Any sign of more activity?" Zane asked.

Nek drifted slightly as they searched, but eventually responded, "No, only local authorities clearing the scene."

Mina thought of the abandoned Comp and expected to feel the same panicked reaction, but nothing came this time. She'd burnt herself out.

"That's good," Steph said. "The others need some time to cool down."

Zane clapped his hands as his suit returned to the Pak. "I hereby decree we take ourselves to the movie room and watch something dumb in the meantime." He pointed to Nek. "You are included in that, by the way."

There was a pause. Mina realized all three were waiting for her to argue about needing to work. Their pending tasks were daunting. Especially if the other three were off the table for now. The urge to encourage them to push on was there, but the words stuck in her throat. She was too tired. Slowly, she pushed herself up to her feet and held a hand out to them both. "Let's go."

15

Those That Can't Do, Outsource

Aldrich made the Comps block the stairway panel with a tattered couch. Word was that Capri was stumbling around again. He'd made the order earlier to drug her after the initial reaction to their testing the virus resulted in matching holes in the walls that the maintenance crew were now repairing, after they'd pulled themselves out. She was being unreasonable. How else were they meant to confirm the new program worked? Two perfectly good Comps floating through his hallways were fair game. The engineers released the infected Comp as soon as they confirmed the trial a success, but even while drugged, she'd hollered for a good while. Why they hadn't put her completely under was beyond him, but they'd done enough to keep her brain mush until he secured his batch of Comps in the suite.

He held no desire for another pop-in. Thus, the couch blocking the door and the elevator remaining fully locked to only his use. Not that he hadn't gotten verbal hits in while she was here, but the restraints remained embarrassing. The shreds of fabric from her stunt sat piled on the same couch, along with the panels that once hung about the room. Tearing apart more of the decor worked as a nice stress reliever after his call with the potential buyers. Aldrich didn't know if Capri's antics or the patron's responses aggravated him more. He'd left the stair runner alone, because at least that served a function. Not to mention his feet weren't modified and couldn't destroy it.

Given the chance, Aldrich would beg his younger self to not be so tacky. Thankfully, this base remained unseen by anyone, outside of the engineers and crew. No one needed their faux pas aired to the universe.

After securing the living area, he moved his minuscule swarm to the office. They rested on the floor along the back wall. The engineers were crafting charging docks fit for them and he didn't want to waste battery life. With his Comps in a row, he sat in the overstuffed chair. Aldrich forced himself to ignore the tearing sounds and enjoy his remarkably comfortable time sitting still in the chair, which would become undeniably ruined as soon as he moved. This was why Lenian standards were all made of the same sturdy materials able to withstand their metal bodies.

Aldrich glanced over his shoulder at the row of dormant Comps. "One of you, come here."

A Comp from the center of the line rose into the air and pushed forward to his side. Aldrich nudged it around to hover in front of him. "Tell me, can you see any rips on this chair with me sitting in it?"

The faint light of a Comp scan rolled over him. *All damage blocked!* flashed along the screen before returning to *Property of Councilor Aldrich.*

"Good, back in line."

Glad to assist! The Comp floated by him.

Aldrich would allow himself to use the chair while he cut together the exciting results from the Comp retrieval. This would be a tasty little package to send out to the interested parties. While Capri was incoherently rambling in her room, Aldrich had filmed brief clips of his Comps around the base. Letting them duck and weave through the floor below his suite. Along with shots at objects he'd thrown down the central opening. His favorite was the group lazily circling the creation being assembled on the telepad.

As he sliced apart the footage, Aldrich couldn't shake a pricking feeling on the back of his head. He turned to see the Comp still floating in the air directly behind him. Without breaking eye contact with its little screen, he reached for the handheld and tapped at the commands. The Comp lowered to the ground and the screen went blank. The program might need a little extra tweaking. Too bad Capri was being childish. He once again could have compensated her for the consultation, but that was another opportunity lost.

To buy him time on the main attraction, he slapped together a teaser and sent it out to his client list. The responses were near immediate, predictable, and promising. Some Collective factions were sending offers. Those like Aris were feigning piety, "ours by right" kind of messages that threatened retaliation for his "thievery". Aldrich knew none of them could trek this far out anytime soon, so he remained unbothered. He marked the more familiar names for priority consideration. Noriko was among those. She was a bore, but always found a way to pay. After that were those who provided little for an initial offer, but included his favorite phrase "something that they could work out down the road". Poor Malia was desperate to keep her small bit of momentum going. After credits, favors were his favorite type of currency.

After the Collective and Warden sorts, there were a handful of interested parties. Most continued to ask for further proof of goods, specifically regarding the Guardians. Gerti continued to almost act offended to be included in such a deal. Aldrich also provided an updated timetable on his creation coming together. The saw-bladed rex would be ready to unleash on the city soon enough. They could be patient a little longer. A message from Mos inquired about any success in retrieving a Pak. Aldrich cut them from the client list out of spite. What those monks would have done with these goods was beyond him anyway, but he paused his work to chew over the problem.

The Pawn count was far lower than desired, due to them throwing everything at that city to become target practice for Comps over the last weeks. His virus might keep the remaining swarm off the playing field for now, but he still needed a way in on the team themselves. He didn't want to divert any more production power to Pawns than there already was, preferring to keep the focus on the creation. They'd blown through most of the birds during the last fight as well. Everything he ordered to be made was another expense sunk into the venture. Aldrich didn't enjoy seeing that number climb.

Regretfully, he admitted the usefulness of Capri's plan of a brainwashed minion. While a teenage girl was hardly a smart choice, having someone take care of business for you was delightful. He pulled up the intel acquired on the team and scrolled through their extended contacts, seeing what better options might be at hand. Aldrich didn't love reaching out to contractors he didn't know, but his hands were tied. Figuratively, this time. His hopes fell even further as he looked over the files, the families were all so tame. The Warden Leader's parents were the only ones who came across as useful candidates.

Within the compiled information was a phone number for the laboratory they worked in, but not their direct extension. He dialed via their translation program anyway, hoping for someone competent on the other end. Cold calling wasn't his favorite, but would have to do for now. The menu programming held no personality and understood nothing more than basic commands. Aldrich wasted several minutes repeating numbers before giving up and ending the call. He would not be trying that again.

Aldrich tapped on Gregory's extension. "Got a minute?"

"Of course." The reply was dry, but that didn't bother Aldrich.

"Some of those birds we have left, they include a sort of speaker function. Correct?"

"Yes, the blue jays are messengers. It's funny you bring that up." He could hear Gregory shifting around. "The planet has a saying. I suppose it got stuck in my head. It's a–"

"Wonderful. Send me the controls for three. Put them down as close to Hephaestus Labs as you can." He sent the location to the engineer.

The end of a sigh came through before, "Right away."

Aldrich shuffled through notices regarding pending deals his coworkers were chasing while he waited. Mundane arms deals filled most of the board. Sales that could be completed in a simple message or two, nothing that took skill or craft to put together. He scrolled a bit slower through the transport listings, already keeping an eye out for anyone buying a ship that might head this direction. None of his colleagues were working on anything nearly as exciting, yet he knew they were boasting to each other all the same. Arriving with Outrider in tow would be a massive delight, for the look on people's faces alone.

His console pinged with the blue jay control program's arrival. The screen filled with their view as the telepad put them down inside a clearing nearby the building. Before heading toward the lab, Aldrich directed them to the crater the ship's departure formed. He sent them on a fluttering loop for a bit of sightseeing. The crater made an impressive little improvised battle arena from what he'd seen in the footage. Aldrich made a note to arrange for a competition to run here. Plenty enjoyed fighting for sport. The bonus of not damaging their own planet would be irresistible. He decided then to broadcast the creation and Guardian fight live. That would give him a gauge for the size of audience such a spectacle could pull.

That distraction of a venture put aside, he turned the birds to his primary target. The Lab was impressive, a sharp cut in the horizon compared to the nature that laid before it. He didn't know where the Willows' office was located, so he sent the blue jays on a pass of the building. With the amount of glass used across the exterior, he expected to see something of the layout. Except he quickly discovered that, outside of the front entrance, the glass was thick and mirrored. The blue jays contained only basic camera feeds and couldn't see through.

Aldrich steered them to the front. He perched his trio on the statue not far from the door. The blue jays registered an unusual amount of heat in their feet, a temperature he expected actual birds would find highly uncomfortable. The people here must heat the thing to keep birds away. What a bizarre aspect to spend resources on.

There were far too many people coming and going from the front entrance for his liking. Slipping through the door would be simple, but there appeared to be a fair amount of humans milling about inside. As he was after a civilized conversation, he preferred to reach the Willows without causing a scene. Additional eyes on him only upped the chances of interference.

As if proving his point, a woman walking by pointed up to the perched birds and said, "Those are a bit in bad taste, aren't they?"

"Yeah," their partner said. "Not the best time to put those out."

Aldrich huffed and sent the birds on another pass of the building. This was supposed to be a simple job. Yet here he was doing surveillance all in the hopes this particular set of parents could be reasoned with.

Back on the side of the building he'd originally approached, Aldrich caught another door opening. He shot the birds toward the building before it could close again. The person passing through dove to the ground as the birds whizzed by, but one bird clipped the man's head and knocked itself out of formation as they entered. The first two blue jays landed on a desk inside, while the desynchronized bird stumbled in a few seconds later.

Aldrich hopped a bird around to take in his surroundings. The room he'd landed in was small, the only furnishings were the desk and a few chairs against a wall. Two halls came off this tiny lobby, but glass doors kept him from going further into the building. He'd come through what looked to be an employee entrance that was currently only occupied by a baffled guard sitting at the desk. The birds' small feet hissed as the still heated metal pressed on cold stone. Leaving little black footprints across the surface.

As Aldrich spoke through his translation program, a bird opened its beak in time with him, "Directions to Jacob and Elizabeth Willows' office, if you would."

"Um, I don't think I can let, uh, birds through." They were reaching for something below the lip of the desk. While also looking around for someone else to magically appear and witness their dilemma.

Aldrich swooped a bird at their hands, making them pull back quickly. The person slid their chair away. That bird settled on the lower level of the desk and opened its beak now. "Clearly, not actual birds."

"Ev-even more so th-then." Their eyes shifted to whatever was under the desk.

He sent a blue jay directly at the person's face. They barely reacted in time to raise their hands and fend off the small, still decently warmed, metal talons. The blue jay scratched all the same, leaving a scattering of red welts across their arms. The person scrambled out of the chair in their effort to get away. Aldrich spoke through the other two blue jays to amplify his point.

"Are simple directions truly worth this trouble?"

The human dove for the side of the desk, reaching for a tablet sitting there. Their bloodied fingers slipped across the screen. "Call off your stupid bird!"

Aldrich stopped the attack. They watched the human tap on the screen with shaking fingers. The door to his right swung open. The guard crawled under the lip of the desk. "The elevator around the corner will take you up. Follow the arrows."

He sent two birds to the elevator and put the final one on the floor to remain with the guard. It stood directly underneath a button for what he expected was a silent alarm and twitched if the guard breathed in its direction. That would keep the human in their little corner. His other blue jays circled the small elevator car as it rose to the third floor. When the doors pulled open, an arrow pointed to the right.

Before Aldrich could direct the birds to vacate the elevator, a clipped voice called out, "The Willows are preparing for their evening appointments. They do not need any pointless distractions."

Aldrich steered his birds out and to the right, immediately hitting the source of the voice in the chest. The human shrieked and flailed in a panicked reaction. The blue jays pecked and clawed as needed to defend themselves. He heard the person stumble and fall into the elevator as he pushed the birds down the hallway. The arrows on the wall ended at a closed door. He used one bird to tap on the glass. No response came. Fully out of patience, Aldrich flung the tiny metal body into the tinted glass paneling. Which cracked but remained intact. The blue jay fell to the floor and was mid-reboot as the door flew open.

Jacob Willows glared out. "Who do you–"

Aldrich opened the beak of his functioning bird. "Hello. I am Councilor Aldrich, speaking to you via one of our creations." He feared they'd assume the bird was a Councilor. "Would you be interested in having a chat?"

Jacob Willows' shoulders dropped. He hitched up an eyebrow as he stepped aside and let the bird in. He gave a glance to the rebooting one on the floor, but made no move for it. Inside the office, Elizabeth Willows rose from her desk to watch the blue jay search for a good perch. Aldrich chose the work table between their desks. The two humans came together on one end.

Aldrich walked his bird closer. "Reasonable to assume you and your colleagues are researching the technology my kind have brought here, yes?"

"Might have given a cursory glance," Elizabeth said.

"Would you be interested in something not broken?" Aldrich fluttered the wings of the bird, assuming he'd need to lay it on thick for the humans.

"An awful kind offer from a stranger," Jacob said. "I assume you are after a trade, yes?"

Aldrich settled into his seat, enjoying the new rips he caused in doing so. "I'd like to talk about your daughter's latest hobby."

He paused to let his words sink in, expecting the parents to immediately threaten him for mentioning their child so casually. Aldrich used those few seconds to frantically search his mind for any clever wording he could use while exposing the Warden leader to her parents. His musing was cut short when he realized neither spoke a word. They looked annoyed to be kept waiting.

The blue jay ruffled itself as he spoke again. "Notice anything strange about her activities lately?"

Another set of blank stares. Elizabeth glanced at her watch, as if he was taking up her precious time. They were giving him nothing to work with. He huffed, "Do you even know where she is right now?"

"Is there a point to this?" Jacob asked.

Aldrich sighed, it came through the bird as a whistle. These humans were taking all the fun out of this exchange. "I simply thought you'd be interested to know she's likely sitting on a spaceship as we speak."

That finally pulled a small reaction from them. Hands at their sides twitched toward each other, but he'd caught it.

"You know where this ship is?" Elizabeth asked.

Aldrich relaxed slightly now that he had a hook in them, but he wouldn't be giving out that information. Last thing he needed was humans trying to scramble together a mission to chase down Outrider before he could claim it. He made the bird idly scratch a small talon against the table, creating tiny ribbons of metal as it did. "No exact coordinates, but we know it's nearby. That's how she's managed these recent little superhero stunts."

This time the pair didn't bother concealing the look they shared. They appeared unconvinced of his statement.

"Mina is highly intelligent," Jacob said. "She wouldn't be out behaving like a brute."

"She wouldn't withhold something like this from us," Elizabeth added.

"Then I don't believe you know your daughter very well." He hopped the blue jay away from them. "Sounds like we all are in need of a little chat with her."

Elizabeth moved to remain in his eyeline. "What do you need to speak to her for?"

"To impress the point of how far out of her depth she is treading. Her and that team of hers are feeling like big heroes here on Earth. The squabble happening here is nothing more than that, a squabble. Greater forces are now aware of Outrider and will seek it out. Her best option is to hand over everything to me and be done with it."

"And what if you're not the only one with interests in that ship?"

"Is that a personal interest? Or are you being a good employee?" Of course these two would have interests in the ship, along with their employer. Aldrich wasn't about to let them have Outrider, but if they could be satisfied with any old ship he could arrange something in exchange. For now, he'd try making a deal with these two directly. Save Hephaestus as a client for another day. He relaxed into his seat, glad to finally have something to work with.

Jacob leaned into the table. "That ship resided on grounds belonging to–"

"My short planetary research informed me your country has a messy history when it comes to land rights. Do you really wish to press that particular point?"

There was a slight tilt to Elizabeth's head that made Aldrich believe she agreed with him.

Jacob waved off the argument. "That aside then. What reason do we have to side with you over our very generous employer?"

"I read up on you two briefly before this call. Both of you with twenty-five years of impressive work behind you. Could have been more lucrative though, if you'd managed to stay still for more than a few years with any company. But you can only stand to be under someone's thumb for so long. Hephaestus must be starting to wear on you already, I expect."

Aldrich caught another glance, this time only Elizabeth toward Jacob. He pressed on, "You prefer to be in control. Free to pursue whatever research fits your fancy. I imagine the knowledge of extraterrestrial life might make a pair like that feel resentful that they've been confined to only one planet."

Jacob rolled his eyes. "Do you not think there'd be a place for us on that ship were Hephaestus to take control of it?"

"And you remain indebted to them for even longer." He made the blue jay give Elizabeth a long look. "Not to mention, you'd be heading out with a target already on your back. Remember those greater forces I mentioned? Do you want them coming after your new spaceship?"

Jacob seemed to agree with the logic, he moved over to stand closer to his wife.

Aldrich wasn't ready to let up. He wanted to be certain they were onboard. With a quick press of a button, he made the blue jay jump into the air. Flapping its wings to stay level with their eyes. "Furthermore, in many regions success depends on the people you know. Having someone willing to make introductions would go a long way."

The Willows now stood pressed side to side. Jacob's eyes drifted over the wings of the bird. Elizabeth stared back at the blue jay as she asked, "And what would you ask of us?"

"Bring Mina in for a conversation. We have a chat and talk some sense into her."

"She's rarely without Zane," Jacob muttered more to himself as he continued to visually inspect the Lenian creation.

Aldrich dropped the bird back to the table, the heavy thunk looked to surprise both of the humans. "I'd suggest against handling two of them at once. Especially without removing their Paks first."

"That oaf is a Warden?" an accented voice asked from behind him.

He turned to see the human the birds had collided with in the hallway. She'd taken some time to straighten herself back out, but there were red tinged slashes in the sleeves of her blouse giving her away.

The woman dropped the damaged creation onto the table and spoke again. "I guess you can teach any dumb dog a few tricks."

Neither of the Willows reacted to her comments. Jacob tapped on the table to pull Aldrich's attention back to himself. "We will consider your offer, but an assurance of your dedication to this partnership would be appreciated."

Aldrich watched him look the bird over again. The leering made him slightly uncomfortable, given that this blue jay was his only point of view on the room.

Elizabeth wrapped an arm around her husband. "We are talking about our only child after all."

Aldrich slumped in his chair, tearing the entire back as he slid down. Everyone always expected free goods. He had a suspicion Gregory wouldn't appreciate losing more of his birds, but such was the job. The humans couldn't see him, so he didn't have to smile, but he did anyway to help keep his tone cheerful. "I'm certain we can arrange something."

16

They are Just the Worst

Zane was impressed that Mina remained conscious through the first Transformers movie. He suspected her general awe of the machinery kept her going. On a normal day she'd undercut her enthusiasm with barbs about the series, but today she'd settled in right next to Steph with her legs stretched out toward him on the other end of the couch and never made a sound. He hoped her head was a good kind of quiet now. She hadn't made a fuss about getting to work or ask to pause everything to check on some task with Nek and the Comps. He took that as a good sign. Mina might be off from her normal self, but she was allowing herself to rest. Not having to fight as much to make that happen was good. Her being cuddled up with Steph was even better.

He hoped it wasn't weird how much he was stealing glances at them. Zane did it mostly to keep tabs on Mina, but they were really freaking cute together. Steph remained zeroed in on the movie, thankfully, so she missed his peeks as well. At the beginning, he'd kept count in his head to space them out, but lost track during a car chase scene.

Not far into the second movie, her legs disappeared from beside him. His next glance found Mina curled up and fighting to keep her eyes open. She was out by the next time he looked over. Zane gave her another fifteen minutes to ensure she was fully asleep before he slowly stood from the couch. While Zane gave his body a quick stretch, he once again found himself surprised at how small she could look when she got all bunched up.

The first time he ever saw her, Zane spent the entire run across their yards thinking he was about to save a little kid from setting themselves on fire. He'd rushed over, intending to put out the flames and find the nearest adult. She'd calmly produced a fire extinguisher to kill the fire as he approached and continued observing the melted robot in her balled up stance as he stood there panting. When Zane finally spoke up, she'd bolted to her feet, completely unaware he'd been there at all. Surprising him by revealing she was someone closer to his age.

"Are you okay?" he'd asked. "What happened?"

"Battery pack overheated faster than I anticipated." She'd reached for the smoldering robot to investigate exactly what had gone wrong, but Zane stopped her.

"Won't your parents be upset you set something on fire?"

Mina laughed, but Zane hadn't known why then. He'd learn later that they'd left her at this new house to wait for the movers and disappeared to their new office. Mina had distracted him from the topic of parents by mentioning having more robots to replace that one with and their afternoon turned into a tournament of fights now that she had a second pair of hands.

He scooped one arm under her knees as Steph gently lifted her shoulders so he could get a grip along her back. Mina didn't make a peep as he lifted her from the couch and headed for her room. He didn't know what to call whatever happened in the landing pad today, but it'd taken its toll on her. Zane had never seen her get that level of worked up before.

His stomach twisted when he recounted the cause. That slight little 'told you so' that tipped everything too far. Zane wouldn't be forgetting that Henrie was on the hook for an apology. Emma too, to a lesser extent, but Sean's argument with her was the more pressing matter there. The last thing he wanted was for this superhero stuff to wreck any of their families. He also recognized that Henrie was dealing with her own sizable problems, but she had no business taking her issues out on Mina. Who was only trying to help everyone.

People never understood that was usually all Mina was after, even if she came at it sideways sometimes. Mina could zero in on their needs and make the perfect thing to fill it. If allowed, she'd repeat that over and over because that was how she showed affection. That was his best friend's MO since day one. By the end of that first summer, his parents had set a boundary against over-automating the house. Sure, she got tunnel visioned on projects, but give her a nudge and she always came back. Simple as that. He didn't get why others found her hard to understand.

Zane held back so Steph could get the bedroom door. She also pulled the covers aside so he could drop Mina directly into bed. They had her tucked in and were out of the room within two minutes.

Steph waited until they were down the hall to speak. "Today was a rough one."

"Very."

"She'll be okay, right?"

"She'll be out for a while. Probably wake up in the middle of the night and go to her workshop. Have something new for us in the morning. Some gadget to help get the Comps back."

"Someone should stay. Not let her get overwhelmed again."

Nek rolled along the wall next to them. "I will assign Comps to monitor her. Ensure she's managing well upon waking."

"Perfect!" Zane put his arm over Steph's shoulders and pulled her along towards the movie room. "I have a lot to teach you about Mina's work to play ratios."

"Do you have a pamphlet for her?"

"Nah, just know it by heart."

Steph laughed as they reentered the movie room. "And she thinks she could make you quit."

His stomach twisted again as he pulled away from Steph. "What are you talking about?"

"Oh, it's nothing. Honest! Just a random thing she mentioned."

"When?"

"After the hard drive, when you walked away. That kind of freaked her out. She said that, um, if this was too much for you, she could make you quit. To help you. Not that she didn't want you here. Just that it might be better for you not to be. Maybe."

"Hey." He gave Steph's shoulder a little squeeze so she'd stop rambling. "I get it. It's cool."

"She really didn't mean it."

"Yeah, I know." He'd brought them back here with the intention of finishing the movie, but no longer felt the desire to do so. "I'm gonna head down now that she's out. Check in with the folks."

"I probably should too." She turned to Nek. "Let us know when she's up?"

"Absolutely," Nek said. "Have a good evening, Wardens."

They both hit their teleports and were pulled away from Outrider. He'd teleported down to the cafe with Mina that morning, so he used the shed waypoint to take himself home. Walking through the backdoor made it seem like he'd been over at her place. Zane gave the Willows house a glare over his shoulder. The dark windows were as expressionless as her parents often were.

She could make you quit, cut into his head as Zane crossed the yard.

No. She couldn't.

There'd been one time, during freshman year, where she tried. He'd been insisting she come hangout with the weightlifting group he'd fallen in with after school. Mina reluctantly caved, and did eventually enjoy herself, but forgot about an assignment for an AP class. She'd finished it the next morning without issue, but that didn't stop her from giving him a hollow speech from the other side of the fence about how she couldn't be distracted anymore. Then walked away like that was the end of everything. At lunch that day, she'd sat far away from their usual table. He'd simply picked up his tray and gone after her, but she wouldn't talk to him. They'd done that for two more days until she asked him to weigh in on a new drone design as if nothing had been going on.

For the last three years, Zane had been proving that he'd always show up for her. Because she deserved someone who would. There wasn't a single thing she could say that would keep him away for good. Zane tried to think of what kind of show she'd put on to push him away this time. All he came up with was her doing a half-hearted imitation of her mother. Maybe some Capri-inspired insults thrown in for flare. All that would do was make him want to hug her. Tell her to leave the acting to her girlfriend.

His parents were watching one of their crime procedural shows when he came in. They raced each other to figure out the killer first. There was a notebook tucked inside the coffee table drawer that kept score.

His dad turned around as he came up behind them. "Hey, bud. What'd you two get up to today?"

"Was gonna check in on the cafe, but there was commotion downtown again, so we stayed away. Kind of bounced around. Was over at Mina's for the last little while." Lying was getting too easy.

His mom turned now. "Rebecca Goza said the Warden fight was a doozy. Crazy birds and those little red ones flying about. They were all over the streets. Good thing you stayed away."

A doozy was the nicest way he'd thought about the fight all day. His shoulders tightened at the realization that this was the same day. An extremely long, singular day. Zane rolled his shoulders and winced at the loud pop one made.

His father's brow furrowed. "You okay?"

"Yeah! Gonna hop in the shower." Zane left the room before any further questions could come his way. Lying might come easier after their last month of superheroing, but he tried not to do too much at once.

Up in his room, he gave his phone a quick glance. His non-superhero friends had moved on from the Warden fight and were now talking about a party coming up, something he'd forgotten about. Zane would have to hope no extraterrestrial issues came up next Saturday. Was hard enough to convince Mina to do social gatherings on a normal day.

They'd been planning a little party too, he thought to himself. Then felt a wave of sadness wash over him again. While reading through Capri's messages he'd found that her team had been talking about making a simple campsite on the planet when they arrived, something reminiscent of their days training together. Forgo the amenities of the ship and rough it to better acclimate to their new world. Supersuit and alien technology aside. They'd be nothing more than a group of friends talking around a fire at night, excited to start their new mission on a far-off planet. The Comps' notations told him those messages happened only a few days before Capri made her pitch to the others about the evil regime. How quickly it all went bad after that.

His team was quiet, a fact he was trying not to worry about. He expected Steph would be the first to pop back into the chat now that they'd come down to Hurst, but she often was the busiest out of all of them and the one who knew best when to give some space. Emma and Sean were probably still together, hopefully on the mend by now. Henrie was certainly ignoring them all; he wondered if she'd try quitting again. Maybe that time he'd tell Mina to keep the Pak and they'd find someone new.

His stomach rolled. Zane kneeled over his trash can and waited for the wave of nausea to either pass or intensify. Facing evil aliens was a regular day now, but thinking mean thoughts was still too much. He hated his nervous system.

Zane pulled in a deep breath, filling his entire stomach with air before pushing it all out. His queasiness lessened with the exercise, along with him internally apologizing to Henrie. He didn't want to be mad at her, not while she was dealing with so much trauma. That didn't seem fair. If he could control things, he'd hold off any Warden problems until she'd been able to fully process what all happened to her because of Capri.

Sadly, that was not a luxury they had. They were all in this fight together, but no one messed with Mina. Not around him. Plenty of others learned the hard way that his best friend was the single topic he didn't mind getting confrontational about. He'd told Emma off a couple times before Outrider happened, and it'd been a major relief when the two started getting along. Which made Emma's recent shift to always siding with Henrie rather frustrating. Their team was already working against crazy odds, all this infighting wasn't helping.

Once his stomach fully settled, Zane got himself to his feet. Pulling the Pak out of his pocket, he tapped a quick code and loaded the armband inside the device. His wrist felt odd without the pressure there. Felt naked.

He grabbed clean towels from the hall closet and headed for the bathroom. This day required a long shower. As long as he'd allow himself to take, which was roughly ten minutes. You never knew when an alert would go off anymore.

Zane mentally skipped through the song playlist in his head as he stood under the hot water, narrowing down his choices for the videos he'd inevitably make for today. There'd be new footage to edit. His night would include pulling clips and sorting them out. A nice, simple task. Mina would approve. Not the content, given how the fight went, but the work in general.

When Zane stepped out of the shower, he noticed the background murmur of the TV downstairs was gone. Usually his parents would be up late on these binge nights, catching up on their saved shows. He changed into a new set of clothes and headed downstairs to investigate.

Zane called out as he descended, "Did an episode trick you guys again?"

Stabbing pain burst across his arm as he came off the last step. He looked down to see bright pink bristles attached to a dart lodged there. Zane pulled out the dart as he turned to the corner of the room it'd flown from. Mel, smirking from his mother's reading nook, was loading another dart into a small gun.

"What the hell?" Zane took a step toward her.

"This is how you put down animals." Mel pointed the tranquilizer gun at him. "You dolt."

"Must we be dramatic?" came from behind him in a bored tone he knew too well, Jacob Willows.

Zane turned around to face Mina's father. His arm felt unusually warm. That couldn't be good. Not with his Pak all the way upstairs and no armband to call for help with. Bad. Dumb. Shit. Worries about his personal safety fell away as he caught sight of his parents unconscious on the couch, darts in both their backs. Elizabeth Willows was crouched in front of his mom while she checked for a pulse.

There was a fuzzy feeling radiating up his arm now, but he ignored the sensation. "Get away from her!"

Mina's mother didn't look at him as she stood. "She's fine. Let's be civil."

His body fought between three separate urges: go to his parents, run for his Pak, or hit one of the three people around him. With the heaviness now creeping through his muscles, he opted to stand his ground instead. "Get out of my house."

Jacob Willows stepped to the side to speak to Mel. "Search his room for the Pak."

They were after his Pak. How did they know he had one, or what it was to begin with?

"Yes, sir." The chair thudded against the wall as she pushed off unnecessarily hard.

Mel made an attempt at shouldering him as she passed. His head was getting fuzzy, but Zane willed himself to remain rooted to the floor. His reward was watching her bounce off him instead. Zane lunged after Mel and grabbed her at the elbow, keeping her from going upstairs. Mel attempted to pull away with little success. He noticed her sleeve was torn and bandages wrapped around Mel's arm underneath. Zane wasn't given time to question the injuries as she fought against him. His joints were starting to feel a little loose, but he won their struggle and pulled her back toward the living room. Mina's parents stood by and watched, making no effort to assist. While his arm was actively turning numb, Zane tried prying the tranquilizer gun from Mel's other hand. She twisted enough to shoot a dart into his thigh, another burst of pain followed by a wave of heat and numbness. He lost enough of his grip on Mel that she slithered away. She put the tranquilizer gun in Jacob's waiting hand and disappeared upstairs.

Jacob Willows took a step closer to him. "Momentary discomfort, I assure you. This was the most efficient route."

"What are you…talking about?" It had taken a surprising amount of effort to piece those words together. What were they going to do with his Pak? What were they doing to do with him? Zane turned to his parents, a move that took longer than he felt it should, and saw Mina's mom step over to his dad. He lurched for her. "Get away!"

Zane wrapped a hand around her arm and pulled. He made her fall to the floor, but tipped himself from the force of his own action. A jab hit the center of his back, a third dart. His body was numb enough now that at least that one didn't hurt as much. He barely avoided tripping over Elizabeth Willows and caught himself on the arm of the couch. She glared up at him from the floor, more annoyed than scared. Which wasn't fair. Zane was trying very hard to be intimidating right now. These two had to know exactly how much sedative was running through his body, yet he was still standing. The least they could do was look a little worried about it.

Elizabeth stood and straightened out her shirt. "This display is rather unexpected. Doesn't fit our current model of him. Do you think it'll throw off the parameters we've set?"

"We should be fine." Jacob Willows answered. "Gives us more to work with. More bite will do him good."

"I have it, sir," Mel called out as she came downstairs.

Zane turned, laborish and slow. His vision wavered and the edges were turning to static, but he still managed to make out Mel handing his Pak over to Mina's dad. While keeping a tight grip on the couch he took a large, wobbling step toward them. "Give. That. Back."

Jacob Willows moved slightly farther away. "We were given explicit instructions not to let you touch this again."

"Who…told…you?" His knees were trying to buckle; he wouldn't let them. He wasn't going down without an answer.

"A little birdie told us," Elizabeth Willows answered as she walked around him. She pulled the dart from his back as she went by. He'd felt the pressure of the needle leaving him, but none of the pain. Numbness overtook the spot of sensation. Zane forced his thoughts off his bodily issues.

She'd said bird. Lenian bird? No. Very bad. His head was heavy. Breathing was weird. Slow. Everything was slow now. His left knee buckled and he leaned heavily into the back of the couch.

"Councilor Aldrich told us about the very interesting ways you and our daughter have been spending this summer," Jacob said. Zane got the distinct impression he was annoyed about how long this was taking.

The new Lenian had sold them out. There was no real grounds for this, but he felt certain that Capri would never stoop to that level. He watched Mina's dad inspect the Pak. Zane's green tint glowed from the pad. So close, but miles away as his body shut down around him. Even with all his issues at hand, he found himself wondering if this was at all what Henrie felt like with Capri in her head giving commands.

Jacob Willows carried on, "Aldrich would like a word with her, sans device, and is willing to compensate us greatly for the aid. We know she's fond of you though. Thought it best to bring you in as well."

Mina. They were going for Mina next. No. They couldn't touch her. He'd promised. She was his family. Not theirs.

Adrenaline shot through Zane's body, the lethargic feeling of the drug fading in its wake. He jumped toward Jacob Willows, desperate for his Pak to clear the junk out of him before he broke multiple bones belonging to these three people. Mina's dad retreated nearly to the front door, but held his bored disposition. Jacob shot a fourth dart into Zane's abs, which he did not feel at all.

Zane's heavy feet caught on each other and sent him stumbling toward the kitchen. He crashed into the island and tried to keep himself standing, but his arms were noodles that couldn't maintain enough hold as his lower half gave out again.

"Is Mina's pet finally going down?" Mel asked.

"Enough of that." Elizabeth Willows casually leaned onto the island next to him. "You didn't need to make this so difficult."

"You." He was fighting for every word now. Breathing was so hard. His head wouldn't stay up. "Suck."

"Impressive endurance and tolerance levels." She looked at her husband. "We should run a genetics screening for fun."

"I'll add that to the report," Mel said.

"Why...do...this?" Zane grumbled as he crumpled to the floor.

"Seems pointless to go into detail now." Elizabeth Willows followed him down. She pressed two icy fingers to the side of his neck, making him overly aware of his own pulse as it continued to slow. "Ask again when you wake up, if you remember."

17

Can't go Home, Can't Stay Here

Capri propped herself up on her workstation and glared at the small flag in the corner of the screen that read "Under Observation". The engineers were ordered to monitor her every swipe after the harmless trick she'd pulled during Aldrich's call. Far as she knew he'd recovered everything deleted, so there was no true harm done. Outside of his already fragile feelings being hurt. The engineers had followed her through the tower, ranting and lecturing until she'd finally run them off with a few well aimed chairs from the dining room.

She didn't want to risk being gassed again so soon, not when her head had finally cleared up for the second time. Instead she opened the feeds for around the tower, catching herself up on the goings on. There was a massive creation nearly finished on the telepad. Maxwell shuffled back and forth as the final touches were being set, making sure the worker drone Pawns kept on pace. They were making a dumb creation. She hated it. Aldrich must have ordered the model since she knew the other two wouldn't have done something so boring.

Aldrich was hiding in the suite with his batch of stolen Comps. Hers currently sat behind her on the cot. Ensuring any booby-trapped Pawn daring to enter her door would meet her first. She'd taken two blasters off a pile of recovered parts that weren't in the best shape, but they'd do. Nothing would get close to her Comps now. As much as she wanted to send them to spy and figure out what exactly the grand Councilor Aldrich was doing up there.

Gregory claimed he was constantly making calls to potential buyers. Or asking the engineers about different aspects of the base. Or Outrider. Or Earth. Basically, anything he could research on his own, were he to bother trying. She wondered if any of those inquiries were about her. What was her going price right now? If anyone out there held interest in an ancient Warden.

"Unfit for duty," she muttered to herself.

Of course she was. Look what they'd turned her into. A raving animal, forced to work with the enemy, scrambling to retrieve what was rightfully hers. Keeping order required hard calls. That's what the new movement stood for. Being brave enough to make those calls, not simply reacting to the actions of others. The original Collective were always losing lives because they waited for the trouble to start, instead of stamping issues out preemptively. Their base here would have been one of legend, if the others had only listened. Outrider would have been the shining beacon of their command. Should have been. Could be yet, if anyone would listen to her.

The aspiration felt hollow to her now. She'd been screaming this plan for so long her own ears were growing deaf to it.

While mildly sedated this last time, she'd taken a dive through the Lenian database regarding the current Collective standing. The drugs helped make everything hurt less, but the ache was spreading through her again. The worst part was that Aldrich was telling the truth. While established factions spread themselves throughout sectors she once knew and beyond, their individual numbers were so small they hardly held any threat. Those that retained a set of Guardians or functional Paks held no more territory than a handful of small, scattered regions across different systems. None were anywhere near capable of becoming the force upon the universe her elders desired. Capri read Lenian reports of their meager stirrings; the majority functioned as independent mercenary forces. Wardens were for hire these days. The only information she bothered uploading to her Comps was the location of the pitiful few faction bases that warranted attention.

Capri leaned on the workstation to watch a Pawn install a fang on the creation, but regretted the choice as a spike of pain shot over her ribs. Her physical aches were returning in force, aligning with her mental ones. She closed down everything on the workstation. If she had to be physically miserable too, she wished to not suffer anymore disappointment for the day.

She sat between her two Comps on the cot. Aware of how unneeded she was by everyone else in the base. Not even consulted on what sort of attack plan might work best this time around. Left to twiddle her thumbs and stay in her room, all because she'd gotten RIGHTFULLY angry at them touching her things. The maintenance crew were fine. Aldrich was being a wimp. She listened to the quiet buzz of the tower for five excruciatingly boring minutes before charging downstairs to Gregory's workshop. He hunched over his workstation and didn't notice her coming in until she jabbed his shoulder.

"There must be something I can do," she demanded.

"Unfortunately," he glanced over the table, taking in a nearly identical layout of work in progress as she'd been observing, "we're rather automated here."

"What are you doing planet-side? What's the plan?" She'd been throwing around the idea of dropping the beast directly into the downtown area. The Pawns did damage every time, but a Lenian creation would decimate the place. Especially with the tail they'd put on this new one.

"Our wise Councilor has requested the crater."

"That's boring. We've done that twice already. You must think that's boring."

He smirked, because he agreed and she knew it, but said, "It doesn't matter what I think. Councilor Aldrich is now in charge."

"Why there? What good does it do him?"

"Vantage points," Maxwell said as he came through the doorway. He swiped something from his tablet toward the workstation. Another new Pawn design unfolded there. "These started production a little over an hour ago. The crater gives him lots of open angles to use. Providing premium footage of the Guardians once they're on the ground."

Capri pulled the blueprint over and stretched the full-scale version up from the table. A hologram of a stripped down Pawn spun before her. The only set of gear left in them were the cameras and a small transmitter. "He's putting them on display?"

Both engineers nodded. Gregory opened a different tab on his workstation, a landing page for a mysterious upcoming broadcast promising "a sight not seen in centuries", but gave no information on when this would happen. He opened the admin access and showed her the preloaded list of contacts who'd be sent a link once the page went live.

Maxwell leaned over her shoulder. "He hopes to have the better part of the galaxy watching."

"All he's doing is making them look good. To what end?" she asked.

"Drives up the price."

"He wants buyers begging to take their money," Gregory said.

In exchange for her ship. Her once home. Thoughts of those unruly teenagers running through Outrider often tormented her, but she rather have it in their hands than some desperate stranger who'd strip it for parts. Her Guardian and Pak, sold off to the deepest pockets. Better they stay with that insufferable Henrie. Capri pushed the holograms away, clearing the station of all his files with it. A rude move, but that was the closest she had to throwing something at the moment. "And you're happy to go along with this plan?"

"Not the first time we've been pressed into compliance," Gregory sighed and began reopening his work. "Remind me, how much agency did we have when you first arrived?"

"I...got better." A weak excuse for herself, she knew. Now they'd replaced her. With a salesman. How insulting.

What exactly would become of her once Outrider was shipped off to some unknown buyer? Was her only sad hope being sold off to the highest bidder too? If anyone wanted her. If they knew she was alive. Aldrich had told her point blank that her and Outrider had been forgotten. She'd been listening in on that call of his, many of them were only giving him their time because they didn't know where he was. They were depending on Aldrich to bring back the goods, or give over the coordinates for a hefty fee.

Capri stood and looked at both of them. "I hope you enjoy your show."

She stalked out of the workshop and back up to her floor. Capri couldn't command the Comps via an armband anymore, but with a whistle they sprang up from their dormant states. "If anyone comes this way, shoot them."

Their small blasters dropped as they snapped into position in the doorway. Capri slapped her workstation awake next. That "Under Observation" flag glared at her from the corner. She paid it no mind as she set to work breaking into Gregory's station from her own. An easy enough task as the two were meant to communicate with each other. Giving her plenty of access points to slip her control programming through without immediate detection. A fact that only won her seconds, until he inevitably noticed tabs opening on their own.

"Capri!" Gregory hollered from below.

She ignored his shouting and focused on reopening the admin page for Aldrich's broadcast site and copying over the contact list. Capri created a new message of her own and pasted the recipients in. Clanging was heard on the stairs. One Comp pushed out to take a shot at Gregory as he ascended.

He crouched low, but didn't retreat. "Must you always be a pain!"

"I think I'm being rather heroic," she responded as she typed out the subject line **Aldrich's Hiding Spot**. "Giving out for free what he'd make people pay for."

This would do well enough to undermine his deal. Aldrich would have time to prepare as the others moved this way, but he'd be on the clock. Desperate to obtain the Paks and ship before his potential buyers arrived to take it for themselves. See how confident he was of his attack plans when the pressure was on. Capri was typing out the coordinates when her station snapped to black, along with the lights in her room. Her entire floor was dark.

Gregory sat on the stairs, his face now lit from below. He looked rather disappointed. "You make it rather hard to keep you alive."

Maxwell called out from below, "Think of this as a timeout. You'll get your lights back when you agree to behave."

Capri grabbed her two Pawn blasters and charged out to the staircase. "When I get my hands on you, Max–"

The suite hatch above slid open. Both her and Gregory watched in silence as the elevator car began to lower. She'd never realized before how slowly the thing moved. Aldrich wasn't looking her way as the car came down. Instead his eyes were glued to his handheld. Before the hatch sealed back up, the stolen Comps flew through the opening and spread out in different directions. They buzzed around the elevator. She gave a sharp whistle and her Comps pulled in close to her sides. Capri didn't know if these were still infectious and didn't plan to risk it. A stolen Comp swooped low, dropped its blaster, and took a shot on Capri. The hit burned across her arm as she barely managed to jump out of the way.

"Hear me out." Gregory moved over on the stairs. "Run."

Capri didn't wait for the Comp to land another shot. She bounded down the stairs two at a time. Aldrich's Comps remained close to him. Allowing Capri to widen the gap between them. Their shots didn't pick back up until she'd cleared another three floors. Hers returned fire, but remained at her sides. Capri let off a wild burst from a Pawn blaster, unable to take the time to properly aim. Every second mattered right now.

"This could have been so different, Capri," Aldrich called after her. "We could have struck a deal."

The lights on every floor blinked off. Only ambient light from the production wings and telepad leaked into the main tower. The already loosed Comp bolts became blue streaks of light through the air. Comps contained plenty of options to function without the lights, but Aldrich didn't know them like she did and he'd need to adjust. She could hear his disgruntled cursing from above as she continued downward. Capri kept up her pace, though it was riskier in the dark.

"Did something happen?" Maxwell hollered from his unknown location above. "The breakers are acting finicky."

"Turn the lights back on, you idiot!" Aldrich rattled the elevator cage he'd inadvertently trapped himself within.

As Capri rounded to the second floor, she heard the elevator stop above. The grate flew open and soon there were other steps smashing down the staircase. A green beam sliced through the air above her, his Disruption weapon. Giving an eerie flicker of sickly light to the tower. She heard the smack of what had to be two of his own Comps hitting the floor below as hers remained pressed to her.

"Even after the grief you gave me," he yelled, "I was going to be merciful! I would have given you this tower! Let you sit by and watch me plunder the planet you failed to win."

She was constantly being attacked by people who insisted on talking while fighting. Did no one simply throw punches anymore? Capri rounded to the final stretch of stairs and took the risk of going over the railing to drop to the main floor. She stuck the landing, but many already damaged parts of her body were angered by the move and she was briefly locked into place from the pain. Two lucky bolts bit into her back before she could recover. Points of lights came on above, Aldrich had finally found the right menu option. They'd be locked onto her again soon. Capri shook off her pain and took off running for the docking bay.

The doors pulled open smoothly as she approached, work done under her command. When the motion lights flicked on, apparently not a breaker Maxwell had tampered with, in unison they almost blinded Capri after her time in the dark. This was more work completed because of her. She'd put this base on the path to a workable standard. A path paved with insults and threats, but she'd gotten results, had she not? Right in time for that arrogant peddler to show up and take all the credit.

Capri rounded the Councilor's transport ship. She spared a short thought to stealing it for the extra speed, but decided against touching anything of his. Instead she sacrificed precious seconds to make one of the Comps etch a rude image into the side of the ship. Her escape pod attached to the scout ship sat on the other side of the bay. Someone had worked on them while she was incapacitated. Neat welds held the two ships together, making the scout now function as a booster for her pod. Which would give her a much larger range of travel. She sacrificed another second to open a side panel, neat bundles of wiring and color coordinated hose lines were running between the two ships. Both engineers' fingerprints were all over this.

A past version of her expected the ship to be rigged to blow as soon as she turned anything on or reached a certain distance away from the base. She knew those two though. Enough to know they'd been only looking for something to pass the time and her leaving the project in pieces had bothered them.

"Open the door," she said to the Comps. They sent their commands to the pod. The doorway opened and the ramp lowered. The interior appeared untouched; the engineers must have focused on fixing the hardware on the outside. She'd gotten the software systems working together practically on day one.

"Want to know what I plan to do with you now?" Aldrich asked from the doorway. The damn thing was so silent now she hadn't heard it opening again.

"Don't care." She walked into her escape pod without looking his way. The Comps hadn't immediately taken up firing on her again, Aldrich wanted the stage for himself.

"I'm going to kill you with your precious Comps. Then I'll find the deepest, darkest part of this planet and drop your body into it. Screw that fire and glory nonsense. You'll be cold and alone and disgraced forever. You'll be as dead as the rest of the galaxy already believes you to be. As dead as the rest of your team."

Capri took a quick step back toward the ramp, ready to make him regret those words, before stopping herself. He'd almost gotten her to expose herself to his firing squad. She backed up and waved her Comps toward the dash. They settled in and began booting up systems. The door began to close.

"You're not much of a fight without your Pak." There was a crackle from outside and then the ship rocked. The power flickered, the door only halfway closed. Aldrich hadn't fully killed her pod with that hit.

"Who tied who up before?" She thought to keep him talking and buy the ship time to recover. Capri kept a Pawn blaster aimed for the partially opened door, but moved to see him out the side of the window. He'd come around his ship and rested an elbow on the wing, oblivious to the graffiti she'd gifted him. Four of the infected Comps hovered above him.

Aldrich spotted her and gave a little wave. "Cheap tactics. All I know is that the engineer's report on you painted a much more striking figure."

Her Comps were working at the dash again, they only needed a little more time. "You want to ridicule me, while you constantly hide behind your little Disruption and stolen goods?"

He brushed off a shoulder. "My modification has put a good number of Wardens on the ground as of late."

"Children." Systems came online along the dash. The door began to slowly pull closed behind her. "If I had my Pak, you'd stand no chance."

He scrolled through something on his little handheld. "You mock me for fighting children, when all you've done lately is lose to them."

Capri wanted to go out there and shut him up, but that was a death sentence. Her shoulders dropped a little once the door fully closed. "I'm done here, Lenian. If you wish me to stay, you'll have to come in here and make me."

Aldrich didn't move, but the Comps drew closer. Their screens flickering *Property of Councilor Aldrich* at her. They each released small cutters, ones that Capri knew could cut through the hull of her ship easily. She eyed the door, realizing that she'd have to risk a shootout in the hopes to save her escape pod. Capri fought Comps several times now, but the act always felt wrong. The fact that these few were being put to work against their will made her feel even worse. The one leading the small pack came to a sudden stop. The others halted as well, but wobbled as if they were trying to move forward. It looked like the first Comp was holding them back.

"What is this now?" Aldrich huffed and tapped harder on his handheld, trying to push through his commands. "Damn things pick now to freeze."

The leading Comp tipped her way, its screen flashed *Leave!* before returning to its previous message. It pulled backward and the others followed suit. The four of them crowded around the Councilor. They weren't turning on Aldrich, but they weren't targeting her either. Aldrich was now cursing at his handheld, as if that would help anything. He seemed more upset that his toys weren't working properly than how she was potentially getting away.

Her engine kicked to life and cut off Aldrich's tantrum. She sat at the dash as the last checks cleared and gave a final glance out the window. Aldrich shoved a Comp toward the pod, trying to force them to fire. A spark ran along his arms, but the Comps were still crowded in close and he called it off to avoid taking them all out.

The dash lit up with new commands prompted by the scout ship's systems. Capri called for the airlock to open, smirked as she glimpsed the Councilor scurrying away. Lenians wouldn't die in open space, but the immediate loss of pressure wasn't pleasant on any kind of body. She'd felt that personally enough times. The Comps drifted along behind him, the one that held the others off being the last to leave the bay.

The pod lifted, shaking slightly from the additional power. Capri worried about her belongings falling until she remembered she'd had no time to take anything with her. Not that there'd been anything left. Outside of her cot. Her eyes flicked to its now empty spot. She'd be sleeping on the floor again.

Capri took over steering from the Comps. Moving them out of the Lenian base and into open space. She wasted no time turning on extra power to get them away. Her exit surely left some kind of scorch mark behind her. She pointed herself toward Earth, but once they left the planet's atmosphere she dropped speed and mainly drifted in that direction.

Which felt fitting for her current mental state. The revolving door of her broken identity kept spinning in her head. Forgotten soldier. Lost relic. Useless partner. Betrayer. What did one become after all that? What was left for her? Where did she go now? There'd have to be a hazardous trip down to Earth for food before she pushed her way out toward the coordinates of one of the pathetic factions she'd saved. Risking another altercation with Nek and their imposter Wardens. To then trek to unknown regions to be labeled as nothing important once again.

Meanwhile, if Aldrich got his way, her history would be stripped and sold to the truly unworthy. More imitators playing at Wardens. The thought angered her more than the children. As aggravating as they were, they stood for something. They were defending their planet against an invader, one more horrible thing she'd become.

Capri rested her forehead on the cool surface of the dash. She'd stopped herself from crying at the base, but alone in her ship, the tears fell free as she sobbed. Her team. Her Rin. Gone. Because of her. The rest of her Collective was long ago destroyed by the inept leaders she'd believed wholeheartedly in. Leaders she'd destroyed everything for. For her team's part, she hoped Nek sent them off properly. Flames and glory, a Warden's ending. Everything Aldrich had vowed to take from her.

Aldrich. Sitting back in that tower, likely feeling smug. Thinking he won something over her. What started as delayed mourning and grief twisted into anger, an emotion that felt much more familiar. The tears turned hot on her cheeks. Her rage overtook her, burned her from the inside out. The need to destroy something consumed her thoughts, but all she had left was herself and her desire for Aldrich to lose.

She sat up straight. "If I'm already dead, so be it. Let it all be gone, then."

Her console only held one glowing beacon, Outrider's location pinging from the same location she'd left it weeks ago. Even at her slowed pace, she wasn't all that far off. Capri redirected her ship for her once home, opening up the new booster as far as she could. As Outrider grew, the pod's system warned of overheating. Fine by her. If she was a ball of fire by the time she hit Outrider's side, so be it.

Flames and glory. Well, less glory, more flames.

Capri's past was gone and her future was stolen, but she could take Aldrich's dream with her. She'd stop anyone from having it. The ship she'd lived on for years, expected to die on one way or another, grew closer and closer. She caught the flash from the deck as Nek registered the approach of her incoming attack. How many of those little Wardens might she catch with this last act? Greedy to hope for the set, but she wanted there to be nothing for Aldrich to turn a profit on.

She could see outside defenses powering on around Outrider. If they hit her, fine, at this speed the remnants of her ship would batter theirs. Enough force to push them toward the moon it hid behind. Perhaps the humans could scramble some sort of force to gather up the remnants. Anything to keep it away from Aldrich.

Truthfully, Capri didn't care what happened next. Let him and the teenagers squabble over all this after she was gone. As long as her fight was over.

Please stop, whispered the imitation of Rin she'd not heard for so long. *You'd only be killing yourself and you know it.*

"You're not here."

And you're not this.

Capri shook her head to quiet the ghost living there. The first blast of defensive fire flew over the top of her ship. There was no reason for those to have missed. Nek had to see the escape pod and know this was her. They were giving her a warning. A chance to change her mind, even after all Capri had done. That wasn't fair. Why show her kindness now?

Nek was part of our team too.

She veered away from Outrider before it was too late. Capri folded over on herself and screamed as the booster cut out. She was not outside of Outrider's defensive range, but no further shots came her way. A Guardian could chase her, but she doubted they'd practiced that yet.

Her ship drifted away from Outrider as the booster cooled, untouched and unbothered. How confused Nek must be. Nearly as much as Capri was. Too much of her hurt. She officially missed being drugged. She set the pod for whatever the last waypoint set on Earth was, something from the Lenian side of the system. The Comps took over piloting as she slipped off the seat and crawled to the space the cot used to fill.

"I'm still here," she said to the empty air. "Hope you're happy."

No answer came.

18

Let Me Put You on Hold

Mina crawled back to consciousness after her overly long nap. Rather than allow herself to stay in bed scrolling on her armband, she went to the deck to get eyes on any updates. She'd hoped for a miracle breakthrough on the Lenian base, but instead watched Capri's escape pod hurtle toward Outrider before changing course.

"Maybe that wasn't her." Mina knew she was grasping at straws, but she wanted to give Nek some kind of alternative. "The Lenians could have automated that ship to dive-bomb us. Then changed their minds. Oh! Maybe they were testing the exterior defenses?"

"Unlikely," was all Nek said.

Fair. Mina didn't believe anything she'd said either.

"She was going to hit us." Mina watched the footage again, not much to look at as Capri's ship had been a decent way out, but a bizarre sight all the same. While her escape pod barreled toward them, the Lenian craft grafted onto the pod bloomed into a beacon of heat as she'd neared. "She had to know that would only hurt herself. Capri had to know that was…"

Mina let the sentence go, not wanting to say the rest out loud.

"She didn't do it." Nek spun, a ball of colorful ribbons on the main display of the deck. They sounded relieved. "She changed her mind."

"That's a good thing."

The two of them watched the small ship cruise vaguely toward Earth. Nek directed every type of radar available at that ship, not wanting to lose it. They didn't know if she'd drop herself to the planet or keep going onward into space. Mina suited up, readying herself if Capri turned for Earth. Maybe she could ask about that death run.

Mina was eager to have a fight on the horizon. At least this was something to do and could provide information about rescuing her Comps. She sent off a message to the group saying that Capri was probably heading toward Earth and they needed to be ready. Nobody answered. Mina felt her panic rising, a flurry of thoughts that they all quit or hated her or both in the aftermath of her meltdown, but then realized that given the time, everyone was probably stuck at a table with their families. She knew from past conversations they all suffered no phone policies, which annoyed her enough on a normal day.

Ten minutes went by without a response. Mina rechecked her message to ensure she'd not omitted Capri's name by mistake. By now someone should have typed out a sly response on their watch. It's why she'd made them. She pushed a long breath out and then pulled a long breath in, then repeated that process until her heart rate slowed. They didn't know for sure what Capri was doing. The escape pod was still within their tracking range. Watching Capri and then sending everyone an update would be fine. With a little more data, she could provide the others a more accurate estimation of the situation.

The odd little ship tipped toward Earth. Waiting for the pod to drift close enough to the planet that Nek could estimate the landing position was a little maddening. Teleporting spoiled Mina regarding the realistic travel time from here to Earth. She imagined the ship could have moved faster if Capri hadn't burned up her booster. As the pod neared the planet, Nek's target radius grew smaller and smaller. Of course she'd go to Hurst again. Capri's estimated landing zone was a surprise though, as she appeared to be aiming for the same clearing between the crater and Hephaestus Labs that Mina and Sean used.

With a few taps, Mina put herself on the edge of the clearing and hid in the treeline. She remained there for twenty minutes as Nek fed her updated tracking on the pod. While waiting, she sent off more messages that received no response. Odds were that Henrie was straight up ignoring her. Emma and Sean could be distracted by their family talk still. What she couldn't figure out was why Zane or Steph wouldn't respond.

Mina typed out, **About to die alone in this field, I guess.** Her finger hovered over the send button when the screen switched over to the tracking. The pod was rapidly dropping into the clearing. She crouched down to watch the ship land near the center, the Lenian booster toward her. The left side opened and extended a ramp down to the ground. Two Comps pushed out into the clearing. Mina's heart jumped at the sight of them, unsure if these were some of hers or ones Capri escaped with a month ago. They swept the area, scans stretching out into the trees. She discovered she hadn't hidden well enough when their blasters dropped and immediately opened fire on her. Mina unloaded her own blasters and reluctantly traded shots, clipping the ship as the Comps weaved through the air.

"Really hate that today insists on me fighting Comps," she mumbled.

She sprinted along the edge of the clearing, keeping the trees between her and the Comps for cover. Mina wanted eyes on Capri. Bark and branches exploded on either side of her as she ran. One shot zipped along her upper back, leaving a burning line across her shoulder blades. She got around to the pod's opening, but became pinned down behind a tree as the Comps shot up the other side.

"Are you going to let Comps do your dirty work?" she yelled, hoping to goad Capri into coming out. She found it strange Capri hadn't charged into the fight upon realizing there was a Warden nearby. Mina tipped out and targeted the joint where the Comps' blaster connected to their deck. One jerked out of the way in time, but her shots landed on the other. The piece broke and fell away. The damaged Comp retreated back into the pod. Her heart sank, she hated having to hurt them. The little robot was only doing what Capri programmed it to. "I got one of yours, Capri. You won't have anything left soon."

The other Comp moved to block the doorway. In the lull of firing, Mina caught a sound she didn't expect. Crying. Close to how she'd sounded earlier that day.

"Nek?" Mina found herself at a loss. "Do you hear that?"

"Yes," came quietly through her helmet.

Mina packed her blasters away, dropped her helmet, and stepped out from the tree with her hands up. The Comp sent off a shot, which she took to the thigh but stayed up. When she didn't return fire, the Comp lowered but didn't shoot again. "Capri, are you okay?"

There was grumbling from inside, but Mina couldn't see her. She took a cautious step forward. The Comp didn't move or fire. Slowly she made her way to the fallen blaster, scooping it up as the other watched. Keeping her hand up to show she wasn't about to use it. Once at the bottom of the ramp, she pushed up onto her toes to peer into the dim interior. The Comp remained in the doorway, blaster leveled at her chest. The other Comp hovered over what must be the control panel for the pod, its screen glowed blue in the low lighting. She caught a sliver of Capri legs. The crying stopped as she'd gotten closer.

Mina called out again, "Could you let me know if you're horribly injured? I'd appreciate not seeing spilled guts."

"Not in the mood, Blue!" Capri snapped. There was a whistle, and the guard Comp retreated into the pod to join the other.

No direct threat had come her way. Mina took that as a sign she could step up the ramp. She held the blaster far out ahead of herself. Once a couple steps up, she slid the blaster across the floor toward the control panel. "Sorry about that. You two are good shots."

The damaged Comp swooped down to retrieve its missing piece before rejoining the other Comp near the roof of the pod. Capri sat balled up on the floor. At first glance, she looked in worse shape than she had by the end of their last fight. Dark circles hung under her eyes and she wore thick bandages over her arms and hands. There was a nasty black bruise creeping up her chest from the top of her shirt. Mina found it slightly interesting that Capri's cheeks got bluer with agitation instead of red. The puffy eyes were the same as humans though.

What had she done to herself out there? Or had Aldrich done this?

Mina slowly lowered herself to the floor in the doorway, but stayed far enough back that she could dive to the ground if another fight kicked off. This was a weird scenario they found themselves in, but she was not about to leave herself without an exit. "Gonna be honest, expected to get jumped walking in."

"I thought about it." Capri glanced up at the Comps overhead. "Oh, calm down. She nicked you."

Mina realized this was the first time she could clearly pick Capri's real voice out from the translated version that came through the suit. The tone was the same, low and annoyed, but her language was interesting. Mina's brain kept trying to think Capri was speaking Italian, but it was more like Capri was making up words that sounded Italian while doing an Australian accent. There was also a lilt to her speech that didn't exactly match up with what Mina expected. Capri would slightly pitch up when Mina expected her to go down. She'd fallen behind on learning the alien language around the ship; there was no app with a vengeful bird to keep her on track.

The guard Comp folded its blaster in and the pair drifted to the other side of the pod. Mina watched the damaged Comp hold the blaster into position as the guard pulled out a torch to weld it back into place.

"How'd you train them on whistles?" she asked.

Capri wouldn't look at her. "Practice."

Well, that went nowhere. "How long did it take to update the ship?"

"Software was simple. I don't know about the hardware. The Lenians…"

"Hmm?"

"Time. It took time, Blue."

Mina was hoping Nek might hop into the conversation, speak through the suit or something, but they remained quiet. People kept leaving her to do emotions all on her own these days. Where to start on the long list of Capri's issues? Childhood trauma, workplace abuse, grooming, loss of loved ones, or–"Oh! I have something for you."

Capri pulled into a tighter ball as Mina reached for her Pak. "I will not fall for a ruse to cuff me."

"No, it's good. I promise." Mina released a small drive from her Pak. "We got into your hard drive. Found, well, a lot of stuff."

During her idle morning, between scrolling socials and playing games, Mina had found herself dragging files into the small drive all the while not really sure what she intended to do with it. The idea that she'd have a chance to attempt winning some favor with Capri by returning her memories seemed outlandish at the time, but apparently wasn't too far-fetched. Mina waved the drive around, noting how Capri's eyes followed the device. "I haven't read or watched all of it yet. We've all only seen parts. But I figured you'd appreciate a copy back."

She set the drive on the floor between them.

Capri didn't move. "What is it?"

"Your team. Everything you saved of them. I think I got everything. I made sure all your messages from Rin were copied first." While Capri's eyes remained locked on the drive and the Comps were distracted, Mina tapped her Pak again and pulled a Lockpuck out, slipping it onto the outside of the ship. There must be intel they could pull from the thing. The puck lit up, letting her know there was something it was chewing away on. Best case, she broke through any protections enough to make a way in for Nek. Potentially gather more of Capri's programming they could then build defenses against.

Capri shot forward and snatched the drive from the floor, pressing it to her chest as she backed into the side of the pod again. "You, uh…I don't know why you did this."

"Because of what I have seen on that hard drive. So, well, I guess I should say–" The call icon popping up on her armband cut Mina off. She glanced down, expecting to see someone finally bothering to answer her, but a picture of Zane's mom smiled up at her instead. "Um, so sorry. One second."

"Okay?" Capri scrunched her face up as Mina slid down the ramp.

"Warden Mina," Nek whispered.

"I know. One second. I swear." She picked up the call from the armband, a small hologram of her phone screen popping up from her wrist. "Hi, Donna! What's up?"

"Hey there, Sweetie," her words were sluggish. "I poked my head…out but didn't see any lights on. I could have sworn Zane said…you were home, but he's…gone. He left his phone. Is he…there? Or did you…two go out again?"

Mina was trying to figure out why she sounded so sedated, especially if Zane was MIA. He never left without some sort of explanation, lie or otherwise. An alarm blared in her head, but she had to tell the truth right now. If she lied and said he was here, Donna would want to talk to her son. "No. He's not with me."

"Well shoot. You two are," she yawned loudly, "usually connected at the hip." Another yawn came from nearby on her side of the call, Zane's dad. "I tell ya, we must…have been tuckered out. Passed out…right here on…the couch. Anyway, is there…someone else he could…be with?"

"I can try Emma."

"That would be…wonderful, dear. Thank you."

"No problem."

"Oh, sweetie, also…we went to the Expo again today…and had a lovely… talk with your parents. They've been in town…for a while. Might be…a record for them." It sounded like she said that half to Zane's dad. As under some unknown influence as she was, Zane's mom couldn't refrain from taking minor digs at them.

"They've been hard at work prepping. I'm sure they'll leave any minute once it's over."

"Let's hope." Donna gave a small gasp; she must have surprised herself by saying that outloud. "Anywho…if you get to him…before I do, tell him to come…home please."

"No problem." The call ended and the hologram blinked off. "Nek, where is Zane's Pak right now?"

Nek spun on her band. "Warden Mina, might you return to Capri?"

"Please. Real quick. It's Zane. Where is he?"

"I'm sure he is…oh, he's nearby." Nek produced a hologram that floated above Mina's wrist.

A map rolled out in front of her, showing Zane's green dot shining from a corner of Hephaestus Labs. Her parent's corner of the building, to be exact. As soon as she'd realized that, Mina shot to her feet and jumped off the ramp. She hit the ground running for the path that connected the clearing to the parking lot.

"Excuse you?" called Capri from behind her. "Are you seriously leaving now?"

Nek was in her ear again. "Warden Mina, might we–"

"They have him!" Mina yelled. She spun back toward the ship, seeing Capri now standing in the doorway. "My pa–bad people have Gre–oh screw this. I don't have time. They have Zane. Stay here and don't do anything evil until I get back."

She turned on her heels and took off in a run again, commanding every boost the suit could produce to move her all the faster.

Before she was out of earshot, she caught one more shout from Capri. "Is this how I rank?"

19

A Little on the Nose

"Warden Mina, I suggest you put the suit away," Nek said for probably the tenth time as Mina hit the edge of the Hephaestus Labs' parking lot.

Mina ignored the request. She was too busy mentally running through the order in which she was going to break everything in her parents' office. Her charge faltered as she realized how many cars were in the lots surrounding the building. She only now remembered that the Expo kept the Labs open to the public later than usual. Which meant a lot of eyes were around. A Warden appearing out of nowhere would draw instant attention. Mina Willows, "beloved" daughter to star researchers, could walk right in.

She dropped the suit, tucked the Pak away in a pocket, and took off in the best run she could manage on her own. One that felt horribly slow after the suit propelled her all the way here. Mina glared at the statue as she passed, hoping that image would reach her parents before she was through the front door. Let them know she was coming, let them think they had the upper hand here.

When the guard inside attempted to put a tablet in front of her, she yanked the device out of their hands and threw it across the lobby. She smiled at hearing the clear sound of a screen shattering as it hit the floor. The guard reached for her arm, but she grabbed two of their fingers and bent them back until she heard something snap. A move she'd learned in self-defense classes before all the Warden craziness started. They cried out and didn't pursue her any further. People nearby rushed toward the guard, and she used the cover to disappear into the stairwell. The tunnel vision inducing rage pushed her up the staircase. A fragment of her mind thought to tell Emma the cardio routine was showing results. Another fraction felt guilty about breaking that guard's fingers. She pushed both away and kept on to her objective on the third floor.

She entered her parent's floor on the far end of the elevator bay. Mina expected Mel to be waiting in the hallway, a stupid smirk on her stupid face as always, but she wasn't there. Rounding the corner to their door, she saw the glass was cracked. Someone had tried breaking through from the outside. Who else had come calling for her parents? Felt good to think they might have more enemies than herself running around.

Mina let herself in, making the door slam open in the hopes the glass would fully break. The first thing she noticed was a set of Lenian blue jays on their standing workstation. Two stood dormant while a third laid on its side. The beak was smashed into the head. She'd found what hit the door. Her father was mid-deconstruction of one wing; she knew because he'd laid the parts out in neat rows. Her hope for an enemy of my enemy situation faded.

The rest of the office was empty. She itched to pull her blasters out and start demolishing everything, but that wouldn't save Zane. As she turned toward her mother's desk, his beacon floated only yards away from her own on the watch.

Nek spun on the armband. "Going forward alone is dangerous. I am alerting the other Wardens to–"

"No time." She'd been trying to reach the others for long enough tonight. Mina wasn't risking Zane's life because no one could check their phones.

Mina didn't pretend like she was oblivious to where her parents were. Didn't have the energy for it, that was being saved for breaking a portion of Mel's face. She yanked the anatomic statue, the one Nek had informed her weeks ago was a hidden switch, forward so hard part of the nervous system snapped off. A section of shelving to her left shuddered backward and slid into the wall, revealing the doorway to their idiotic lair. Mina expected creaking stairs or a shaking elevator when she stepped over, but found only a short passageway. Yet another disappointment from her parents. Some of the offices she'd always assumed belonged to other researchers must be fake.

Mina crossed the hall, coming out to a wide room. A larger version of their home lab. Arranged so similarly that she found herself briefly disoriented. They were sitting in relatively the same places. Neither looked away from their work as she entered. Why bother with this hidden doorway situation if they didn't care about someone coming in?

Maybe because the table holding a strapped down Zane wouldn't have fit as nicely in the other room. There was a metal bar bent over his head. She saw a set of lights running along the inside. Given their recent stunt on her, Mina assumed they were doing some kind of mind-altering work similar to the box she'd stolen. More access points meant better results. Her heart plummeted into her stomach as she took in the sight, but his feet wiggled and she knew he was alive. Mel stepped around from a much smaller workstation in the corner, his Pak in her hands. It dimly glowed his mint green. She wasn't concerned about Mel accidentally attuning, there was no way she'd be acceptable Warden material.

She ignored the minion and stepped toward Zane. "Let him go. Now."

"In time. We're behind schedule," her mom said and waved to a monitor showing a long red progress bar which was only filled an inch.

"Transport took longer than anticipated," her dad added, glaring past Mina to Mel.

"I don't care." Mina didn't look at either of them, only reached for the first strap around Zane's ankles. She yanked on the buckle until Zane gave out a cry of pain. Leaning closer to see what hurt him, her hand rested on the table's edge and a spark of electricity bit into her. The jolt made her jump back a step. Mina then noticed a set of wires along the side that disappeared below the edge. They were running a current through the table. She glared directly at her father. "Turn that off."

He didn't move. "We found consistent stimulation helps."

"Sets things more into muscle memory," her mother added.

"Who knew. All that ridiculous body mass turned out to be good for something," Mel said behind her.

Mina ignored them and traced the wiring along the table. Secured to the back leg was a fully encased power box. There weren't any switches, their annoying remote triggers again. She gave the box a kick, which did little as it was bolted to the leg.

Her mom sighed, "Settle yourself."

Nek spun into a ball on her watch. "I'm almost in."

"Who was that?" her dad asked, leaning forward. The first bit of movement either made since she arrived.

Zane groaned again. He seemed unconscious, but she didn't know if that was from being drugged or the electricity or whatever they were trying to do to his brain. How long had he been here? How long had they been messing with him?

She sensed Mel moving in closer behind her. "Call down, Mina. Animal testing is standard protocol."

Mina turned, throwing a punch directly for Mel's nose. No suit involved. There was a loud, wet crack as Mel's head rocked back from the hit. Mel let out a string of British sounding insults as she stumbled backward. She dropped Zane's Pak to the floor as she moved to cover her newly broken nose. Mina's knuckles were bloody, but the ache was satisfying. She now understood why Emma liked punching things twice.

"Good form, Warden," Nek whispered.

Mina made a mental note to brag about the move later as she scooped up Zane's Pak. She tried loading it into her own to free up her hands, but nothing happened.

Nek whispered again, "No Paks within Paks."

"She hit me!" Mel whined, hands pressed over her nose. "Tell her that dog isn't–"

Nek flashed white on the watch. "Helmet up, Warden Mina."

She hadn't needed the clearance. Mina rushed at Mel as the suit rolled out and grabbed the baffled minion by her collar. Throwing Mel into a cabinet while Mina's helmet closed around her head. "Call him a dog one more damn time."

There were disapproving sighs from both her parents behind them. She used a small assist to pull Mel's feet off the ground before tossing her aside. Mina turned to her mother. "Turn. It. Off."

Her mother rolled her eyes as she reached over and pressed a command on her keyboard. "We're determined to be dramatic then?"

The electric hum of the table cut off. Zane's legs stopped twitching in their restraints. Above his head, the row of lights blinked out as well. Mina kicked the power box again, this time breaking the bolts holding it to the table. Giving them no chance of turning the current back on. All the while, neither of them gave any reaction to her standing there in a Warden suit. Given the birds, she expected the Lenian Councilor sold them out. Capri would have bragged about it back in the clearing.

"She hit me!" Mel yelled again from the floor, blood running freely down her face.

Her father typed on his keyboard. There was shuffling from the front room. The two Lenian blue jays flew through the door carrying a box of tissues, which was dropped onto Mel's legs. Mina thought if this were someone else she'd be yelling for her to leave and get a better job, but Mel deserved her parents. Instead, she unloaded one of her blasters and took the blue jays out with two shots as they circled the room. The updated tracking from the Comps worked wonderfully. The birds fell together through a glass cabinet door, smashing several containers. Something started to bubble and smoke as whatever was stored inside mixed.

Her mother tsked at the same time her father huffed. She'd finally annoyed them. That was the most emotion they'd shown so far in this encounter. Even if they knew her secret, she would have appreciated them being a little surprised she was good at this. Mina dropped her helmet in order to glare at them.

Her father rose from his chair. "I never thought you to be so emotional, Mina."

"I'm surprised to hear you've thought of me." She crossed over to the top of the table, breaking the straps on Zane as she went. He was blinking up at the bar above his head. Mina grabbed the bar and pulled, bending the metal away from him. A move mostly done for show, but she was being emotional after all. "I consider being aggravated a rather rational response to you experimenting on my best friend."

"We were unlocking potential," her mother said. "We knew he was capable of more. You must too. You wouldn't have continued associating with him if not."

"He's perfectly capable of whatever he wants. Without your meddling!" She gave the bar a hard enough pull to break it fully from the table. She chucked the piece toward the dead Lenian birds, smashing more containers and gear. "You're the ones who apparently needed help from outside sources."

"One does not turn down someone owing you a favor."

Mina tried not to gag at the sentiment. She pulled the groaning Zane up on the table and pressed his Pak into his hands. "Nek, can you get a better read on him?"

"One moment." Nek spun on her watch.

Her father stepped up to the other side of the table. "Be practical, Mina. Give us the Paks. Councilor Aldrich has a very reasonable offer for you. For all of us. We," he made a point of gesturing to only himself, her mother, and Mina, "are meant for greater things. Beyond this planet."

"But we knew you'd want your friend along." Her mother stood behind her desk. "We were simply making him more optimized for the journey."

"He doesn't need to be optimized!" she yelled. Mina held her father's eye for longer than she had ever managed before. "You're right, I am meant for things bigger than this planet. So is Zane. And I will make it my personal mission to ensure you never get a foot off Earth."

Zane pressed his Pak to his chest, and the suit quickly spread along his body. "Mina, my parents…they were…"

"They're good. Your mom called me."

He took a deep breath in, comforted by that. "My head feels weird."

"We're gonna get you taken care of. I promise." She relaxed slightly as his helmet enveloped his head. "Nek?"

"There's high levels of sedative in his bloodstream. The suit can detox that quickly enough. His baseline brain waves are off from standard, but that might be the drugs. We'll need him on the ship to fully assess."

"Is it not hypocritical of you to be using an outside source right now?" her mother asked.

Mina turned only enough that her targeting system could lock on to her mother's computer. As she raised a blaster, her mother quickly stood and moved away from the desk. Mina shot bolts until the machine was a pile of rubble. A more or less pointless act, but one that felt good. She turned back to Zane. "How's the stomach feeling?"

"I'm fine." He leaned a little too far to the side.

"I'm setting a new teleport waypoint now," Nek said. "Warden Mina, I attempted to seal the door, but there are–"

A bang came from the front office. The door sounded like it shattered with this latest hit. Her parents looked smug. They must have called reinforcements before Nek was inside the system.

"You're going to make other people deal with me?" Mina asked. "Why am I not surprised?"

"Come with us to have a chat with Councilor Aldrich," her father said. "We're your safest bet out of here."

"It's out of our hands once they come in," her mother added.

"Hephaestus Labs has it out for me over your stupid box?"

"You took far more than that from them, Mina. They want everything you stole from The Park."

Stole. That's what Hephaestus was telling themselves about a ship they never knew was there until she helped turn it on. Someone else trying to take her ship from her. Sure, Mina could give something back. She'd drop her Thunderbird through the roof once they were clear. Right on top of those Warden investigation display rooms. See how they enjoyed that.

She looked between the two of them. "You'd let those guards hurt me?"

"Course not," Zane mumbled.

Her mother sighed. "The theatrics are growing tiresome."

"You either come willingly," her father said. "Or we waste time waiting for the guards to subdue you and take you then."

As she heard the first guard entering the passageway, she knew they were stuck. Nek couldn't lock on them while they were in a fight. Mina pulled her helmet up and unloaded her second blaster. She didn't hate the idea of breaking more things before they left.

20

Pizza Boxes and Fire

Capri could tell the building ahead of her wasn't a good place. That was a weird sense one gained from walking into too many hostile areas. The people leaving weren't in a panic. They appeared more annoyed than anything. Capri also felt annoyed. She'd pulled an oversized jacket from the escape pod's supply hatch before following Blue. Mina. Who'd left her rather briskly after giving Capri's team back. The drive sat heavily in a small inside pocket. She wasn't about to let Rin's messages get far from her. Her Comps were pressed against her back under the jacket, keeping themselves out of view from anyone going by.

Capri pulled the hood up and lowered her head as she stepped out of the way of the oncoming group leaving the building. A set of guards inside waved people toward the exit. One, sporting a series of scratches across their arms and face, halted her only a few steps in by gripping her arm. She glanced at the hand and then slowly up at the human standing there. He took in her inhumanly hued face before looking behind her. Capri followed his eyeline to see a different guard getting their hand splinted. Had Blue done that? She was on a little rampage of her own then. The guard released her arm and followed the next set of people out the door. He was opting out of whatever else was about to happen here tonight.

She continued forward into the hallway beyond. Another guard, who'd missed her first interaction, called out, "Ma'am, you need to stop!"

Yet again a hand was on her arm, fingers tight and pulling her backward.

"Get ready," she commanded the Comps. They lowered to her thighs as she spun on her heel. Breaking the human's weak hold was simple, as was using that arm to turn the man around and twist it behind his back as she moved. There was a pop as she pulled the arm up higher than necessary. Her hood fell during the spin and she heard scattered gasps as the remaining civilians caught sight of her. She bent the guard forward until the Comps' blasters were right in his face. Capri pulled one of her Pawn weapons from the front pocket of the jacket to press against the back of his head. This wasn't her preferred situation. Mainly because weaponry that required ammunition was annoying. She never liked that blasters needed to recharge after too long of use, but she couldn't complain much at the moment.

The civilians noticed and now the panic kicked in. Most ran for the doors they were already heading for, but several ran back into the building. The guard being bandaged, and their helper, both stilled on the couch. Two other guards appeared and pointed their weapons at her.

"What the hell is going on today?" the injured guard asked.

"One of you do something!" ordered the man she had in hand.

Capri kicked a leg out from underneath him. She enjoyed the smack that echoed out as he went down. "Shush. You're the one touching people you shouldn't."

The guard tipped his head enough to see her. "Oh, shit."

She eyed the other guards. "You all should leave. I'm not interested in this fight."

One inched closer. "Stand down."

She whistled for the Comps to move. They pushed to sit level with her head. "Do you think your reaction time is better than theirs?"

One Comp performed a quick scan. *Five active targets* appeared on its screen. There must be more in the hallway behind her. She'd need her other gun soon, which meant letting go of this hostage. The other Comp switched the blaster for the small plasma cutter usually reserved for working on Outrider. If the Comp got close, that would slice through the human weaponry in seconds. The little things were getting crafty. Capri felt proud.

The injured guard called over, "Leave it, man. You've seen the news."

The guard closing in didn't break eye contact with her. "There are scarier things in this building than an alien."

Capri ignored being called 'an alien' and smiled. "Sounds intriguing. Care to point me in that direction?"

A door behind her swung open. Capri kicked the man in front of her away. He smacked into the floor as he'd been unable to catch himself on only one good arm. She moved to put a wall at her back. The other guards around her shifted closer, but the Comps emitted a garbled amount of static that kept them away. Their own version of growling. Capri pulled her second gun to aim toward the newcomers. Employees, based on the badges hanging around their necks, stepped out into the hallway.

"Hostile takeover, sweet," one said, while barely glancing away from the device in their hand. "Whatever you want is probably on the third floor."

"Come on!" came from a guard down the hallway.

The employee shrugged. "Judge me if you want, but I'm staying on the good side of aliens."

More employees came through the doorway. The elevator doors pinged and opened to release more people. Everyone took on various degrees of caring upon seeing the drawn weapons. This was getting far too crowded for Capri's liking. The frantic civilians sounded to be nearly cleared out, but she wanted that panic back.

"Take out who you can," she commanded the Comps. In a flash, they pushed off toward the lobby, blaster bolts rapidly releasing as the pair closed in on the nearest guard. His shot missed by a mile. Nearby employees either dropped to the ground or scattered. A burst of sparks poured out from his hand as a Comp got close enough to use the cutter. The guard leapt back and dropped their useless hunk of metal as the Comps zoomed off to their next target. Capri watched the employee who'd sided with her take a swing for the guard. An unexpected ally, but she'd take any help she could get.

Bits of stone on the wall behind her exploded, shots from down the hall missing her by inches. Capri returned fire, the Pawn blasters releasing bursts of bolts that forced the humans to disappear behind their corners for cover. There was a groan that let her know someone was down. A kick hit her leg, knocking her aim off and making her miss her next shot. Capri looked down to see her hostage had crawled back to take a cheap shot while she was distracted. She shot him in the shoulder, thigh, and knee in one quick burst. He wouldn't bother her again.

A female employee rushed her from the front, shoving her back into the wall. A second joined her and they tried pinning her arms down. Capri struggled long enough to make sure they were straining to hold her before dropping herself to the floor, pulling the two women together. Their faces bashed into each other, three teeth joined Capri on the floor, and the two women fell away. She lost one of the Pawn blasters in the fall. It spun out of reach before getting kicked off into the lobby by a fleeing employee.

Her human ally was shoved to the ground by another guard, landing right next to the blaster. They twisted for the weapon and sent off a burst of shots to keep the guard back. Capri noticed they were smiling, which was a fact that concerned her slightly. Along with their following shout of, "I welcome our alien overlords!"

She was cursed to have unusual comrades.

Glass shattered across the lobby, the guards fired erratically on her Comps, doing more damage to their own building than their targets. Panes crashed to the floor as the Comps circled around to her. She sent a long series of bursts down the hallway as she stood and moved toward the stairwell door. The fleeing employees, who seemed wise enough now to not fight her, provided enough cover to get through the doorway and out of any guard's eyeline. Before losing sight of the front lobby, she spied her ally disappear out the front door. Pawn blaster firing off into the sky.

Capri was officially tired of this planet. She elbowed any descending humans on her way up the stairs. Most were fine to step out of her way once they saw the weaponry. Shouts came from below, guards coming after her, but she shot over the railing to keep them on the ground floor. A bullet pinged off the wall behind her from above. Capri peeked over to see a guard waiting on the third floor, where she was told all the fun stuff was.

"Sic 'em." She nudged the Comps into the open air and watched them zip up toward the guard. There was a flash of bolts and more pings from bullets as she jogged up the stairs. The guard who'd shot at her, along with two more she hadn't seen, laid unconscious by the time she reached the landing. Part of a Comp's casing was torn open; she imagined one bullet must have gotten lucky.

There were more sounds of shots firing on the other side of the landing's door, specifically the sound of blaster bolts. Capri felt oddly certain Blue wasn't far away. She pulled the door open, tipping around the edge enough to see Blue holding her own against a set of five guards. This group must not have been cleared to kill, as they only held electrified batons. Green was there, but leaned against a wall rather than help fend off their attackers.

This whole firefight she was caught in was nothing but a hassle. Blue had clearly walked into a trap, Capri should leave her to it. The drive felt warm in her pocket. Pictures and videos of a previous life she didn't expect to ever see again. Capri sighed and shoved the Comps into the hallway. "Help them."

A Comp instantly shot one guard in the back, knocking them toward Blue, who performed a decent wide kick to put them down. Timid, but minorly impressive from the efficiency. While not dead, that guard wasn't a threat anymore. The other Comp pushed forward and took a different guard's knees out, giving Blue a clear view of Capri as they fell.

"Did you follow me?" Blue called down the hallway. She ducked to avoid a swing, throwing an elbow into a guard's ribs.

Capri was certain she heard a crack with the hit. "I needed to see what you deemed more important than dealing with me."

A guard jabbed Green in the side with the baton, electricity spiked across the suit. She knew only a small percentage of that would get through to him, but Green groaned loudly and swayed from the blow.

Blue shifted to catch him, losing one blaster wielding arm to keep him upright. "I need you on your feet, please."

"You don't...need...me," drawled Green, now trying to push her away.

Capri stepped back inside the doorway as one guard turned to run down the firing Comp, tucking her remaining blaster away to free up her hands. When they came even with the door, she tackled them into the wall. Her troubled shoulder took the brunt of the impact. Capri wondered if that wound would ever get the chance to fully heal as they crashed to the floor. She stayed on top of them, grabbing their arms as they attempted to jab her with the batons. Electricity sparked near her face. The Comp fired shots near the human's head, distracting them enough for her to gain more control and bend the batons down toward their neck. Their skin burned as she held the batons there. She didn't let up until their kicking stopped. This one wouldn't be getting up either. Probably ever.

Capri kept the batons as she stood and turned to Blue, who had two and a half guards on her. The one on their knees was attempting to reenter the fight. Capri gave that one a kick to the head and two shocks to the back once they were down. Green took a swing at another guard. The hit landed, but he did more damage from his entire body following the punch. They both toppled to the ground. Blue smacked the remaining guard across the face with one blaster before knocking them backward with shots to the chest.

Capri crossed over to Green, who was slowly getting to his feet, and tucked herself under one of his arms. She pulled him the rest of the way up, crouching slightly as he was several inches shorter than her. She gave a nod to Blue. "You take point. Clear the stairs."

"No one is going to believe me about this." Blue looked down the other hallway, at something Capri couldn't see. She raised a blaster, but seemed to think twice about whatever she'd wanted to do and moved toward the stairwell door.

Capri kept Green, Zane if she remembered right, up as they stepped behind Blue onto the landing. Blue shot down the gap at the guards waiting on the first floor. Capri's Comps added their own bolts for good measure. Blue's foot dangled over the first step, but she stopped before moving forward. There was a familiar tilt to her head, Nek was talking to her.

Blue twitched toward the stairs and then to Capri, like she couldn't decide which way to move. "The others are here. They're almost at the front now. I don't think they should see you."

"Well, this truce was short-lived."

"You severely messed up He–Pink's head. She's gonna–" Blue grunted and tapped the back of her helmet against the wall. "Whatever. She's already mad at me. There's probably a second staircase across the floor. Can you get to your ship?"

There was commotion downstairs; it sounded as if they were pulling away from the staircase. Capri knew she was putting Blue in a rather hard position. Her team wouldn't be happy she'd let Capri go without a fight. Though Blue seemed more focused on getting Green to safety than anything else. Teams were messy. Everyone was supposed to be equally protective of each other, but they all held favorites. Cycles repeated, the good and the bad.

Capri nodded to her Comps. "We got in fine. We'll get out."

Blue examined her teammate, who was taking deep breaths and appeared to be shaking more of whatever was ailing him. She must have decided they could risk another moment here. "Were you going to hit Outrider earlier?"

Capri's stomach twisted. It took her a long moment, but she finally muttered, "No."

"Do you think you'd try something like that again?"

Her hand drifted up to the pocket with the drive. "No."

Blue sighed and did something they'd trained Capri over and over never to do. How many Elders drilled it into their heads? Never unattune a weapon. Never leave something an enemy might pick up and use on you. She watched as a shimmer ran over one blaster, stripping away the band of teal running along the side. Blue turned the weapon over to Capri. The girl was doing a rather grand gesture, as she didn't know that Capri was hiding a Pawn blaster.

Capri pushed the weapon back. "You're not supposed to do that."

"I know. Nek said so too." She glanced through the doorway they'd entered from. "If I'd been through what the Collective did to you, I'd want to burn down a world or two myself. I can't let you have the world, but if you want to take out this specific building, I won't stop you."

Capri shoved the other baton into the stomach pocket of the jacket, a rather ridiculously large pocket now that she thought about it, and took the offered blaster. She stepped toward the doorway. "You truly hate whoever is back there."

"They tried to..." Blue looked at Green again, failed to hide a hitch in her breathing. "They hurt people. For no reason other than mild scientific interest. They claim to be helping, but they hurt people because they think they have the right to."

The knot in Capri's stomach pulled tighter; Blue struck a sore spot with those words. "Are they anyone to you?"

"My parents."

"Your parents suck," Green mumbled.

"Oh." For all her homeworld's faults, at least her parents had been patriotically brainwashed the same as her. They'd never personally done harm to her, only believed harm was the standard price to pay. "Do you want me to–"

"I don't care. Whatever you do. I don't know if that makes me less worthy," Blue gave a cautious look to her Pak as if the entire suit might turn to smoke on her right then, "but I sincerely do not care."

Capri realized that maybe the true talent of the Paks was finding broken children that needed them the most. The suit held together all their parts until they figured out how to do it on their own. She could have used more time with it, but she'd need to sort that out for herself now. Capri blurted out, "Councilor Aldrich. He wants to strip all this off you and sell it."

"We figured. He snitched on me to my parents."

"Lame," Green said.

"Some buyers claim to be remaining factions of the Collective or independent Wardens. In truth, there's nothing left. It's all broken bits and scraps out there. When Aldrich fails, they'll come for you. Eventually. They're starving out there and you have a feast." Capri wasn't sure why she was talking so much, giving away all this information so freely.

Nek, for the first time in this entire conversation, spoke up from the suit's armband. "Thank you for the warning."

Capri backed into the hallway. "Get them out of here, Nek."

They spoke freely now, "The others are outside the lobby, holding for you and Warden Zane."

Warden Mina nodded to Capri, hooked an arm around Warden Zane, and the two started down the stairs. Capri watched them descend, in the chance anyone came from below again. They'd have a nice, quick fight out of here and then grab a ride home to Outrider. She missed Outrider's teleport. The Lenian one tugged too hard because it was calibrated to pull on metal. When the Warden's cleared the stairwell, Capri moved into the hallway. She took her petty gripe about teleports out on the guards trying to get up, sticking her baton into their backs and sending a few hundred volts through their systems.

She followed the trail of unconscious bodies leading to an office. Inside the room, she found a disassembled blue jay laid out on a table. Since the space was clear, Capri scooped up the parts and shoved them all in the pocket of her jacket. Capri would need to find a larger carrying container soon enough. The jacket was beginning to weigh on her. There were more guards leading into the next room. Warden Mina had performed a fair bit of fighting before getting surrounded in the hallway. Capri stepped over them and crossed to the next lab, blaster out ahead of her. Unsure what condition these atrocious parental figures would be in. What she found was one sniveling person on the ground and another open doorway across the room.

The human gaped up at her, blood running down her face. "What the bloody hell now?"

"Bad day?"

"I did everything for those two." She threw a hand toward the empty desks. "I did CRIMES for those two. Their stupid daughter comes here wearing a super suit, breaks my nose, and I'm suddenly 'disappointingly inadequate.'" The woman pushed herself to her feet. "They took the time to fire me before sneaking out their backdoor."

Capri realized they might have talked in that stairwell for too long. She'd leave a note on Outrider's window. *Sorry, we chatted too much and I missed out on killing your parents.*

The door across the room shifted, Capri and her Comps both aimed for the opening. The deep blue of a maintenance crew head poked out of the darkness. Capri huffed and lowered her weapons. "And where were you hiding?"

"Storage."

"Why?"

The other crew appeared beside them. "Saving snacks."

"Councilor eats too much," the first added.

"What are those freaky things?" the human asked.

"You do not talk unless spoken to," Capri snapped while giving the crew a hard stare. She sighed and spoke to the human again, "Where does that come out at?"

"Back side of the building. Near researcher parking."

"Direct to ship," the crew said together.

A decent escape route, putting her in no real rush. Especially if the Wardens were putting on a show out front. Capri spied two more broken Lenian blue jays, one slightly melted, inside a cabinet that was giving off concerning odors. She held her breath, picked the less damaged one out, and handed it to one of the crew. "Hold."

Capri leveled the blaster at the woman. "Quickly now, tell me what's valuable around here."

21

Reunion Rumble

"Just a couple more steps," Mina coached Zane down to the ground floor. His balance had much improved since she'd pulled him off the table in her parents' lab, but she kept hands on him out of caution. "When we get to everyone, you stay behind us. Okay?"

"I will be punching." He pulled his fists up and readied himself to swing if anyone tried coming through the door.

"We don't know your full condition. I need you to be careful."

His hands fell to his sides. "Do you? Do you need me?"

That was the second time he'd made that kind of comment. Mina didn't know where that was coming from. She feared whatever they were trying to alter in his head was the cause. Before she could ask, Emma came across their team channel. "Sound off. Where are you two at?"

"Just hitting the ground floor by the elevators. Where are you?" She kept a hand on the door handle, ready to run.

There was an explosion from the other side of the lobby. She heard glass shattering. Steph laughed as she said, "Just opened the front door."

"A very Mina-esque special," Sean added.

Everything they'd done together and her legacy remained one explosive. She couldn't help but smile as she stepped into the hallway. The door stopped halfway open. Mina peeked out to see it was pushing on the leg of a Lab

200

worker, who was unnervingly still. A dead guard laid not far away from them. Her stomach gave a little twist, which she took as a good sign of her morality being intact. Mina believed what she told Capri; she didn't care what happened to her parents anymore. Wouldn't bat an eye about whatever ill fate became of them. She didn't want to become that numb about all people though. That felt dangerous.

This whole fight felt more threatening. Their enemies weren't lifeless robots programmed for their destruction this time around. You could tear apart a MegaPawn and not feel guilty about its family back home. Her fight upstairs had been hard. Pushing back what felt like an endless line of guards. As soon as she knocked one down another would take their place. She'd almost asked if the paycheck was really worth the trouble. Reaching the hall with Zane in tow felt like a miracle until she saw the fresh batch of guards waiting for her there. Capri's arrival had been surprising, but heavily appreciated. Then Mina had watched Capri take the fight further than she dared to, killing any guard she came near. Capri made it look simple, just another part of the job. One Capri was very good at. Mina didn't want that for herself or for her team.

Bullets pinged against her door. Mina tipped around to see a guard crouched low and aiming her way. She really needed to take a look at the benefit package Hephaestus was offering. The cafeteria was great, but didn't outweigh all the horrors going on elsewhere in the building. Certainly wasn't worth dying over. Zane slipped through the door behind her. More shots whizzed by, one clipped the top of his helmet. As he pressed against the wall, she raised a blaster and sent two bolts the guard's way. Her second shot snagged their leg, and she heard them cry out as they retreated around the corner by the lobby's reception desk. Mina checked the hallway behind them, clear for the time being. She moved away from the partial cover of the door, keeping an eye out for that guard to reappear from behind the lobby desk.

"Mina." Zane took a deep breath in. "Bodies."

"I think most are just unconscious." She stepped over another Lab worker, this one groaned and looked to be coming around, and headed for the lobby.

"Keep your eyes on the team."

He slid along the wall behind her. A saber bolt sliced through the lobby toward the desk. The bolt was bright neon purple. When it collided with the desk, the stone exploded into rubble. Larger damage than a simple scorch mark being left behind. The guard she'd sent crawling behind the desk would be regretting that decision.

"I love bomb-blade," Sean said on their channel. He was fighting inside the seating area where couches were tossed, shot, and broken. Sean had his batons connected and extended to their full staff length. Mina watched him hook a guard with the scythe bladed end and pull them toward Emma, who was waiting with her gauntlets to knock them out.

A good combo, but she didn't feel comfortable with how close they had to get with enemies. Integrating ranged attacks into everyone's weapons jumped to the top of her to-do list.

Nek spun on her display. "I've locked down the elevators and any doors possible. They shouldn't be able to send more reinforcements from within the building. Unless they blow through them physically."

"So we only have to clear the problems here." Mina stepped out next to the broken desk and tried to get an idea of their numbers, but everyone was moving a little too much. The targeting system tried, but the multiple pings shifting around were overwhelming.

Steph caught sight of Mina and Zane first. "You two okay?"

"We need to get him to Outrider," Mina answered.

"I'm fine," Zane protested. He took off in a run for a Lab worker closing in on Emma, who was duking it out with another guard. The worker held a long nozzle attached to a tank on their back. His mace appeared in his hand and he took a wide swing toward their weapon, knocking it upward as the worker pulled the trigger. A long pillar of flames erupted toward the ceiling.

"Why do they have flamethrowers at the ready?" Steph asked.

"I don't know, but it makes fighting them easier," Henrie said.

Mina felt herself jump slightly at hearing Henrie's voice. She'd not expected her to come this time, but Henrie was holding her own on the other side of the lobby. Henrie had also commandeered a set of electrified batons. Mina watched Henrie toss one to connect with a guard's head, then ran forward and slid across the floor to sweep their legs out from under them. Catching the baton on its descent to jab the guard with a second burst of volts. Mina knew she could never tell Henrie how similar her and Capri's fighting styles were. Especially when she couldn't tell if that was Capri's direct influence on her, or something they'd naturally had in common.

Zane bashed the flamethrower again, smacking the nozzle into the lab worker. They screamed as the fuel lines broke and flames erupted along their arms. Zane's mace disappeared, replaced by a large fire extinguisher. He doused the worker as they scrambled to free themselves from the compromised tank. Zane then used the extinguisher to knock them unconscious.

"When did you make that?" Mina asked as she took shots at a set of workers trying to come up from behind. The extinguisher was his green, meaning it came from Fabrication.

He switched back to his mace. "Like week one. Sean found them in the catalogs. Figured it was best to keep some on hand."

"Some? Who else has one?" Amid their individual fighting, everyone else raised a hand. "I don't set that much on fire."

"I was told they were precautionary," Nek said.

A crash came from down the hall. Two workers stepped out of a display room through the window they'd broken. One raised an arm and a more familiar buzz shot by her side, grazing her arm. They'd broken out the Pawn exoskeletons. She should have been concerned about the Lenian weaponry they'd also commandeered, but all she could think about was that wire breaking through the man's arm.

Mina ran at them. "Take those off!"

More shots went by on either side of her. One bolt hit her left thigh, nearly the same spot the Comp had shot her earlier, but she kept going. The other worker was holding a normal gun, a bullet ricocheted off the top corner of her visor. They might kill her before she figured out how to save them. The worker using the Pawn blaster ran at her, like they expected to knock her backward instead. A pink blur went by, Henrie had run from across the lobby to catch up. The worker made it three steps before part of the exoskeleton extended out from their forward foot to give them a longer stride. The metal pad hit the floor fine, but when the human foot came down the new support rods of twisted metal had nowhere to go but into their leg. The worker cried out and fell. Henrie was quickly on top of them, sending a hard hit into their head to stun them. That was one way to keep them still.

The other worker stopped moving, they struggled between aiming at the two Wardens or pulling at pieces of their exoskeleton. Mina watched the metal dig in along their arm as they panicked. The Pawn parts were trying to form together like they did when creating the MegaPawns. The fact that a flesh and bone person was wearing them wasn't going to stop their programming. She switched her blasters for the mini-torch she'd copied off the Comps and kept her hands far out ahead of her as she neared the worker.

"Don't struggle, it only gets worse if you do." Mina meant to sound calming and helpful, but the worker pulled harder at the Lenian metal along their leg. She watched a length of wire loop around their shin, the frayed end started to dig into the skin.

"Have you seen this before?" Mina asked Nek directly.

"Warden Mina," they sounded slightly bewildered, "from my knowledge, no one else has been reckless enough to try this."

"Stay back!" The worker shot once between Henrie and Mina, but then abandoned the gun to focus on the exoskeleton trying to bond with them.

"Stop fighting!" Henrie shouted.

Mina grappled one of their arms, running the cutter along a joint positioned on their shoulder. She burned the worker, there was no way around it, but they didn't seem to mind as she pulled the entire piece off their arm. The minor burns and scratches were better than what their unconscious co-henchman was dealing with. The worker stilled and allowed her to circle them, finding every weak point in the suit. With a series of quick cuts, she set them free, albeit slightly bloodied. The worker glanced at their discarded gun on the ground and back to Mina. She sighed and unloaded one of her blasters, putting two quick bolts into the floor at their feet. They ran for one of the broken front windows and leapt into the night.

Henrie had started on the Lenian parts trapping the other worker, yanking wiring and weak pieces away as she could. She spoke only to Mina as she crouched down. "Is this, um, what Capri's device was doing to me?"

Mina had seen those barbs digging into Henrie's back, at the time she'd thought Henrie's movement had caused the damage. Maybe it'd been this unusual reaction, but she didn't want to freak Henrie out right now. "I didn't get a great look at that box while activated. I can't say for sure."

"Either way, thanks for getting it off."

"Anytime." That didn't sound right. "I mean, I'm glad to help however I can."

Mina checked in on their other four teammates. They appeared to have the remaining Hephaestus employees and guards corralled at the other end of the lobby. Steph sent a charge toward a trio trying to break for the hallway. Two guards were knocked into the wall, while the remaining employee dropped to their knees and put their hands on their head unprompted. So there was a limit to what Hephaestus could ask of some of them. Sean was taking big swings with his staff. Continuing to herd enemies toward Emma and Zane, who rushed in and knocked out their targets time and again. Emma did some move where mid-jump she put her back to a guard as she wrapped an arm around their head. As Emma fell on her back, the guard's face smashed into the floor below.

Sean's whoop could be heard across the lobby. He was on the team chat a second later. "Wind yourself with that one?"

"A little," Emma groaned. "But did I look cool?"

"Very."

"Worth it."

Henrie laughed a little at Mina's side. "She's such a dork."

"You might be the only one that can say that to her face," Mina said. She got to work with her cutter. In short order they removed most of the suit, but the lengths running through the worker's leg remained a problem.

Henrie spoke their shared worry out loud. "Those are going to bleed a lot."

"Yeah."

"But they have to come out."

"Yeah."

"Awesome."

"Yeah." Mina clicked her cutter to a lower setting. "Okay, first gross step. Rip off the pant leg."

Henrie didn't question her, only grabbed a torn spot and yanked. The pant leg split, revealing the two rods stabbed through the worker's calf.

Mina tried to ignore the blood pooling beneath the leg as she pointed to a rod. "You pull. I'll burn them shut. I can't fix whatever damage is in there, but at least they won't bleed out."

Henrie put a hand on the first rod, but hesitated. "We're really trying to save people here?"

"Only way to prove we're better than they are."

Henrie nodded and yanked the rod out. Mina jumped forward and cauterized the two newly opened wounds. She caught the tiny flash of a notice saying Nek had switched them over to recirculated air, effectively sealing the suits shut. Mina was thankful to avoid the smell of burning flesh. The pain catapulted the worker back to consciousness. Henrie shoved them down. The two of them made quick work of the second rod; the worker passed out again after the pull.

Henrie tossed the rod aside. "My dad made me do this extremely intense first aid class three summers ago. What you just did was way cooler than any scenario they ran."

Mina didn't know how to respond because she was stuck on the fact that Henrie might have actually complimented her. Additionally, Henrie had revealed a small bit of information about herself. All in one go.

"We're clear!" Emma hollered from across the room, pulling Mina out of her stunned state.

"Doors below are being forced open," Nek said, "but I'll have you in five seconds."

"Do we have time to steal our cutouts?" Sean asked while already stepping toward the hall where their display rooms were.

"No," all five answered him.

He stopped. "Fair enough. Had to ask."

Mina took in the fully destroyed lobby of Hephaestus Labs. Rubble, glass, and people were everywhere. Her team remained standing and everyone looked good. From where she stood, she could see the statue had been sliced cleanly in half, Steph had done a little extra damage on their way in. She still felt the urge to call her Thunderbird, but this would be a good enough message for now.

Each of them gained their faint colored auras and were pulled out of the destruction. As soon as they reappeared on the landing pad, a Comp pushed into Zane's space. *Please lower helmet.*

Zane did as requested with a quick, "No problem."

The Comp unloaded a syringe and stabbed Zane's neck, pushing something faintly yellow into him. Mina stepped over to catch Zane as he stumbled a step to the side from the surprise.

She dropped her helmet and gave the Comp a tight smile. "We need a little more heads up before needles happen, okay?"

Noted.

Nek rolled into the room on their panel. "That will flush the remaining drugs from his system. We'll need to scan him for potential brain alterations."

"Brain alterations?" Emma asked.

Zane rubbed his neck. "They didn't do any brain stuff."

"They held you for a while, Zane," Mina said. "We don't know what they all tried."

"They tried insulting me a lot. They tried leaving me with Mel, but I kept barking. I think they were waiting for you to do the actual head stuff."

And they'd complained about her being dramatic. She pulled his arm toward the door. "One scan, for my peace of mind?"

His shoulders slumped. He smiled and allowed Mina to pull him along. "Yeah, let's go."

Steph appeared on Mina's other side, hands wrapped around her upper arm. "I am so sorry for missing your messages! I feel horrible."

Mina felt herself stiffen slightly, remembering how long everyone had left her unanswered, but made herself shake it off. "You all got there when we needed you."

"See, I was working on my saber moves out at the junk warehouse. Because I didn't want to bother you on Outrider. I thought it'd be nice to have something new to show off. I planned to try out some new spin tricks, but then I realized you could spin up the charge too and do bigger damage. That's how I found out there were highly flammable and explosive things left in that building. There might be a hole or two in the warehouse now, by the way. Then my mom called while I was literally putting out fires. There was a whole thing with her new boyfriend she needed to rant about. I'll tell you about that later. I got trapped on the phone with her. Which isn't an excuse. I should have been paying attention to the armband." Steph sucked in a breath after her long ramble, hands tight on Mina's arm. "I need you to know I wasn't ignoring you."

"It's fine, Steph. Honest." Mina could tell from the rate Steph talked she was panicking. She pried a hand off Zane to loop her arm with Steph's. "Bomb-blade seemed pretty worth it."

"It absolutely was!" Sean hollered behind them. He slapped hands on Zane and Mina's shoulders as they entered the medbay. "We also owe you an apology."

A Med hovered over the first bed, Mina nudged Zane to lie down.

"Yeah, real bad time to go on Do Not Disturb," Emma said.

"You can do that on the Paks?" Mina watched data filter to the framework as the Med scanned Zane's brain. She didn't really understand medical chart data, but it gave her somewhere to look other than the people around her. As the rush of adrenaline from the fight left, Mina felt her agitation returning.

"That's more of a shove under a pillow and forget about it thing," Emma trailed off as she answered.

Sean threw an arm over his cousin's shoulder. "We were pretty deep in family talk. Then Henrie came banging on Emma's door and got our attention."

Mina looked away from the scan results to Henrie, who was sitting on the next bed over. Henrie rolled her Pak between her palms. She locked eyes with Mina. "I was ignoring you. Figured the others would come help. When no one answered, I went over to Emma's."

"I'm surprised you would pass up a chance to fight Capri again," Zane said from under the Med.

"Yeah, me too." She set the Pak aside and twisted the covers up in her hands. "I have a few specific things to apologize about. But I want to start with saying I am sorry, for all of it."

Mina was about to say everything was fine again. About to start the apology she owed Henrie in return. About to let this mess get behind them, but then Zane spoke up first. "It's for the best that you didn't come. Capri helped us get out."

"What?" Henrie stopped twisting the cover.

"We saw the ship in the clearing," Sean said. "We knew she was there."

"Yeah, I assumed they'd run her off."

"She, um, followed me to the labs." Mina steadied herself, deciding right then not to regret her decision. If they were going to be mad at her again, so be it. "She could have ran after I left for Zane, but she didn't. And like Zane said, she helped us."

"Why did she do that?" Steph asked.

"I gave her a copy of her team back. All the pictures and videos and messages. It didn't feel right for her to lose everything from that drive."

"She's just out in the world then?" Emma asked.

"Unless she got to the ship. Could be anywhere now."

Steph started hopping on her feet. Letting out short 'oh!'s as she jabbed her code into her Pak. A Lockpuck fell out into her hand. "I saw you'd put this on the ship! Did it grab something useful?"

Mina wanted to kiss her, but didn't think this was the time. Nek had, no doubt, become too distracted with the fighting to register any notices from the Lockpuck coming through. A Comp appeared from a tunnel and took the Lockpuck away, up to the deck where Nek could directly tear into any new data they'd acquired.

"You let her go," Henrie said.

Mina pulled up the hologram from her armband and played the footage from earlier. Letting them all watch the ship speed toward Outrider before giving up. She then switched to the suit's recording of her short talk with Capri. Leaving it on a frame where they could see her current condition.

"She almost killed herself by smashing into Outrider. I followed her down, and she was crying. She doesn't look good. I don't know if her injuries were Aldrich's doing or her own. Capri does know what the Collective became after all these years. She said there's nothing left other than squabbling factions fighting over their dwindling resources. I think," Mina was taking a bit of a leap here, "she's finally acknowledging what all she destroyed in their name. She knows what she did here was wrong. That what she did to Henrie was horrible. She'll probably never say so to our faces, but I believe she feels sorry."

"That's something, I guess," Steph said.

"I also, sort of. Maybe. Kind of. Told her she could ransack the Labs and do whatever she wanted to my parents."

"That's pretty badass," Sean said.

"While being murdered by Capri is something your parents totally deserve," Emma said. "Are we really supposed to forgive and forget the rest of what she's done?"

"It's the only way to prove we're better than they are," Henrie answered as she stood from the bed and tucked her Pak away in a pocket. "That said, I reserve the right to have one street fight with her, if the opportunity arises."

"I'd say you get four, at minimum," Sean muttered.

Mina was afraid Henrie was going to leave, so she stepped into the girl's way. "I need to apologize to you, too. I've been judging you for how, um, intensely you react."

Henrie's face remained a level of neutral that Mina expected was a physical effort on the girl's part.

"You think I'm emotionless, right?"

Henrie looked over her shoulder towards Emma, who gave some kind of silent response. "I, um, thought you could be a little, uh, calculating. Yes."

"You thought I cared more about the Comps than any of you."

"I said that. Yes." Another pleaful glance to Emma, who didn't seem to give Henrie the response she wanted. She scuffed a shoe on the floor. "That's one thing I'm sorry about. Tonight showed me I was wrong. You charged into that building alone to save Zane. Then helped those workers who'd literally just been shooting at you."

"I do care a lot about the Comps. Possibly an unusual amount. I can't say you're wrong there." Not with the full on meltdown she'd thrown over 2876 earlier today. This very long, no good day. "Before all this, I made my own drones and robots. Way simpler stuff, but I worked really hard on them. Until Zane came around, they were all I had for friends. I do hear how sad that sounds, but it was true. As a result, I get a little over protective about the Comps now."

"I get that." Henrie fussed with the hem of her shirt. "We moved bases a lot. Dad was kind of a fixer, they sent him wherever the problems were. Made it hard to make or keep friends."

"We've all got each other now," Steph interjected quietly.

"We do." Mina gave her a smile before turning back to Henrie. "Though, back to your previous comment on me being calculating. I am rather analytical. That's just how my brain works. I think you and I come at things very differently and we're going to need more time to get the hang of each other."

Henrie's eyes went to her feet. "Yeah. Yeah, that sounds fair."

Mina realized she'd forgotten a major part of her whole apology. "I was going to drop my Guardian on Hephaestus. How's that for being overly reactionary?"

Her head snapped up. "You were?"

"Yeah. Once Zane and I got out. Planned to tell Nek to drop the Thunderbird and level the place. Not very in the spirit of trying to be better than them, huh?"

Henrie smiled. "Would have looked awesome though."

"Maybe next time. And you can melt it with me."

"Deal."

"Nobody move," Sean whispered. "They're getting along."

Henrie snorted out a laugh as she looked at the others. Mina turned to see Emma, Sean, and Steph all frozen as if midconversation. Zane, who'd been cleared by the Med, pretended to be asleep on the bed. Nek turned themselves into a series of straight lines along their panel. Even the Comp remained frozen in place, hovering halfway out of the Med.

She felt Henrie lean over her shoulder. "I can make them pay, Captain."

"Show no mercy."

Steph let out a small scream and ran for the door as Henrie shot around Mina. Sean wasn't far behind her. Emma stopped in the doorway, making herself a barricade. She kept Henrie inside the medbay while yelling for the others to hide. Sean reappeared and wrapped his arms around Emma's middle, pulling her into the air and away. Henrie was laughing as they all disappeared down the hall.

Zane sat up and gave her a little clap. "You're getting better at that."

"Hold your applause. I have a question for you." Mina sat on the end of his bed. "What did you mean when you said I don't need you?"

He sighed and closed his eyes. "It was the drugs talking."

"Well, what were the drugs trying to say?"

"Steph told me you said you could get me to quit."

"What? I never–oh. No, Zane, I...okay, hold on. Look at me. Please." Mina waited until he did. "I know the hard drive stuff bothered everyone. You included. And I knew if the others couldn't reconcile that and wanted to leave, they would. Except you. You'd stay, regardless of it hurting you to do so. For me. So I...I said I'd run you off from me, if that meant you were happier elsewhere. Because I don't want you hurting." She laughed and held her arms out to him stretched across the bed. "Which I am doing horrible at."

"How do you think you could run me off?"

"I, um, I didn't figure that part out. I guess I would–"

"You couldn't do it." He shifted down the bed to sit next to her. Now she was the one avoiding eye contact, but he forced her to look at him again. "We're not just best friends. You are my sister. I know family is a dirty word for you, especially right now, but I'm trying to fix that. You aren't shaking me. Ever."

"What if they're right?" Mina discovered she'd developed a little catch in her throat. "What if I am like them? What if I go wrong one day?"

"You? Never. Absolutely not. And I never want you to ask that again. You understand me?"

She wrapped her arms around him. "I desperately need you here."

He smiled and squeezed her tighter. "I know."

Mina pulled away from him. "Should we go join the chaos?"

"Five bucks says Sean is already hanging from something."

As they left the medbay together, Mina pulled up local news on her armband to check on any immediate coverage of their fight at Hephaestus. She was surprised, and happy, to see that a fair portion of Hephaestus Labs had caught on fire after they'd left. While they were reporting a few deaths discovered when firefighters entered the building, they remained busy with putting out the flames and hauling away the injured survivors. The corner that used to contain her parents' office was nothing but a column of black smoke now.

"Do you think Capri got them?" Zane asked.

"I think that's asking too much out of today. If anything, their plans are way off schedule and we kept them from being able to take Aldrich's deal." That was good enough for her right now.

She closed the feed as they zeroed in on the noise coming from the movie room. Sean was accurately hanging from the ceiling with a seat cushion in hand. Emma stood atop the loveseat with her own cushion held high. While Steph was keeping the couch between herself and the circling Henrie, who was clucking like a chicken at them.

"Come on," Henrie teased. "Someone at least try to fight me."

Nek faded in across the panel. "Good news, Wardens."

Mina spun to face them. "The Lockpuck found something?"

"It pulled data from both Capri's system and the Lenian ship attached. We found the coordinates for the base and the key required to bypass their cloaking."

Mina turned to her team. "Anyone up for a visit to Councilor Aldrich?"

Everyone gave a whoop as a response.

"I love that energy. Really. Seriously, though. Is everyone good? Today has been a long one and they don't know we're coming. If anyone needs a short rest, we can hold off."

"I could use ten minutes to down a quick snack," Sean said.

"I want to melt their base with my Cerberus as soon as possible," Henrie said.

Zane interjected, "But let me hit the bathroom first."

Everyone dispersed for their small bit of prep before their space adventure. Mina was the first down to the Guardians. She climbed her way inside her Thunderbird to wait for the others. Nek's newly updated map glowed on her dash. The Lenian base sat near the top of the planet. They were going to Mars, her brain wasn't entirely wrapped around that fact yet. They were going to put an end to this new threat. Most importantly, they were going to save their Comps.

22

Someone's at the Door, Hide

"I called you all to quiet your concerns about my ability to produce results," Aldrich said to his wall of clients. The batch of Comps floated behind him. The two he'd accidentally killed were out of sight on the floor until the engineers finished the charging stations. He'd set the remainder on an interweaving pattern with their screens changing color as they moved, giving himself a more dynamic background. Much better than the dreary spaces others were calling him from. The movement and flashing colors also helped distract from the scuffs the Comps acquired during their standoff against Capri through the tower.

"Have you stolen another pinch of Comps?" Getri asked. His ticking seemed louder on this particular call. Aldrich didn't know if that was something the Empyreans could turn up or if Getri was that naturally insufferable.

Aldrich was about ready to drop him from the call, but his money remained on the table and spent better than others. He'd lost several Collective factions and Warden groups since the last call. One spouted about feeling "dishonorable" after reviewing the footage and seeing the team more directly in action. Others, he assumed, were merely planning their own voyage to either coerce the team into joining their ranks or take it by their own force. Best of luck to that lot. Even if he sold the planet's coordinates off to anyone,

215

they were looking at months in Earth time before arriving. Without the coordinates, it could be years before they stumbled across this place. Either way, they'd be far too late.

For now, he smiled and shook a finger at the Empyrean. "Soon enough I'll have an entire swarm in hand."

That was hopefully not a lie. Aldrich was waiting for an update from the Willows. Even with his warnings about taking on two Wardens at once, and reminding them that he truly only needed them to secure Mina for their deal to be valid, they'd assured him that acquiring two Paks would be simple work. Hours later and he'd yet to hear a peep. He'd tried spying on them with his backdoor access that remained on the birds, but all three were offline. The humans probably broke them five minutes after he'd given over the controls.

Getri crossed his gearwork arms and tipped back. "More grandiose promises, I see."

"And still no Guardians," Aris piped up, sadly not one of the faction leaders to drop from the call. His yellow stars continued to flash in what Aldrich believed to be an intentional beam of light aimed at the helmet.

Aldrich switched the feed to his camera Pawn and pulled it to the balcony window. The creation stood tall, as tall as possible on the telepad anyway, and gleamed during its final adjustments. "We are tightening the last few bolts now. Your confirmation will begin soon."

He grinned as a row of blades spun on the back of his creation. Not something he'd timed, but it was lovely when things worked out. Aldrich aimed the Pawn back at the Comps. He walked through the grouping, nudging them around as he needed more space. "I know you've all been rather patient. I want to show that I appreciate your interest in working with me. How about I send these lovely little things out? Free of charge."

Everyone always wanted freebies. Aldrich watched figures shift in their view screens, clearly interested in getting their hands on the vintage Comps. They'd all be so excited about their new toy, nobody would check the programming for a little bug he'd leave in the system after he cleared the Comps of his ownership virus. A small string of code feeding Aldrich with any interesting bits of data that the Comps might overhear with their new owners. He preferred working with tangible goods, but everyone needed a little intel in their back pocket. Necessary part of the job these days.

"I know we've all been using encrypted channels for peace of mind." Aldrich tilted toward the Pawn; the Comps continued circling around him. "The first seven to send me verifiable coordinates can have one of these dear little antiques."

"Keeping some for yourself?" Noriko asked, as Aldrich's handheld pinged with the first direct message coming in. She'd of course have to find something to be a stickler about.

"Always hold a little back. They taught us that in training." Aldrich stepped over to the handheld, letting his investors keep eyes on the Comps. The first message contained coordinates from Malia, the do-gooder was quick on the draw. She beat Getri by only fractions of a second, judging by the timestamps.

There was a popping sound outside. He assumed a last test was being performed on the creation. Maybe the beast had snapped a Pawn in its jaws. Gregory sent him a message, but he swiped it away without reading. The engineers were still needing questioned regarding their performance earlier, but he didn't have time for that right now. He noticed one Comp was out of rhythm with the rest, drifting toward the window instead. Aldrich tapped on his control program and changed the Comps' pattern, moving them into a row that floated up and down in a wave along the wall behind him. The trouble Comp took up position at the end of the line. A series of pops went off outside the window. Maxwell messaged this time, but Aldrich cleared the notification without reading again. The tower gave a little shake. His window rattled in its frame.

Aldrich crossed his office to peer out. Above his creation, beyond the glare of the working lights on the glass, a ball of electric blue light hung in the air. He watched the light grow until it collided with the telepad dome. The glass held, but the hit shook the entire tower again. Another blue light formed out in the darkness, while a glowing red joined it off to the left. As his eyes adjusted, the outline of the three headed Guardian came into view not far outside the telepad. One by one, out of the dust cloud they'd stirred up upon their arrival, the Guardians took shape all around the dome.

He stepped back into frame for the call, his smile cemented in place. "One moment, everyone."

Aldrich muted the call and switched his feed to his previously recorded footage before anyone could ask questions. Just in time to avoid them seeing the lighting change through his office as the fire breath from that Pink Guardian hit the glass and rolled up the side. His handheld nearly snapped in his hand with how hard he hit the call button to the engineers. "Send the creation out!"

"That's what we were trying to ask!" Maxwell said.

"Why wait for me?"

"Are we not held to the orders of our Councilor?" Gregory asked.

"Just send it!" Aldrich ended the call. He wanted to leave the room, move as far away from the incoming damage as he could. Yet he found himself rooted to the spot, his eyes locked on the Warden onslaught.

A spiked tail swung from out of the dark, aiming for where the fire had been hitting. That would be Silver trying to help break through. Lenian glasswork was a major export due to their fine craftsmanship. He knew the damage threshold on these telepads were the highest in their market. Watching the Guardians send attack after attack made him hope it would be enough. An alarm sounded and lights flashed across the different cranes. A second hit came from Silver's tail, more sharp scrapes along the dome. After the next burst of flames, he feared sections of the glass were becoming a little droopy. A sudden flash of white overtook his vision. When his eyes cleared, the creation was gone. From behind the Guardians, a roar ripped through the dark.

The attacks on the dome stopped. He heard a Guardian answer with a roar of its own. Aldrich leaned a little further into the window. His creation, now outside the telepad, was drawing the attention of the Guardians. All the damage they'd inflicted on the glass hindered his view. That was a problem easily fixed.

Aldrich made another call to the engineers. "Send the available Pawns out to cover the fight."

"You want to do that now?" Gregory asked.

"Does this remain a priority?" Maxwell asked.

"We only have one shot at this. Send them out and direct the feeds to me." He ended the call again.

Annoying pair. Aldrich could see why Capri became violent with them. He watched the workstation fill with different camera angles as the Pawns came online and moved out to the fight about to start. Giving a quick scan to the airspace around the Guardians, it appeared they'd not dared bringing more of their Comps around. A regretfully wise decision on their part.

Aldrich recentered in his video frame, took a deep breath, angled his personal Pawn to the degree he preferred, and reentered the call. "Good news! Our main event is starting! I didn't want to waste your time with a preamble. Let's get right to the fight, shall we?"

He once more hit buttons before anyone could say a word, helped that he'd never taken them off mute either. Aldrich started them on a feed circling the fight high up. Six Guardians were closing in on his creation. He didn't know when the last time six Guardians were on the same battlefield at all, much less on the same side. There hadn't been proper time to research those types of facts, but he assumed most others wouldn't know the answer either. On his handheld, Aldrich tabbed over and hit send on the mass message he'd drafted earlier.

ONE NIGHT ONLY!

Witness a full Guardian team, the likes of which not seen in centuries (and NEVER in these forms), take on the newest and deadliest Lenian monster on the market. Join* at the link below before it's over!

***entry fee required**

23

This Fight Should Have Been an Email

They were on a different planet right now. The stars were different. There were far more of them out here. No, they were the same. Mina was the one in a new position. While her Thunderbird took shots at the glass dome connected to the Lenian tower, she'd been leaning over her control panel to see as many stars as possible. Barely an hour ago she'd told her parents they'd never make it off Earth and now she was on Mars. Technically she was hovering over Mars from inside her Guardian, but the rest of her team were on the ground so it counted. Her reverie was cut short by the creature inside the dome disappearing and shortly reappearing behind them. Now there was a giant T-Rex staring her down. Stargazing would have to wait.

"Anyone else kind of disappointed with this design?" Sean asked over the comms.

"They could've made Rumbleroar, and they blew it," Emma added.

"Let's break this one so they can have a second try," Mina said as she pushed the Thunderbird toward the monster's head. Talons and fangs locked together, keeping them at a stalemate as she attempted to pull away and the beast wanted to yank her down. The Lenian creation stretched taller as she struggled to free herself.

Zane came in from the side, ramming his antlers into the leg of the creation.

220

They didn't catch any plating, but dug grooves along the side. The tail whipped around in his direction. A small set of saws snipped the edge of one antler. The piece flew off, kicking up a trail of red dust as it skidded away. Zane whined over the comms, "Very not cool!"

Mina sent an electric shock rolling down her wings, directing both right at the creature's face as she allowed it to pull her closer. The Lenian robot shook and broke its grapple. Two of the Kitsune's tails immediately wrapped around the snout and attempted to wrestle the head down. The T-Rex's tail whipped in Sean's direction, but Emma's Drake caught the end between its teeth and held it in place.

"Think this will pop apart like the first one?" Steph asked.

The monster's arms stretched farther than they should've been able to claw at the tails on its face, shoving one tail off and freeing part of its jaw. At least the Lenians had bothered to find a workaround for the big head, little arms issue. Henrie's Cerberus came in from the side, attempting to grab an arm with one of its three heads.

Steph landed two hooves on the monster's back, but pulled away as the saws there spun up. "We might need you to melt these, Henrie."

"Need a little longer on the recharge," Henrie said as her Cerberus was knocked away. "Then I'm on it."

Mina moved to angle herself over the back of the monster, thinking her blast might at least jam up some blades. Something smacked one of her screens. She thought she must have hit a bird until she remembered they were on Mars. She watched a Pawn roll across her screen, that disgusting yellow haze around it, before correcting itself and pulling away from the Guardian. The Pawn was the same smaller version that the Lenians sent before and appeared to be carrying that virus. Nothing on her dash lit up or indicated issues within the system. "Nek, that virus can't infect the Guardians, can they?"

Nek spun on her display. "No. The Guardian system is far too complicated for that to break through. They'd need to get through the framework first."

"Wonderful." Mina twitched the Thunderbird's wing and snapped the Pawn out of the sky. It smashed somewhere below on the ground. Now that

Mina was looking for them, she realized they were surrounded by those Pawns. None were helping the creation, instead they all hung back in a wide circle. She spoke to the team channel, "I don't know what these Pawns are doing, but if you get a chance to knock some down I'd go for it."

"Say less." Steph shot off into the sky, running down the set nearest her while the others currently had the monster surrounded.

"With this kind of coverage, I think we're on camera," Zane said. His Jackalope antlers caught the edge of a plate and peeled it away from the monster's side. The creature howled as much as possible with its mouth held shut, but ripped its tail away from Emma's grip to defend itself. The Jackalope barely dodged that hit, saw blades instead clashed against rock and sent sparks into the air.

"Is this a good time to bring up the pose?" Sean asked.

"You gotta let that one go," Emma answered.

More Pawns fell from the sky, the Pegasus sending them plummeting with the burst from its wings. As the Kitsune tail was pulled from the mouth, the beast grabbed hold of a length and went for a bite. Fangs sunk into the Guardian's metal. Mina felt newly disappointed she hadn't figured out how to deafen metal-on-metal sounds yet.

"Get clear!" Henrie called out. "Breath is hot."

Sean pulled his Kitsune back as far as the creation would let him go. Emma's Drake had lined up for another bite at the tail, but she stepped off. Zane did the same. Henrie pushed her Guardian in, running at it from the side and getting her front legs right up on the thing. The beast didn't fall, but tipped from her hit alone. Mina watched as the left Cerberus' mouth glowed before pouring flame onto the back of the Lenian monster. Blades spun under Cerberus's paws, making Henrie pull away and direct the remaining fire toward its head.

The creature pushed upward as it roared again. The full height of this thing was uncomfortable. Hot metal rolled down its side. Mina saw a set of blades looking rather pliable and pinged them for Emma. "Give those a few hits before they cool off."

"On it," Emma said as she took a leap at the creation's back. Her Drake's claws ripped into those weakened blades, leaving gashes where the saws once sat. She backed off as others spun up, clipping one of her silver spikes as she moved away.

The robot turned toward Henrie, appearing unfazed by the loss of the blades. The creation roared again as it dropped lower, eyes locked on the Cerberus. As Mina moved to line up another energy blast, she noticed more Pawns coming out from one wing off the tower. They filled in the small gaps her and Steph had created. She refocused on the fight in time to catch a glow coming from the throat of the creation. A slightly familiar soft green that built up and leaked between the fangs.

"Henrie, move!" she shouted, but the blast beat her. Whatever that Councilor hit them with before in the parking lot apparently came in a size 500XL.

Cerberus tumbled across red dirt, slamming against large boulders several dozen yards away. Henrie's comm vanished from their link.

"Nek, is she okay?" Mina asked.

Nek was a tight ball of colors on her display. "Vitals are active. That hit knocked out systems. She'll need time to reboot."

"Anything broken from the hit?"

"Slight cracking across her right screen, but the suits are self-sustained. She'll have air."

The Lenian monster moved for the downed Guardian. Zane's Jackalope cut it off first, sending two thumping feet into the chest and knocking it back. Mina flew in, grabbing the top of its head in her talons. Saws chewed away at the innermost claws, but she held on and flung herself backwards as hard as possible. Steph came around front, taking Zane's spot and sending her own wing blast into the chest, knocking the creation further away.

"We need this thing to tip over!" Sean said as several of his Kitsune's tails wrapped around the monster's singular tail and pulled. Saws spun, causing further sounds of metal grinding as he did.

Claws batted at her talons, trying to pry her off the creature's face. Her Thunderbird sent an energy blast down into its head. That briefly shorted out the saws and let them give another good joint pull. The Drake took a run for the exposed stomach area, claws tearing into the plating. The monster swung for the Drake and tried to protect its relatively softer middle.

Mina's dash flashed with a notice that the talons were cut from her Thunderbird. Her grip slipped and the monstrous T-Rex shook her off to the side. The Drake pulled away as the beast crashed forward, catching itself on those remarkably strong front arms. The creation pushed off the ground and broke into a run for the Cerberus again. The Kitsune still held onto its tail, though the Guardian was now missing lengths from three of its own tails. Steph ran in and stomped down more blades, rendering them useless along the tail and giving Sean better grabbing points. He adjusted as he could and dug himself in deeper, but got dragged along by the Lenian beast.

While Mina's blast was still recharging, she snatched Pawns up in her remaining talons and flung them at the monster's head. She might not be able to stop it, but maybe she could annoy it into changing targets. The glow in the creature's throat returned. She called out to the team, "Breath weapon just reactivated."

She threw herself at its face, jamming her talons into the fangs again. Hoping that if the creation couldn't open its mouth, it couldn't use the blast. A fact she was feeling rather sure about until the beam cut through the fangs and slammed her Thunderbird. Her control room went black around her and the heads-up on her suit shorted out. As the beast tossed her off to the side, Mina was thankful the straps on her chair were mechanical and not something energy-based. They kept her secure as the Guardian tumbled through the air and hit the ground, her screens nothing but red dust. Small blessing, she landed upright. Extra bonus, she was officially now on Mars too.

Her team was yelling for her, she was sure, but all she heard was the grating of metal-on-metal. Nek said Henrie had only needed a few minutes. She was likely almost up when Mina got hit. Waiting this out would be fine. No time at all. Once she had eyes on the team again it'd fly by.

The dust settled and Mina discovered she wouldn't be watching the team because she'd landed facing the Lenian tower. Such an obnoxiously bright and shiny building. Felt like a blight on the face of Mars. Which was where she was right now. Staring at an alien fortress surrounded by endless red rock, with her team fighting a monstrous robot dinosaur behind her. What a fun sentence.

Who knew chasing good footage for her now abandoned website would lead to this? One day she'd spied a little hidden ledge up the side of a mountain and now she lived on a spaceship. Also, she had friends who fought aliens alongside her. With robots big and small, when stupid aliens didn't hijack them anyway. Also also, one of those people was now her girlfriend. Which felt like a cherry on top of this already insane summer. They might have also confirmed her parents were evil, but she'd mostly suspected that already.

"Warden Mina," the crackled voice of Nek came through her suit.

Mina snapped out of her thoughts as her heads-up flickered on with a dozen different notices. "I'm good. All good."

"Your Guardian…booting. Standby."

"Are the others okay?"

"Warden Henr…online…ack in the fight. They…damage to the Len… Taken out…saws. Warden Em…caught arm…dian's teeth. Warden Z… breaking a leg…bring it down. They–"

"Thank you, Nek. Sorry, I didn't mean to make you give me a play-by-play. Please go to the others. I'll be up soon." Her dash flickered with a glint of power as the Guardian worked to right itself.

Mina tried to keep her ears open to the sounds of the fight behind her, tried to guess what hit was which one of her teammates landing a good blow. The dash pulsed with blue light, but faded out. She scanned the tower, reluctantly admitting the dome that originally held the creature was a neat design. All the glass glittering in the tinted light of Mars' twilight was upsettingly pleasing. Better yet was the sight of the scratches Emma and Zane created earlier. Her eyes went up the tower, finding only one long window built into the side. There was a figure there; she thought they might be looking back at her. Or her Guardian, at least. They moved away into whatever room was beyond.

There was a short list of options for who that was. Councilor Aldrich, who'd come down and insulted all of them. Or one of the two Lenians that also lived in the tower with Capri, Henrie had told the others about them. She'd need to get through those three to retrieve the Comps they'd stolen. Which didn't feel like too hard of a task.

Her dash flashed blue again. The Guardian held a dim bit of power this time. Crackles of the comms filled her ears. She picked out enough to put together that they'd taken a front leg off and heavily damaged a back one. Part of the tail was gone and Steph had landed an impressive flyby stomping, crushing part of the neck. Seemed that energy blast was having issues firing up now.

Mina punched her dash in excitement, happy to hear her team was kicking ass. Even if it was without her, a thought that didn't bother her like she expected.

"Mina," a static filled Zane came across, "Ne…says you…almost back on…shout…u can. Please."

"Can you hear me?"

Static covered cheers responded to her. A pulse of energy ran over her wings. The Guardian shifted and pushed itself up, unbalanced because of the missing talons, but stayed upright.

Her comms came back in full to hear Sean calling out, "…down! It's down. Emma, break its neck."

"Gladly!" Emma replied.

"Out of context, this would sound horrible," Henrie chimed in.

Mina turned her Thunderbird around to see her team was indeed dogpiling on top of the Lenian monster as it was now knocked prone. Zane's Jackalope took an impressive leap into the air in order to land directly across the head. Sean had tails wrapped around the final working leg and the remaining chunk of tail, but the beast wasn't putting up much of a fight anymore. Emma's Drake dug claws and teeth deep into the throat.

Mina called out, "Careful of that weapon! Damage might set it off."

"She's right," Henrie said. "Go for the base of the neck."

Mina's heart jumped a little at Henrie agreeing with her. That was going to take getting used to.

"Roger that." The Drake backed off the direct attacks and moved lower to work on separating the head completely.

Mina waited to see the joints coming apart before turning the Thunderbird to the tower. "I'm going for the Comps."

"Give us five more minutes," Zane said.

"I got this." She flew around the glass dome, knowing she wouldn't get through that alone, and kept low to the ground. Mina expected there must be a loading bay built into the place. Her suspicions were rewarded with gleaming orange doors set into the opposite side of the tower. The Guardian would never fit through, but breaking open the door was all she needed. She had a super suit, after all.

With two quick snaps of energy blasts, there was a dent large enough that she could have fit, but the spot quickly filled with debris as the chamber beyond lost pressure. Mina was a little surprised that the tower didn't have any defenses built-in like Outrider did. She suspected the Lenians never thought someone would come knocking.

Mina was waiting for another blast to charge when the bay doors took on an opalesque shimmer. The debris pressed against the gap fell away and the doors pulled open. They must use some sort of shielding to hold pressure. Her brain was yelling "TRAP" over and over, but her brain was also telling her to get in there before the doors closed.

She leaned her Thunderbird forward to make for an easy jump to the ground. Dust kicked up around Mina and she felt an increase of pressure on her suit before it rebalanced. The urge to hop her steps as she neared the tower was strong, but the suit kept her grounded.

Nek spun on her heads-up. "Might I convince you this time to wait for the others?"

"You're with me. I'm good." She pulled her blasters though and was forward thinking enough to peek into the room before entering. She couldn't see anyone inside. Only the loose items pulled toward the door and what she assumed was a ship. This Lenian ship was larger than whatever had been attached to Capri's pod, and far more angular. Didn't feel right to her, seeing something meant for space travel with so many pointy parts. Mina walked slowly through the bay, using the ship to cover her from anything coming from the left. She came to a quick stop when she spotted a patch of scratch marks in the paint. Either drawing dicks to deface property was a universal thing or being on Earth had truly affected Capri's brain in her short time there.

Mina was considering adding something to the designs when a faint hiss from the other side of the ship pulled her attention. She dipped low and poked her head around, finding another door standing only a couple of feet open. The main bay door was still open and shielded; her exit hadn't disappeared yet. With her blasters held straight out in front of her, Mina jumped through the doorway and into the dim hall beyond.

An emerald green Lenian stood several feet away with a tablet in hand. "Doorbell must be on the fritz. Took a moment to hear you knocking."

Mina heard them speaking; the language clipped and even. The automated voice translated directly into her ear matched. She pointed both blasters at the Lenian, while trying to think if she'd missed an actual doorbell outside. "Uh-huh."

They stepped off to the side of the hallway, an arm stretched out to the rest of the tower beyond. "He didn't lock down the elevator this time, because he's an idiot. I called the car down for you."

"Thank you?" She took cautious steps toward the figure, blasters held high. Mina passed them and surveyed the empty center of the tower. A wrought-iron type elevator ran up the middle. There was a similarly designed staircase circling the tower. "Might take the stairs though."

"He blocked that entrance. The elevator will take you right into the suite."

Nek became a tight ball of white on her heads-up. "Wardens Zane and Steph are coming."

"My teammates are on their way." She stepped out further into the space, remembering to check behind herself as she went.

"The bay will remain open." The Lenian followed along casually, tapping on their tablet. "I'll point them your way. Remember to send the car back down."

She moved one blaster from them to point at the elevator. "And you won't kill me once I step in there?"

"I refrained from ever shooting Capri. Also, we're quitting." They pointed a corner of the tablet at something behind her.

Mina spun to see a second Lenian, this one a deep yellow, coming up behind her with what appeared to be coolers hung over each arm. "Raided the fridges. The springhead won't have a morsel left to cry over. Did you convince her to let us go?"

"Working on it." Green came around to her other side. "We sneak out on a measly little transport ship. You lot do whatever it is you're wanting to do here. Sound like a good trade?"

Mina muted herself to them, speaking only to Nek. "Um, is this normal?"

Nek unspooled to a ball of colored ribbons again. "Nothing has been normal since I came to this system."

She backed herself up toward the elevator, again only speaking to Nek. "They dealt with Capri for weeks, kind of a punishment in itself."

"And made the creations that have threatened your city for the past month."

"Fair." Her back hit the elevator door. She gulped and hoped she wasn't making the wrong call as she opened her mic out to the team. "There is going to be a ship leaving the tower. Leave it be."

"Who's on it?" Zane asked.

"Lenians. Employees, kind of. I think."

"Engineers," Nek supplied. "The ones crafting those monsters."

"They're letting us in the tower," Mina said. "Pointed me toward Aldrich. I think we've determined the universe is far too gray to be making calls on people."

"As long as you tell them they suck for me, one time," Henrie said.

Mina pulled the door open behind her and stepped into the elevator car. She turned her mic out to the Lenians. "Henrie says you both suck. I suggest you get moving before she arrives."

They got right to it, disappearing down the hallway she'd come from. Mina shut the door and flipped the only switch in the car. The lift rose all the way to the top. A hatch pulled open for her as it moved past what she'd assumed was the ceiling. She kept her blasters aimed out, waiting for something to hit her as she came to a stop in the open room above.

A space littered in tatters of fabric. Mina wondered if Capri had done this in a temper tantrum during her stay. The destroyed couch blocking the stairway, piled high with more bits of fabric, made her reconsider that this must have been Aldrich's work. She flipped the outside switch, sending the car back down below. There was noise coming from up the staircase.

"Oh wow, we're on Mars," Zane said on the comms, his voice sounding a little heavy. "Like standing on it."

Mina stopped with her foot on the first step. "Nek, do you have readings on the air inside the tower?"

"Oxygen levels are good once you get by the airlock," Nek answered.

"Hear that, Zane? You wait until you're inside to lower that helmet."

"I've got eyes on him," Steph answered. "He's running."

Mina started up the stairs, taking them at a run as the carpeting softened her footfalls. This floor only held a couple rooms, with the noise coming from the door closest to her. She edged up to the side, listening closely.

"My creation put up a good fight," the Councilor was saying, "but I didn't want to scuff your new Guardians too much."

She peeked through a crack left in the door. The Councilor wasn't visible, but her Comps were. They did a wave along the wall as their screens flashed different colors. The guy had put them on some sort of party mode. How insulting. There was no way of avoiding the Comps in this room. Mina didn't want to fight them, she'd hoped to contain them somehow.

Aldrich spoke up again, "I'll let you enjoy the view of the Guardians for a short while longer. Then we'll get to the serious business of talking prices."

There was a bang. It took Mina a second to realize the sound was her shoving the door open. Councilor Aldrich sat in a tattered high backed office chair, smiling at someone on his screen. In his surprise, he shoved away from the desk, rolling into the wall with the Comps. Bits of foam pulled out behind him as he jumped from the chair. The Comps didn't move, only kept their rolling pattern. His eyes shot to a handheld on the desk corner nearest her. Mina shot it twice as he lunged. The device exploded and fell to the floor. Second one of those she'd taken out. She moved between the Councilor and his computer.

"This was an incredibly stupid plan," she said. A Comp pushed forward and bumped into his head, Mina wondered what command made it do that. They were supposed to be under his control.

Aldrich shoved the Comp away. "It was an excellent demonstration of the available merchandise."

"Of which you have no right to sell!" Mina was over this guy. At least Capri wanted to kill them and take over the planet for a cause. Not sell them for parts.

His eyes cut to the side of her. "Not true."

She shifted enough to see the screen he was looking at. There was a ticker running, symbols she didn't understand until her suit translated, a viewer count and a running total of profits. "You made us a pay-per-view show?"

"Opportunities are abundant on this planet. If you gave me a chance to explain the benefits…"

Mina stopped listening once Nek started whispering in her ear, "Wardens Zane and Steph are on the stairs. The others are reaching the airlock now."

Aldrich was now looking at the screens behind her. "…all can win. Perhaps one of you might persuade the young Earthling into a peaceful deal? I'll give you a discount."

Mina shot him three times in the chest, knocking him into the wall. "Not for sale."

His hitting the wall broke the Comps from their pattern. They pushed forward into the center of the room. She noticed one move closer to her. The Comps weren't marked with their numbering, but she knew it was 2876. Her best robot was almost in reach.

"Everyone is," he grunted and pulled himself up. That green spark ran along his arms. "Some merely choose to pay with their lives."

She took a run for the wall to her left, putting the batch of Comps between them. 2876 would forgive her. Turning on the adhesion, she ran straight up the wall as the blast went off below her. The Comps fell to the floor, one problem sorted. Mina shot him four more times from the ceiling, pushing him toward the window she'd seen from outside. There was a set of cheers from the screens along the wall, their show going into overtime. While hanging upside down, she spotted the Pawn pressed into the corner, broadcasting her out to whoever Aldrich was trying to sell her team off to.

Zane burst in, mace high and ready. Steph was close behind, saber glowing. They both nearly tripped over the deactivated Comps before spotting her on the ceiling.

Zane gave her a thumbs up. "Way to use the room."

"Oh, now it's a good move," Mina said.

Steph cleared her throat; saber pointed at the bad guy. "This is where you surrender, I believe."

Mina caught him twitch his right hand before another spark ran over his arms. She sent off two more shots, aiming for the presumed trigger on his hand, and Steph let her bolt loose. Aldrich turned out of instinct to protect his front, Steph's hit left a red hot slash along his side. As well as shattering the window behind him. His blast went off, but aimed at the wall it did nothing but dent the metal. Both of Mina's shots hit her target. Aldrich's thumb sat at an ugly angle now. Black oil dripped down his hand. She supposed organic metal would bleed. She wondered if inside his arm was a skeletal structure similar to a human's, only made of metal. Mina backed far away from that thought, which felt like a grisly rabbit-hole.

She felt the pressure building in her head and took the brief pause in fighting to walk herself to the floor. Glad she could clear the dots from her vision privately, thanks to the helmet. She leveled her blasters on him again. "How about you stop trying that?"

"I'm not sure he's got much else for moves," a voice called from the screens, their actual language making a sort of double lair with the translation.

"Can someone move the feed?" another asked. "I can't see that sniveling salesman anymore."

"Loyal customers," Zane scoffed.

Aldrich glared from the floor. "They want what I have."

"You don't have anything!" Mina shouted, nearly in time with a third voice from the screens.

Councilor Aldrich pulled himself up on the frame of the window. "I will take every single scrap of worth from this planet. For no other reasons than to leave you rotten Wardens standing in the ruins aft–"

He grunted and stopped talking. Aldrich slowly turned, revealing two sais shoved into his lower back. Chains hung from the ends of the sais and trailed down to a figure in the bottom portion of the broken window frame. In the same moment Mina registered the pink band and realized it was Henrie, the other girl dropped away. Mina's instinct was to lurch after her, Zane and Steph did the same. Aldrich did as well, as the chains snapped tight and flashed a bright pink. He stumbled backward to the window, catching himself on the splintered frame. Hands came in from either side of the window, grabbing onto his arms and pulling him backward. Mina watched his eyes go wide as he fell into the open air and out of sight. Emma and Sean tipped around the sides of the window. Henrie poked up from the bottom as Aldrich hollered the entire way down. They were quiet until they heard the hit below.

"Henrie remembered part of the layout," Emma said. "Thought this would be faster than the stairs."

"Oh, forgot to send the elevator down," Zane said. "Our bad."

"Can we leave now?" Henrie asked. "Kind of freaking me out being here."

Mina turned to the fried Comps. "Yeah! We'll scoop these up and meet you guys at the airlock."

Sean pushed off the wall and glanced down. "Um, hate to say it, but he's gone."

"How?" the rest shouted.

"That's some horror movie bullshit," Steph grumbled.

Mina heard a snicker from the screens. She gave a glare to the Pawn filming but knew they couldn't see her expression. "Get after him!"

The three Wardens outside took off in a run down the side of the building. While the other three sprinted for the elevator, a horribly slow moving elevator. Mina grew impatient and stopped the car only two levels down. "I think we can take the fall damage."

"Don't bother," Emma called through the comms. "Apparently the one other skill that guy has is moving fast."

"He was already in his ship by the time we hit the airlock," Sean added. "Didn't even try stealing your Guardian sitting there."

Mina regretted not adding to Capri's graffiti. She hoped he didn't catch the damage, that someone else would point it out to him down the road.

Nek spun on their armbands. "Guardians confirmed the visual of a ship taking off. It's an unknown model, moving very fast. The odds of catching him are slim."

"Well." Zane softly kicked a nearby wall. "At least we ran him off."

"Speaking of." Mina stepped into the elevator. "Anyone want to threaten aliens?"

"Yes!" Emma called over the comms. "Send that down for us once you're up."

Mina thought she heard Henrie grumble, but it sounded like she was coming along. Steph and Zane pressed in with her, and they returned to the suite. They kicked a chunk of foam around while waiting for the other three to come up. The team reentered the office, finding the screens now black. Everyone must have assumed that the show was over once Aldrich got yanked out the window.

She tapped around on the interface, slow going as she kept having to wait for the suit's translation to catch up, but eventually found his call list. Which included a handy little feature to call everyone at once. Boxes began opening one by one along the wall. Aldrich's buyers appeared surprised to get another call so soon.

"I don't want to actually talk to any of you because this has all been rather aggravating," she started. "But I do want it fully known and understood that we are not for sale. Not our ship. Not our Guardians. Not our Comps. Not us. None of you will take any of this from us."

A Warden with yellow stars across their helmet, or at least a being wearing a Pak suit, leaned in. "Perhaps we can talk about a partnership. The Collec–"

"We don't want any part of your Collective. We are Wardens, but we do not stand with you."

Some of the alien faces before her rolled their eyes, or eye stalks, or fleshy parts that she was taking to be eyes. She was trying not to focus too much on individual faces. If these were some of the beings Henrie had in her head, it was no wonder she had nightmares.

Mina stepped back, falling into line with her team. "I think we can all agree that Aldrich–"

"Al-dick," Emma muttered behind her.

"Wasn't up to the task. This," she pointed to the Pawn hovering in the corner, "whole broadcast is insulting. None of you appeared to have much faith in him, either. So I'm not acting like putting him down was a hard-won victory. I mean, honestly, we fought a bunch of normal humans who put up a better fight earlier tonight. My parents were more intimidating and all they did…"

Mina let that point go before she started rambling about her personal life too much. "I will say the engineers that were here, they made decent monsters to throw at us. They seemed to care about their craft. They were creative and weird as hell. And you know what they did? Opened the door and let us in while they slipped out the back. They were smart enough not to mess with us."

She hoped that was the case anyway. They hadn't acted extremely intimidated.

A male figure made of shining bronze clockwork gears shifted in his frame. His voice was metered out by the ticking coming from him. "I'm sure what you've done so far has felt impressive, but–"

"What we've done so far is square off with one of the best from your Collective's glory days several times." She stared at the Yellow Stars figure and hoped they could tell. "Learn your own history. Look up Outrider. They sent some of their best out here. Capri was one of them. She killed her team for your twisted Collective. Put together a mad plan to take over our world on her own. She underestimated us. We took her Pak."

That statement seemed to hit with the few Warden types on the call. Mina held onto that fact. "I'm sure you think you could do better. Let Aldrich rip you off by buying our coordinates from him. Or hunt us out yourself. Then waltz in and take everything from us. You can certainly try. My suggestion, forget about Earth and save your resources. But if you insist on coming here, I beg you, make the fight worth our time."

No one responded to her, Mina realizing she needed to end the call somehow. Walking over and hitting a button seemed anticlimactic. Mina pulled a blaster and shot the setup and Pawn, sparking up the room and dropping them into darkness. With her comms set to internal, she asked, "They're gone, right?"

"Yes," Nek answered. "Only the broadcast outside remains active."

Steph wrapped an arm around her waist. "Very dramatic. I loved it."

Mina patted Sean on the back. "It was somewhat pose inspired."

"I'll take it!" Sean bent over and scooped up a Comp from the floor. "Everyone load up on Comps, we have to get these guys home to recoup."

Everyone followed his lead. Mina made sure to grab 2876 first.

"I believe I found the original programming saved in Aldrich's system," Nek said. "I can contain them on Outrider and reverse it."

Mina saw Emma giving Henrie's arm a squeeze. She was probably dying to get out of here. "Henrie, would you want to head back to your Guardian? Maybe work on knocking out those camera Pawns."

Henrie nodded. "Sure, but what are you all going to do?"

"Well, I want to get what we can from the place. But don't want you stuck inside it more than you have to be. Then I was thinking we knock the thing over."

Zane clapped and started for the door. "I'm gonna pick out souvenirs for everyone."

"Be careful," Emma said as she followed him out. "That's a slippery slope to your people making museums filled with stolen goods."

He gasped from the hallway. "Hurtful. But true."

Henrie grabbed Mina's arm, letting everyone else go out before them. "Thanks."

"No problem. Go catch your breath. You did amazing. Also. Love the sais for you, by the way. You did way better with those than I did."

"Thanks. I stumbled on those chains when digging through the weapons locker. I put this together quick before we came here. Worked well enough, but do you think we could make a sturdier version? The weight is a little off for me."

"Absolutely!" Mina stopped herself from grabbing Henrie and shaking her in excitement. Now wasn't the time for that. All the same, she felt thrilled to finally have a weapons project for Henrie. "Also, real quick. Once again, sorry for blowing up on you."

"Not like I wasn't pushing buttons with all the crap I've been giving you lately. That wasn't fair. I'm sorry too. Again."

"Honestly, you're not the first to call me out for being a little overzealous about my robots. And you won't be the last. Don't tell the aliens I just tried to intimidate, but we're all still figuring this out. We're doing it together, though. Might get bumpy, but we get by."

Henrie lightly punched her arm. "You're pretty good at this. Captain."

"I'm trying. And I know you are too. Don't forget we got your back."

"Just not like how I got Aldrich's, I hope. How did his face look?"

"I'll play it in the training room later. Maybe print it for a poster."

The two caught up with the rest of the team, who were opting to unblock the hidden staircase and take that down instead. Henrie, Emma, and Sean headed for the main floor. The cousins would walk Henrie to the airlock before starting their search from the bottom up. Mina, Zane, and Steph started from the top down.

As far as the actual raiding went, their physical findings were meager. Most of the tower was untouched. They found what appeared to have been Capri's quarters, and got by her lock with the programming from the Lockpuck, but there wasn't much there they didn't already know. The next floor down only contained two workshops that looked lived in. Nek pulled data from the workstations, glad to update Outrider's database with more current information about the universe at large. Mina spotted designs she wanted to try out for herself in the batch as they scrolled by. One workshop had a desk littered with sensors of various sizes. After Spud gave them a scan, Nek determined the parts would fit in Outrider and replace existing sensors. They presumed these would give the ship an extra boost to close more of that five hundred year gap. Nek also advised that the materials the

Lenians used were compatible with the Fabrication forges, meaning they could plunder the place for materials if needed. Mina was concerned about that option, having seen what the MegaPawn exoskeletons did to those Lab workers. She'd do some extremely small scale testing before using it on anything the team would interact with directly.

They'd run into more Pawns on their way out. As Henrie knocked them down outside, a handful more turned on in one of the side wings and drifted into the tower. The batch hovered on the main floor as the Wardens made their way back down. None of them reformed into MegaPawns or attacked the Wardens at all. Aldrich had stripped them of anything but their cameras and the command to observe. All they did was broadcast out to whoever Aldrich had suckered into paying for the show. Steph started reciting Shakespeare directly into one before Emma punched it away. They made short work of the few inside before heading out to rejoin Henrie.

The materials being reusable didn't stop them from knocking the base over. They could pick pieces out of the rubble down the line if needed. Breaking the glass surrounding the telepad, their new intel told her that was the name, became a game. They took turns and hoped they'd be the one to break the dome. Felt right that Henrie, opting to smash all three of her heads into a set of previously created cracks, was the thing to shatter the structure. The team watched glass shards bounce and fly away over the surface of Mars, along with the cranes and machinery pulled away by the lost pressure.

The tower itself was more of the same. Bashing, beating, and melting sections in tandem until it collapsed over into the red dirt. Zane took extra time thumping down the top, flattening the suite section as much as possible.

Their last game was picking off the final Pawns, which were lazily floating around as no one remained to direct them. Nek said the broadcast remained up the entire time and that people joined the stream right up until the end of their demolition. Apparently, the wider galaxy missed the entertainment of a full Warden team in action. Mina hated knowing Aldrich made a buck off of them, but she considered the recording of him falling out the window her own payment.

With the last Pawn destroyed, Nek confirmed the broadcast shut down. They all sat in their Guardians, happy with their work, and let Nek bring them home.

24

To the Beaten Goes the Spoils

Capri wasn't upset with her haul. Weapons, nasty chemical concoctions, and intriguing little inventions were coming with her. She'd also nabbed Lenian and Comp parts found in a different office. The human assistant, who'd repeated several times her name was Mel, had supplied a set of carts once Capri's acquisitions surpassed the carrying capacity of her and the maintenance crew. She'd hoped to raid the kitchens that the human told her were below, but there was far too much commotion down there. Capri thought the Wardens were going to make a quick escape, but apparently they'd made quite the mess to compliment the one she'd left upstairs. The human pointed her to a kitchenette area well-stocked with pre-prepared meals and a variety of snack foods. Capri settled for taking everything from there. Between that and taking anything from the personal fridges of the other offices around the floor, one cart was decently packed with food.

Her last moments in the office included ordering the maintenance crew to douse the place with anything that was marked flammable. Not quite dead parents, but she thought Warden Mina might appreciate the gesture. Her parents' secret exit was an elevator. Before stepping into the lift, Capri tossed a match and watched the lab go up in flames.

They strolled along outside with no one bothering them. Capri even dropped her hood at one point and drew no attention. Everyone remained focused on the building that was now on fire. The assistant grumbled once they reached the end of the paved parking lot and headed for the wooded area. The maintenance crew shushed her before Capri said a word.

Once at the ship, Capri pointed to the assistant. "Start loading things inside."

"Sure, why not?" The human grabbed an arm full and walked up the ramp.

Capri turned to the maintenance crew. "I have no plans of returning to the tower. This was a bad call on your part."

They both shrugged. Capri realized these two must always assume abusive work environments were the status quo. Her own behavior never dissuaded them from that. She made a mental note to try being a little nicer. Try, a little. When they weren't being overly annoying.

"Help load. Don't let the human touch anything."

The pair disappeared inside the ship; she immediately heard a yelp from the human. Mel. She should probably bother using names if she was going to be nicer to people. While alone, Capri carefully removed the heavy jacket from herself, not wanting to lose any bird parts from the large front pocket. She tied up the arms to keep everything bundled inside. Not that she could do anything with the blue jay parts, but she'd brought the junk this far already. Might as well keep everything together. Maybe she'd get close enough to the tower to dump the birds nearby. Let Gregory hunt through the dirt for pieces. Or keep them and let the Comps puzzle out rebuilding the hardware, bringing her number of little minions to a whopping four. Six, with the crew onboard. Seven, if she brought Mel along too. The number stuck in her head like a dare.

Mel's morals appeared to be rather loose, if not outright abysmal, given the sort of tasks Warden Mina's parents put her up to. Which could be handy if Capri headed in the direction she'd been considering. Capri had her list of mildly interesting factions and she was sure they'd come across more on the way who needed someone to get them into shape. Having a person beside her willing to get the job done no matter what would be useful. No Mock Pak on Mel's back required.

Capri came around to the ramp as Mel walked out with one empty cart in front of her and the other behind.

Mel walked the carts several paces away from the ship. "All loaded. What next?"

Before answering, Capri walked up the ramp and surveyed the pod's interior. These escape pods weren't meant for many people, which was why Outrider had a bay of them, but the two larger beings and assortment of robotic entities could make due for a short time. Their scavenged trophies were stowed away in the compartments. The only item taking up space was the food. There was an emergency stash of rations she'd barely touched hidden away in another compartment. Along with whatever the crew had stashed. All that would cover them for a good while, but she thought they might hit up a store on their way out to be safe.

"Helloooo?" Mel called from the bottom of the ramp. "Earth to the alien who hasn't bothered telling me her name yet."

Capri's hand twitched to where a blaster would have sat on her side, but she'd let the crew tuck those away with everything else. A good decision on her part. She was trying to be nicer after all. Instead she took a breath and turned back to the human. "My name is Capri. Come inside and get cleaned up."

Mel climbed the ramp in a flash, giving Capri no time to have second thoughts about bringing her along. Capri hit the interior panel for the doors and sealed up the pod behind them. She made Mel and the crew stand in a line as she ran through all the compartments around the pod and what was not to be touched by anyone but Capri. They then watched her demonstrate how to access the compressed bathroom facilities. The human scrunched her face about the arrangement, but Capri advised she could get over it or get out. Mel withheld her complaints after that, though Capri caught the lift of an eyebrow when she'd mentioned they'd be sleeping directly on the floor. Perhaps sleeping mats were something else they could pick up on their way out too.

Capri pulled out what was left of the med supplies and left Mel to patch up her own nose. With a whistle and point of her finger she got the Comps to start up the pod. The maintenance crew tucked themselves under the dash as the system ran through its checks. Capri settled into the chair, her bundle of Lenian bird parts sat in her lap. When the pod launched, she heard Mel stumble behind her and tried not to laugh.

"Perhaps a warning next time?" Mel asked.

"Mmhmm," was all Capri managed to get out.

She'd set no immediate direction for takeoff, only steered them into the lower atmosphere of the planet to hover while she decided where to go next. Capri considered doing this last small heist in another city. Hurst had brought her nothing but bad luck. She was done with it. Which could also be said about the planet as a whole.

While they hovered, the dash pinged two ships on the radar. The main signal was Outrider, turning the same as ever behind the Moon. Capri wondered what those little Wardens were up to after their fight here. Celebrating another minuscule victory, she imagined. She thought about passing close enough to send Nek a message, but decided against it.

The second blip hung around near Jupiter, a Lenian craft from the designation. Had Aldrich taken to his ship to hunt her down? How far would he dare chase her and leave his treasure trove unprotected? Mel had barely stayed standing during launch. Capri didn't expect she'd handle a dogfight very well.

A message came through via the Lenian side of her ship.

We've been waiting for ages. - G

One of Capri's hands covered her mouth, concealing the smile that had broken out there, while the other typed out a reply. **Running behind, have to stop for snacks. Send any requests. I have the maintenance crew with me.**

Wondered where they got off to. - M

I also grabbed two of your birds, Gregory.

That was kind of you. After the food, do you have a destination in mind? - G

Another world you want to try taking over? - M

I hit him for you. - G

Thank you. I have ideas. We'll decide once I catch up, but it has to be somewhere a human can breathe.

Whyyyyy? - M

Later.

Capri felt a long tied knot come apart in her gut as she locked on to the next town over from Hurst and set a course for their general store. The maintenance crew were already snoozing below the dash. She laid out the Lenian blue jay parts and set the Comps to work on them. See what they could put together before meeting up with the engineers. Mel had taken it upon herself to begin reorganizing the food, unsatisfied with how the crew had stacked everything. Capri rolled the drive between her palms, once the Comps were freed up she'd use one to privately read through some of Rin's messages again. With Mel around Capri didn't dare connect directly into the pod's system.

Her dash blinked again with an incoming message from the engineers, this time a large video file. The thumbnail showcased the full team of Guardians assembled outside of the Lenian tower. Capri tipped and grabbed a bag of chips out of Mel's hands. She found herself excited to be only a spectator this round.

She studied the Guardians as the file finished loading, trying to align her team with these new forms. Rin wouldn't approve of Warden Mina's selection, she'd never pick a form that stood anywhere but the front line. Caro would also dislike her Guardian flying because of Warden Steph, heights were never her thing. Jarden would have been chaos in the form Warden Emma put together, enjoying the hitting power almost too much. Capri imagined Ali and Camden would have settled in well with the forms Wardens Sean and Zane picked, respectively. Though Camden would have needed more practice getting the hang of those antlers. As for her own Guardian, Capri still couldn't say she liked the three headed beast. Of course she preferred her version better. The fire was a good touch though.

They'd had a talk once, while sitting around the common area, about what it'd be like passing on their Paks. That was the point of their original mission after all, foster the next generation in a new region. The rest didn't know about Capri's real motive yet, that fight was ahead of them. At that moment they were still all on the same side and contemplating their future. Jarden had waved off the idea, saying they'd be taking his Pak off his corpse so he didn't care. He'd never know how right that prediction was. Rin disagreed, she wanted to know who was taking over after her. Wanted to look them in the eye and know they were worthy of the responsibility that came with a Pak. She wanted to see what they'd built in action before she was done. Capri had taken that from her.

We were a great team, whispered her ghost of Rin. *And so are they.*

Capri sighed and squeezed the drive a little tighter. Yes, she supposed they were.

25

And Now, We Chill

Her parents weren't dead, that much Mina knew. She had complicated feelings around that fact, but a fact it remained. She knew this because their deaths weren't included with those reported by Hephaestus Labs. Who were working endlessly to spin the entire fight as being started by the Wardens unprompted. Their representatives were telling everyone that it seemed suspicious how right as the Lab announced their investigation into the Warden identities, the team had come through to destroy the building and injure so many of the employees. Pictures of Capri were everywhere now. Mina suspected she wouldn't hate that people were assuming she was a Warden. She also was telling herself that the fire was Capri's doing, a bit of good destruction on her way out.

Another sign her parents were alive was the clothes missing from their house when Henrie and Emma snuck in to poke around. Wherever they went, they expected to stay for a long time. Their office was cleaned out, but the cameras had been cut before anything happened. They didn't know if that was her parents' doing or Hephaestus Labs. The team kept watch on the house for the next couple of days. Nek set up a small program to turn lights on and off around the house, to keep up appearances that at least Mina was living there.

For now, her parents were simply gone, and them being gone wasn't anything those around her would question. Zane's parents would expect her over for dinner most nights, and she'd do so happily. Then pretend to walk to the house until she could teleport to Outrider. Even with them gone, she wouldn't stay in that house again. She only stomached it long enough to clean out the kitchen.

She also kept expecting someone else from Hephaestus Labs to come after them. The Lab wanted the Wardens and their ship. Her parents knew about Zane and her. They could have guessed the others had they paid any mind to her small social circle. Mina came up with two theories so far. The first was that her parents remained so confident in their own abilities that they'd not shared the intel with anyone else. Maybe they even still thought Aldrich's deal was on the table, unaware that he'd been run off. The second was that someone else did know and was biding their time. Making a new evil scientist plan to come after them that probably included strapping more clueless henchmen into Lenian exoskeletons. Nek discovered Mel was no longer on the Lab's register, but she didn't know if that meant she was in the wind along with her parents or off doing something slimy on her own.

Even now, as they took a break from their training up on Outrider to have lunch, she swiped through the camera feeds the others had agreed to have installed around their homes. No one was going to sneak up on her team or their families again. She was still trying to figure out a way to subtly make up for it to Zane's parents.

The Comps were working through all the data pulled from the Lenian base, filing intel away that would be helpful. Nek was picking through that to create a highlight packet for the team, adding anything pressing they needed to know first. No one had given the document much of a look yet. They were still riding high from breaking down the tower. Along with still waiting to hear if their recovered Comps were okay.

They'd dropped the infected Comps directly into the containment units once back. Nek had cut off another team from the main framework and set them to the task of cleaning out the virus from their programming. Now that they had the original code on hand, they knew what to hunt out and delete. But it was long work and last she checked they still hadn't dared turn one of the infected Comps back on yet.

Steph crumpled up a plastic wrapper and lined up a shot to the trash can on the other end of the kitchen island. "Think I can make it?"

"You can certainly try," Sean said, pretending to shoot her with his fork.

Mina rolled her eyes at what must be the hundredth time someone used that line since she'd done it. "Ha. Ha."

Steph took the shot. The light ball of plastic fell a good foot short of the targeted trash can. "Well, that is embarrassing."

Sean scooped the ball up and dropped it in the trash. "Nah, you made it. We all saw."

The other four around the room clapped. Steph took a little bow. "Thank you for supporting my delusion."

Nek rolled into the room, bright waves bouncing high. "Attention all!"

A couple hands went toward their Paks. Zane spoke around his mouthful of popcorn, "Of course evil doesn't respect lunch breaks."

Nek laughed, "Oh, no. Nothing serious like that. I have an update for you. I've been keeping certain tasks off the main framework in hopes to surprise you."

Mina was about to ask how they kept tasks off the framework when Comp2876 came flying around the corner. Its screen flashed *Surprise!* and from below dropped Mina's tiny horn that gave a short tooting sound. She lunged forward and grabbed 2876 out of the air, hugging the small robot tight to her chest.

"Buddy!" Mina was immediately trying not to cry in front of everyone. Her best robot was back. "I'm glad you're okay."

"How'd you get the horn in?" Steph asked.

"Removing the self-destruct component," Nek answered. "I've scheduled the swap in the rest of the swarm to happen over the next few days. I think we've moved away from needing that functionality."

Comp2876 gently pushed away from her so its screen was visible. *Glad to be back!*

"Okay," Henrie called over. "Hold them up and say cheese."

Mina smiled and held 2876 up as their screen flashed *Cheese!* and Henrie snapped a picture of them. She released 2876 and attempted to wipe her tears away undetected. Steph caught her and handed over a leftover fast food napkin, giving her hand a squeeze as she did so. Henrie's face paled as she looked at her phone.

"Is the picture that bad?" Mina asked.

"Sam is calling," Henrie said quietly.

"Who calls people these days?" Sean asked.

Emma waved them all to be quiet as she pried the phone from Henrie's hand and accepted the call. She switched the call to speaker and held it out for Henrie.

Henrie tipped forward. "Hey, Sam."

"Hey," they answered without going on. Which baffled Mina because they were the one who'd made the call.

"Um, how's today been?"

"Got the windows replaced. Good to have the plywood out of the front." They sounded like they were shuffling papers, probably sitting in the office at Restoration. "The evil birds haven't been around for a few days, so that's a plus."

"Totally!" She paused. Emma gave her side a squeeze and she spoke up again. "I, um, also saw Megan posted that downtown was done."

"Yeah, back to normal downtown noise."

"And it didn't take crime."

"No crime." There was another pause on their end. "We were going to grab pizza tonight at Sax's, if you and Emma would like to join."

"Yes," Henrie said rather quickly. "I mean, I technically have to check with my mom, but I think she'll say yes. Emma is still more on her good side than I am."

Sam laughed a little, Mina thought it sounded genuine. "Good to hear. I'll text you when we're going over."

"Sure. Awesome." She, along with the rest, waited as Emma ended the call and set her phone down before she dropped her head to the countertop. "That was so awkward."

Emma patted her on the back. "But you got the first awkward one out of the way."

Mina's watch flashed with another update on the Comp's information dump. She swiped the notification open on her armband to see they'd gone through and identified some of the people on her call. She'd told off some interesting beings across the universe. Oh well.

Nek had also taken the time to chart out their relative locations and confirmed it would take a while for anyone to reach them here, even with the coordinates. Until then, they'd train. They'd be ready for whoever came next. The team had taken up running Guardian drills on Mars now that the planet was vacant. The space gave them the privacy to look a little awkward as they learned and held no threat of knocking over buildings. They would also keep an eye on Earth issues. As they'd previously discussed, now that the space problem was on hold, they could try helping planetside as it seemed necessary. Given what they knew about Hephaestus and their actual intentions now, she expected the Wardens would be needed sooner than later.

Zane jabbed her in the side, speaking of coming back to Earth. Mina closed the document and gave him a smile. "Sorry."

He smiled back. "You're good. We were deciding what the four of us wanted for dinner."

Steph leaned into her other side. "My vote is also doing pizza, but wearing disguises. I'm being told that might be too much."

"You could never be too much," Mina said, and after Steph smiled she continued on. "But yeah, we should probably not crowd them."

"Everyone be on call though," Henrie said. "If this goes horribly, I need you all to come through and act like there is an attack going on. Save me."

Emma laughed, "It'll be fine."

They began talking about food and what was the best cross section of sounding good to eat and allowing them to leave at a moment's notice if needed. Mina thought about the list of new potential enemies coming together right now. Of all the new questions and answers piling up while they debated ramen or barbecue. Instead of panicking, she made her case for the Thai place the next street over from Sax's.

There was plenty of summer left. She'd worry about the superhero stuff later.

About the Author

Tara Brazee is lost in a cornfield somewhere in Nebraska, but it's okay. There's wifi and D&D actual play shows to catch up on. When not writing about a group of quippy teens in her superhero series, she's tapping away on one of the many other tales trapped in her WIP pile—knights learning magic, newly sentient robots, and demonic bartenders trying to make rent coming soon. If she's not writing a book, she's reading one. Odds are that one day she'll be discovered crushed by the weight of her TBR pile.

Also by Tara Brazee

In With A Bang

The first Outrider Adventure. Mina and her friends uncover a long dormant spaceship with alien life still inside. They soon find themselves fighting to save their city with the help of supersuits and giant robots.

New Fighter Unlocked

The second Outrider Adventure. Capri's after intel on the team, but she needs someone who can get around unnoticed. Unfortunately for Henrie, her summer is about to take a dive.

9 7 9 8 9 8 8 9 1 9 9 5 7